The Egyptian Coffin

Jane Jakeman

HEADLINE

First published in 1997
by HEADLINE BOOK PUBLISHING

First published in paperback in 1998
by HEADLINE BOOK PUBLISHING

10 9 8 7 6 5 4 3 2 1

ISBN 0 7472 5604 7

Printed and bound in Great Britain by
Clays Ltd, St Ives plc

HEADLINE BOOK PUBLISHING
A division of Hodder Headline PLC
338 Euston Road
London NW1 3BH

PART I

Malfine, 1831

CHAPTER 1

The Narrative of Lord Ambrose Malfine

When I finally relinquish my grip on life, I shall have done little to increase our family inheritance of Malfine. I appear to be a tough-sinewed sort of specimen, likely to stay firmly in this world in spite of all fortune's attempts to mow me down beneath her iron wheels and hurtle me out into the next, but I confess that I have not made many additions to this great and crumbling estate, where I reside amidst the unswept marble halls and acres of tangled woodland which my father bequeathed to me. My grandfather and my father hustled about improving this world – at least, my father did so till madness overtook him – but I have not inherited their capacity for inordinate busybodying. I fear I should never have made that good and faithful servant of whom St Matthew speaks, who doubled his master's investment of five talents to ten. I am by temperament one of nature's prodigals.

But there is one gift to posterity for which I am responsible, though my heirs may require some explanation of an extravagant and puzzling piece of their inheritance.

In the entrance hall of this great mansion of Malfine, in the heart of the English countryside, is a curious and exotic object, which generations as yet unborn may ponder over, if it remains undisturbed after my lifetime.

It is an Egyptian coffin.

For a coffin, it has some odd features.

Air-holes, for example.

I am looking at the coffin as I write these words, gazing into the hall through the open door of the library, where I sit at my customary table. The colours of the painted wood are still bright after two thousand years: red, peacock blues and greens, ochreous yellow. The lid of the coffin is in the form of a human being with a tranquil carved face, gentle and full-lipped, and a headdress of lapis blue and gold. The swaddled body that would once have lain within was, I conjecture, protected by the scarab beetles, the winged creatures, necklets and collars, which adorn the surface of the coffin. Painted eyes and black shapes surround the base; creatures with jackal heads are busy with their peculiar task over the breast.

In the chaste black-and-white marble hallway of Malfine it is a fantastical apparition, I grant you, for the decoration of Malfine is decidedly in the cool classical style. The coffin speaks of dark old gods and strange lives, of doors broken down and bats fluttering suddenly away towards the black interiors of rocky tombs, of sand drifting till it buried the very entrances to that cavernous world.

In these papers my heirs may read a thumbnail sketch of the truth about that coffin. This will doubtless be very different from the tale they will have heard from some pious elderly relative or flattering parson, just as the real history of Malfine is very different from that which will no doubt be solemnly presented for public consumption.

The truth is that this great mansion was created by my grandfather, old Hedger, who made a fortune on the stocks in the time of the late King George the Good and Mad, of pious memory. My grandfather was too shrewd to lose his money in building mania, but by accident employed a genius for an architect. It was the young man's first commission, so my grandfather got him cheap.

Before this talented fellow died of drink, to which some say he was driven by old Hedger's contentiousness over the payment of fees, he set the house amongst sweeps and curves of lawn, with lakes and streams flowing around it, and created a white portico with a pillared façade and curving wings, so graceful and sweeping that it looks as if the whole great marble caboodle had just floated down from heaven and settled in the English countryside. This, sparsely furnished, was the inheritance which my grandfather passed to his son George.

George, my father, would no doubt have led a blameless, brainless, life, as did the surrounding country boobies, roaring to hounds and fathering children to chirrup away in the surrounding countryside like so many hedge-sparrows. Like the neighbouring squires, he would doubtless one day have expired of apoplexy when perusing the sins of government in the *Morning Chronicle*. He would, as did so many other affable country fellows, have diligently maintained the work of his father, keeping the vast acres of Malfine's roof intact, and perhaps have even have made some modest additions, a conservatory, for example, to ruin the pure Palladian lines of the house. Or he might have married a lady of fashion, who would have employed some jobbing plasterer to stick topsy-turvy wedding-cakes upon the ceilings.

My father did none of these virtuous things, though there are some classical statues dotting the grounds, which were acquired by him on the Grand Tour and sent back in crates from Pisa, Florence and Rome. They are not, I believe, of any special artistic merit, but were purchased by my father on the advice of an agent, and are those which might be thought suitable to adorn the property of a gentleman of means – goddesses with their arms snapped clean off and scanty shreds of drapery, young men with arrows and lyres and stark-naked barnacles – that sort of thing.

Those are his contributions to the house – sculptures and a name, the name of Malfine, the result of the first time in his life when my father failed to conform. The first, but it was in a major respect, for he married my mother.

My mother, Eurydice, was an exotic flower transplanted to the English countryside. She was the daughter of a Cretan family, exiled when their castle was lost and their island captured by the Turks, a romantic history, but one which resulted in penury. All my mother had to bring to the marriage was her ancestral claim to the castle of Mala Fina, in Crete, and the wild peninsula on which it stands, a claim which I inherited. It is from that place that the present name of this English mansion derives: my father insisted on calling the house and the barony which old Hedger's financial dealings had procured for him after our Greek inheritance, so that I should at any rate have something from that ancestry, even though that something be no more than a name and the crest, an outlandish wolf's head, that goes with it.

Eurydice bore two children, myself and my sister, Ariadne, and died soon after the birth of my sister, leaving my father, that outwardly phlegmatic English squire so mad with grief that he nailed up the doors of her rooms with his own hands. He then sent my sister to be reared with relatives in London and allowed me to run wild in the grounds. He died very shortly afterwards of grieving and mad riding.

Of my own subsequent adventures in my mother's country, I may tell the world anon; at present, let it merely be said that I volunteered to fight for the liberty of Greece in its revolution against the dominion of the Turks, that I was wounded and given up for dead, and that I was brought home, barely alive, to my silent and shuttered inheritance of Malfine, where I have slowly recovered my strength, though not my taste for society.

And since that time my only positively enduring acquisition, the only addition I have made to the mansion of my father and grandfather, has been, oddly enough, this Egyptian coffin.

They are quite fashionable, of course – Egyptian antiquities, as were Greek and Roman vases and marble sculptures a generation or two ago. Mr Belzoni, the explorer, only recently created a fashion for Egypt with his 'Egyptian Hall' in Piccadilly, to which an avid public thronged to see such things as Mummies Inside Their Tombs, and learned personages now collect stone reliefs carved with those strange calm-faced gods and goddesses, or heavy blind-eyed heads of dark serpentine or red porphyry. The trinkets of Egypt, too, beaded necklaces and tiny sky-blue figurines, adorn many a Cabinet of Curiosities. More ghoulish objects, pathetic bandage-wrapped creatures contracted into desiccation, have been sold as souvenirs to those visiting the Land of the Pharaohs, and brought back by travellers to excite sham horrors in those at home.

But the story of how this particular specimen was acquired must begin, not in that exotic and far-flung land where the coffin was made, but here, in this great house in a remote corner of England. The recounting of this narrative involves

a tale of human wickedness such as I had hoped never
to meet on British soil, expecting it to be outlawed and
repugnant both to our justice and our conscience. But it
was neither, as the reader of these documents will ultimately
recognise.

We cannot foresee the future, whether our own or that
of others, although there are those in Cairo who scry into a
pool of ink and see reflections of the future passing in the
blackness. In a room in the heart of the city the fortune-teller
will look into a black mirror and see a man in his desert tent,
the heat shimmering in stony grey waves below the glassy
surface, 'through a glass darkly'. But who can tell what the
future may require of us? What provision should we make
now for those faces that will peer at us through the glass
of time?

It may be that a legal record of events will at some time
be required and I have therefore placed with this narrative
of mine some letters and records that will substantiate my
evidence, should that ever be necessary in case the matter
comes before a court of law. These papers include certain
private letters of my own, including correspondence from
one particular personage. She and I will be dust long before
any other eyes read what we have written!

CHAPTER 2

To a gusty September night last year I date the commencement of my entanglement with a piece of cruelty such as nightmares might conjecture, the record of which I have endeavoured to set down and preserve.

And Elisabeth, with her usual wit, discerned later the innermost reason for my placing these papers under seal – which reason is not that which I might give to the world, speaking of the need in this case for legalities and proofs, of the privacy of our correspondence and the like. No, she went straight to the heart of the matter, when she had read through these pages.

'But who killed him?' she asked.

It is now almost a year ago that the strange events described in these papers commenced; she and I were deliberating what we were to do with our lives – as if we truly possess the powers of controlling our affections and our fates! That evening is lodged within my memory as sharp as if it were an engraving. And it is limned in my mind in black and white – the colours of moonlight.

Malfine at night: we have been walking in the grounds. The great white portico, the columns and the steps, the lawns and the lake, all are beneath the clear moon of the fullest phase. In the woods, the creatures feel the first frost of winter. The candle shadows flicker in those parts of the house which are inhabited: the rest are left to moonshine and darkness in rooms where the great mirrors reflect only emptiness and no sleepers lie within the curtained beds.

We entered the house and made our way to the library, where a fire had been banked up. The watcher from the dark world outside would see lights and movement confined, so late at night, to this long room, where we are still talking, as we have been all evening, serious, intent, our voices low. Shadows pass and re-pass before the windows and quiet murmurings drift across the lawns.

We are pitting their wits against our passions. That is the cause of all our talk, and little difference it makes to our hearts. You, Elisabeth, you the cautious one, were willing to throw all prudence to the winds, for my sake. I, the temperamental and fiery soul – I, who once ran away to fight in a distant world for the sake of abstract concepts, of ideals, for freedom and honour – why, I have turned preacher, I counsel caution, for your sake!

'But do you want me to remain here? Here, at Malfine?'

Your tall form moves along the room as you speak. Your hair is loose and flowing around the shoulders, and your skirt of silver-grey cashmere swings heavily, silently, from side to side, like some pale soft-winged creature of the night, fluttering down the length of the room and then drawn back to the pool of light.

Staring into the fire, without turning my head, I say, in a low voice, 'Of course, I want you to remain! You must not doubt that! But I fear it harms you.'

'Being with you cannot harm me. Leaving you – ah, that would be harm indeed.'

'I did wrong to ask you to come here. When that dreadful business at Crawshay's farm was over – when the murderers were made known and you were free to go where you pleased

– I should have let you go. The world could no longer suspect you of any guilt and you had no commitment to any person living, save for the natural bonds of family affection. But you are now alone and your reputation is damaged by living in this house with me.'

'Where would I have gone? My parents would not have taken me in, and my husband was dead. What care I for society? And you, Ambrose, surely what the world thinks is of little significance, caring as little as you do for gossip and tittle-tattle! No, I will stay here. Let our neighbours say what they please – let their tongues wag!'

'Yes, but my dearest Elisabeth, you should try to be reconciled with your family, for your own happiness – I know that you are deeply attached to your mother, and she will not countenance this present situation whereby you reside under my roof. You are living with a man to whom you are not married, a man, furthermore, from whom the whole county is estranged. And I cannot offer you marriage – there would be no honesty in such an offer from my lips. I was barely alive when I returned from Greece, and I have scarcely begun to live again. I do not know if I shall ever be fit to share my life with another human creature – at least, not for such a pledge as marriage implies – "as long as we both shall live". No, Elisabeth, for your own sake, I cannot propose marriage, cannot make you an offer as hollow and false as a cracked pitcher.'

You pace up and down again, your shadow brushing past the alcoves of leather-bound books, passing between the windows and the light of the candles. It is not the least of the attractions which you hold for me that the workings of your mind are often impenetrable, disguised behind your smooth and masklike beauty; you can keep your own counsel, you are a free and independent spirit. Sometimes, as at that moment in the long library in Malfine, this knowledge can fill me with jealousy; sometimes, as then, I wondered if you were thinking of him, that dead husband whom once you must have loved and for whom you left your parents and your home.

Well, he is dead and gone, like the ghosts of my own past, and we two are alive and warm, your flesh and blood vibrant and feeling, part of this world, not of the next, not of the past.

Returning once more down the darkened length of the library, you put your hand on my shoulder. For a moment, we are diverted from the subject of our talk.

You were like a lovely moth in that pale, silently moving dress.

When I was a boy, I studied moths. It seems quite irrelevant, does it not, yet the topic is not so far removed from the subject of these papers, after all. In my youth, I used to run through Malfine woods at night in search of different species, following some light-winged creature fluttering ahead of me through the darkness and I knew all the old country names for moths. The Star Wort, the Lute String, the Ghost Moth that hovers above the grass on summer nights. The Cream Wave that flies through the Maytime woods. Have you ever seen the sepia filigree on the wings of a Pale-Shouldered Brocade?

What useless stuff I crammed my head with, when I was young!

And I kept silk-worms, and fed them on mulberry leaves. But moths, no, I could not breed them like the silk-worms. I tried, once, collecting up the caterpillars and keeping them in a flask, but it is never successful, breeding them thus.

From a captive chrysalis, the adult moth will often emerge deformed.

On that night those images of my boyhood were overlaid

by others, the thought of another child, pale and solemn. He sleeps now in a small chamber above me as I write, not one of those gloomy mirrored grand bedchambers but a room suitable and unfrightening for a little boy, and he has gone quietly to bed. He is a child who will never disobey, never go running through the woods at night. I long for some signs of spirit in this sad little creature. Whatever we decide for ourselves, we have young Edmund Crawshay, the heir to Crawshay's farm, to consider.

Well, I have fixed upon my course with regard to him, at any rate. I shall adopt him. He has no one else in the world except for us, after the deaths of his mother and father in that charnel-house at the farm. The least I could do was to bring him to Malfine and undertake his care and education. I shall not abandon that resolve. He goes away to school, to get a gentleman's education, and spends the holidays here at Malfine. I believe that this plan meets with Elisabeth's agreement, for boarding school is undoubtedly good for him, as it is not for many children. There he has small companions to amuse him and perhaps bring some smiles to that quiet and obedient face. He is too old for a governess now, and I think he will be happier away from this district, where the shadow of his parents' deaths must still hang over him.

But what are we to do, then, Elisabeth the former governess to young Edmund, now no longer needed by her charge, and I, her quixotic rescuer?

On that particular evening I knew it would please me greatly if, for her own sake, she would try to achieve a reconciliation with her family in Bristol. Elisabeth's disastrous marriage to Richard de Carme, of which they so disapproved, was over – her husband's death freed her from it, and her parents might welcome her back as a widow – such

13

a description is the small coin of respectability that eases all transactions in society.

As for my affairs, did not Dr Sandys recommend that I should undertake a journey for my health's sake? He said that my wounds have healed marvellous well, but he would like to see me spared the rigours of an English winter and I therefore arranged to set out on my travels, which would doubtless brighten up my spirits from the grievous state of lack-lustre which Elisabeth's absence would cause!

So we reasoned our lives apart, but we two are bound together by a passion which, for all our intelligence and wit, we cannot, and would not, talk away.

'In the spring,' I told her, 'I shall return, and if we are of the same mind as now, and find our passions unchanged, we could take up our lives here again, although there is nothing simple between you and me! What difficult creatures we are! We cannot flee away into the night like the lovers on St Agnes' Eve; we live in the world, we have ties and duties to consider.' Yes, I preached this, I who shut myself away like a hermit, and shun human society. I thought of her, my Elisabeth: I would not demand that she shared my isolation. She would want friends, the natural companionship of her relations. And I – even I, feel from to time the pull of old ties that still bind me to the world beyond Malfine.

Yes, I wrote to her, as I had promised. I made a tardy correspondent, I fear, for some of my letters were sent through the deserts in the care of some rough Bedouin hand, and crossed many seas and enter many harbours before they came to her. But never did I forget to write. Whenever we were separated, no matter what befell me, as long as there was some strength remaining in my hand, I endeavoured to scrawl a few lines to her.

*   *   *

How came I to go to Egypt? This is a tale which I would rather have ignored from the outset. If I had refused to meddle in the matter of the Westmorland estate, why then our lives might have attained that hermetic peace and tranquillity which is my goal.

Ah, but the girl! It is only that she is of the same blood, that she has the same look, that very devilish turn of the head, that pale face and dark-red hair, of my dear friend. I see him again, that vanished companion, when I look into her face. All that I owed to my own youth, to our friendship, the bonds of memory and affection – these told me that I must intervene in what befell her – and having once waded in the shallows, so as to speak, I found a deep and muddy river, in whose treacherous currents many innocent creatures would perish if I drew back.

The truth is that I owed a debt, to life, to my young self, and that debt was reclaimed of me, though my physical strength was recovering fast, for Sandys is well enough for a country quack. He studied at Edinburgh, and the Scots breed good doctors. At least he does no great harm to his patients, unlike those fashionable London leeches who fairly blow their patients apart with clysters or contrive to kill them off with blood-letting. He is a serious-minded fellow, busy and skinny, with wispy brown hair and a quick grey eye that takes in a good deal more than he will let on.

Sandys, as I say, visits none of the indignities of fashionable medicine upon us – for I count myself among his patients, since he tended the wounds I had got in Crete, the sabre-slashes on my face and body. It would be truer to say that Sandys took over the management of my scars, rather than the care of my wounds; Belos, my manservant, had cared for me first, bringing me home on a stretcher to die, as it was thought. But I lived, to confound them,

15

so Sandys had little to do but cluck when he took over my care.

In fact, I told neither Belos nor the good doctor that I had a third physician: the gypsy woman whose caravan was camped in my grounds. The scar on my leg was healing, yet it troubled me greatly, burning and itching, and she brought me a salve, very odd-smelling, which straightaway cooled the inflammation. I did not ask of her the compounds which had gone into her receipt; I know that the Romanies have some remedies which they inherited from the Arab physicians who have passed their skills down for centuries. At any rate, after a few days, my scar seemed to be less angry, and it began to heal into a thin line, so I suppose the witch had something efficacious in her noxious unguent, but I did not care to mention this preparation to Belos or Sandys, for fear of being mercilessly harangued into the path of medical righteousness.

But to return to Sandys: I will set down here the gist of a conversation which turned out to have a bearing on a far more important matter.

'Damn it, Sandys,' said I on this occasion, pulling my shirt back on, when he had come to inspect the progress of his patient. 'My wounds are healed! Can you not see that, man!'

'I still fear for your lordship if we have a hard winter,' says he, in that prudent Scottish voice. 'You were much weakened by fever, as well as by the wounds, so your man tells me!'

'Ah, Belos is an old maid! I'm as fit as a fiddle, Sandys!'

'Not quite, if I may contradict your lordship. I would like to see you taking care this winter to keep out of draughts and chills.'

'Keep out of draughts!' said I. 'Why, Sandys, you sound like a old beldame muttering beside the fire! But I tell you what, Sandys, and this will please you mightily, I have a notion to travel. I long to go East again, and cannot settle here at Malfine amongst the turnip-heads and clod-hoppers.'

'I agree that English country-dwellers are not always the most stimulating company,' says he, 'but I most earnestly desire you not to jump from the frying-pan into the fire!'

'A cautious metaphor, but not well-chosen, Sandys, since I propose to leave a cold climate, not one that might be alluded to as a frying-pan! But into the fire, yes, for I long to feel desert heat again; perhaps it is because my mother was Greek that I have a taste for hot climes. I would travel again, and to the Levant. What think you?'

'If you would not be too precipitate, my lord, I would encourage you in this enterprise. Be sure to take plenty of warm clothing, for I understand that nights in those climates can be cold indeed.'

And so he went on to give more such tedious advice, till I was near bursting out at the ears. I was to be in the East before either of us might have predicted and without time to follow most of Sandys' instructions, but in one respect he did advise me well, and there I was somewhat surprised. He had heard of the way of preventing the smallpox contagion, which was first practised in this country by the good Doctor Edward Jenner.

'He was, like myself, if I may compare with such a distinguished practitioner, a country doctor. He observed that the milk-maids who contracted cowpox did not fall victim to the dread disease of the smallpox, and so he concluded that a greater disease may be averted by the infliction of a lesser – the principle of inoculation.'

'Aye, I know of it, for I have read upon the subject and heard of it from medical men in London, but I did not think it was practised in this part of the world.'

'The country people do not trust these new ways. But I am

having a small laboratory built on to our house, and there I hope to keep up with my scientific studies.'

'And you intend to practise the art of butchery on our innocent rustics?

'Your lordship pleases to be merry.'

'Yes, by hell and tommy, I must be quite recovered!'

I strode out into the hall, while Sandys turned for a moment to collect up his instruments. At this juncture Belos entered holding a sheet of paper.

He, too, would doubtless cluck away at me. I decided to take the initiative.

'And what is that letter you have in your hand, Belos? If it is addressed to me, you may save me the trouble of perusing it. Read it for me, will you? Oh, I perceive you have already undertaken that duty without my instruction, so you can merely tell me the gist.'

'It is a request for assistance in a local matter, my lord.'

'Well, send five guineas to missionaries or aged grandams or whatever good cause one of our neighbours may be soliciting for – and keep that smile off your features! The charitable ladies in these parts may solicit wherever they wish provided they make no intrusion into my peace and quiet.'

'As your lordship pleases.'

'Yes, my lordship does please, so there's an end on it.'

'But it was not a charitable matter that engaged my attention in this communication. At least, as I understand it, the young lady is in no urgent need of financial assistance.'

'Young lady?'

'Yes, my lord. Miss Lilian Westmorland, of Westmorland Park.'

'The house about ten miles hence, off the turnpike road? I remember poor Westmorland died long ago. He was my friend once – we were boys together, you know. But I had not

18

seen him for many years – I believe there was some scandal about him, though not, of course, approaching anything like the scandal I have caused in these parts. Dame Rumour will never stop clacking her tongue, and I am frequently tempted to live up – or rather, down – to what she says about me. But to go back to Westmorland – did he not drown in the river after some drunken jape?'

'Yes, my lord, that is the family. The child—'

'Must have grown into a woman. Westmorland's death occurred before I departed for Greece and I have seen nothing of her since my return.'

'Yes, and the girl is now seventeen, and left an orphan by the recent death of her mother.'

'Well, that is sad indeed, but what am I to do about it? I should cut a sorry figure as a stepmother.'

'You would indeed, my lord. And I do not believe your financial assistance is required – not, at least, with any urgency. Westmorland Park is a very considerable estate, and its revenues would in all probability be quite sufficient for Miss Lilian's maintenance, even after the depredations caused by the unwholesome activities of her late father. No, it seems there has been a riding accident at the Park, and they beg you to send Dr Sandys over to attend Miss Lilian, as soon as he has finished waiting upon your lordship.'

'What, has the girl met with some ill chance?'

'It seems her horse threw her, and she has lost consciousness, my lord. There is no physician except for Dr Sandys within an hour's ride from Westmorland Park.'

'Well, dammit, Belos, it grieves me to show a neighbourly decency amidst these rustic surroundings, but I suppose I've no choice in the matter. Sandys has finished his advice on my convalescence, in any case. Here, help me with my shirt. The sawbones is still here, packing away his instruments, having

19

pronounced me hale and hearty – at least, as hale as any man who was unseamed through the middle by a Turkish cutlass and left for dead might ever hope to be. Very well, I'll tell Sandys he's wanted at the Park. I'll take my obligations that far – but mind, no appeals for widows and orphans!'

'Yes, my lord. And while we are on the subject of charity, may I ask whether we are to continue to give sustenance to those gypsies who are encamped in the grounds?'

'Yes, send them something out from the kitchens, will you? They won't be here much longer – they'll be moving south soon. They're like the swallows – when the cold weather comes, they're off to warmer climes. I've a good mind to do the same, since Sandys has given me a clean bill of health – a few months in some sultry climate would just suit me now. Oh, by the way, Belos, I heard they had some fine horseflesh in the stables at Westmorland Park. How did the accident happen?'

'The messenger who brought the letter told me it occurred as the young lady was riding along the path through the woods in the grounds.'

'The horse suffered no harm, I trust?'

'The horse had to be destroyed, my lord. A fine mare, as I understand, though I know nothing of horseflesh myself.'

'Destroyed, eh? Now, did it really, Belos? Did it really?'

I had not thought of Sam Westmorland these fifteen years or more. He was the son of our neighbours at Westmorland Park; he and I had played together, had run wild together, and, we thought, should grow up together. Yet he died alone.

I had shut Sam out of my mind these many years. Now I recalled him, the dark red hair, the face always laughing, always thinking of some new adventure or absurdity. We were twins in that, we two, urging one another on with dares and bets.

When Sam had married, he was in his eighteenth year and I in my seventeenth. I had thought our friendship should end then, at least that part of it where we caroused and jested and ran after women. But, I suppose about a year after the wedding, he rode over to see a new dog I had got at Malfine, and before we knew it, why there we were, drinking a bumper in the cellars, another on the steps, riding through the grounds, betting on who could leap the hazel fence, on who would be first to run headlong, breakneck from the top of Wayland's Mound! I can hear his voice yet, calling out 'I dare you! I dare you!' in some absurd challenge or other, as we raced wildly towards some new danger or other, embracing fear as we embraced life itself.

I do not remember which of us bet on who would be first at the river, but I do recall which of us conceived the insane notion of swimming to the weir.

I did. How painful it once was to remember this, how difficult to forget, and how hard now, after close on eighteen years, to recall it!

Sam died, of course. That is why I now record our foolish long-forgotten dares, for this death also forms a part of the story that follows. I did not expect to think of it again, and yet I find myself now recalling, moment by moment, those last minutes of his life.

Sam was a strong swimmer, but he was trapped by some malign underwater weeds, and his body was knifing out of the water and then falling back like a gaffed fish as he struggled. The brown weeds were tangled round his breast, at the last moment I saw him alive, being myself swept over the weir and unable to reach him. His cries mingled distantly with the roar of the water as I was borne away, to be washed up against the further bank, and crawl to safety at the bend below the weir.

I heard two months later that his widow was delivered of a girl-child. There were rumours that young Westmorland was running up debts that might have ruined the estate, had he lived – apparently, his marriage had not altered his way of life. So prudent voices said that the heir might be lost but the estate was saved. I said that I was too grief-stricken – I was really, as I understand now, too ashamed of my part in his death – to ever call at Westmorland Park again. And in any case, very soon after I left for Greece.

The story that I now heard from Belos, of the riding accident suffered by Sam Westmorland's daughter, revived my memories. Possibly, just possibly, I should take an interest in the child of my dead boyhood friend. She now, perhaps, had no one left in this world to advise her, and though I suspected that I, a radical spirit in my youth and a hermit in my mature years, would make a most unsuitable guardian, still I could offer her some protection.

But her immediate need was for medical attention.

'Do you go to Westmorland, now, Sandys,' said I. 'I have no more need of you – go and mend the child's head with vinegar and brown paper, or whatever the latest sawbones fashion would have.'

I might perhaps myself ride over the next day, or the next after that, and take a look at Sam Westmorland's daughter.

That night I slept uneasily, and woke to find my candle had guttered down, and my pillows were scattered in disarray.

Suddenly there was a sharp sound, as of hard rain or hail driving at my window. Yet it was a calm enough night; a few minutes later, when the sound came again, I rose, pulled a dressing-robe about me and crossed the room. There is a balcony outside my bedroom window, which overlooks the great lawn at the back of Malfine.

There were two figures on the lawn, one in the act of picking up a small handful of earth or twigs, which had presumably been the source of the sound that had roused me.

The moonlight gleamed on unkempt locks tied up in ribbons, on draggled skirts, their flounces sewn with coins and bits of glistening metal and pale shiny bone.

'*Raia, raia!*'

That is the title 'lord' they have given me in thanks for a service I have performed them, and I had rather be called by their gypsy peerage than have a dozen fat knights of the realm bowing and scraping to me, for I have earned my Romany lordship, whereas I am Lord Ambrose Malfine of Malfine solely because my wily old devil of grandfather became exceeding rich and lent some money to a greedy prince.

The voices mouthed their whispers from below the balcony, floating up from the dark world outside the room. 'The *grasni*, lord, the *grasni*! *Balansers . . . balansers . . .*'

I could partly understand their Romany language, having acquired some of it in my travels abroad, and long been interested in that strange and secretive tongue – for they do not care, as a rule, to let outsiders learn to understand their conversation. I knew enough to tell that what the gypsies were saying had something to do with a mare. And money. *Balansers* are guineas.

More murmurings. Then the gypsy voices again, agitated. 'The *gry, grychoring*!' Which is to say, there was some agitation about horse-stealing.

Horses, guineas and theft are the three most common entanglements of the Romany world, and they occur in many and various colourful conjunctions. I was inclined to take no notice and dismiss the business as some foolishness that could soon be settled and might easily have waited till daybreak, without rousing me from my bed. But this was something of sufficient importance to agitate the gypsy woman and her daughter so that they would come to me in the middle of the night.

I got a little more of the story from them, and looked down on their moonlit faces, sharp-boned and finely featured, and promised them I would do what I could.

'Very well, let me speak to your man. Yes, if the matter will not wait another minute, as you say, then tonight. Will you fetch him here?'

Now I was well entangled in the net of events. I should have stayed in my bed!

The next day, Belos brought me my breakfast as I yawned in the library.

'Your bacon and mushrooms, my lord.'

'Ah, perfect, Belos. Any coffee?'

'Yes, my lord – shall I pour it now?'

As he poured the bitter and enlivening black fluid from a silver pot which was grand but somewhat tarnished, like so much at Malfine, Belos added; 'The gypsies have cleared off. And they may have cleared off some of your lordship's possessions, for aught I know – I never did think it was right they should be caravanned on your land in the first place.'

'Belos, you were once yourself a strolling player, were you not, so have you no sympathy for the vagrant life?'

'None whatever, my lord. And I was not a vagrant. I was an *artiste*.'

'Well, I'm sorry to have offended your feelings, Belos – watch out with that coffee – you'll have it on my lap! There now, you've got it all over this paper I've been writing.'

'Beg pardon, my lord. Is it aught of importance, or was your lordship trifling with verse again?'

Really, Belos is not made for a servant, which is, I suppose, why I take pleasure in employing him.

But as to the paper from which I was wiping a pool of coffee even as he spoke, I will let it speak for itself later on.

CHAPTER 3

Some few days after I had heard of the accident that befell the young heiress of Westmorland Park, I decided to pay my respects and offer suitable neighbourly assistance. This was, of course, entirely out of character, and I must confess it was prompted, not solely by concern for the daughter of my boyhood friend, but by a certain curiosity which the tale of the gypsies had aroused.

Here at Westmorland Park, it seemed, there had occurred a riding accident in conditions which I, as an experienced breakneck hell-raiser in my youth, can personally testify are unlikely to foster such an event. There was Miss Lilian Westmorland, a skilled horsewoman, there were horse and rider well acquainted with the track they were following, the terrain being easy going, the weather perfectly fine. The horse, a valuable thoroughbred, had been so badly injured it was shot immediately after the event.

Could these oddities fit together snugly to make a whole, like those wooden puzzles children turn over and over in their fingers, till, suddenly – *click!* – and the whole toy glides into place? We had a few strange happenings – no more, but the puzzle they would make when fitted together – ah, that aroused my interest. Sufficiently to propel me into the saddle and give Zaraband a good canter out towards the locality of the accident.

At Westmorland Park, the door was opened by a small maid – who presumably was not accustomed to such duties, for she could not have noticed that her hair was escaping from her mob cap and falling round her thin face, as her arms struggled with the heavy weight of the front door. I assisted her to propel it open, and she squeaked in alarm. I tried to reassure her.

'I am merely paying a friendly visit, I assure you! Is your mistress at home? I am Lord Ambrose Malfine.'

This elicited yet more cries of alarm, and the little maid gasped out that she would 'fetch Mistress Jennet straight away', but this proved to be unnecessary, for an elderly female personage of the most damnable respectability was advancing down the hallway, in a black gown that clearly constituted an impregnable fortress of virtue, with a steel hussif's chain clanking at her waist.

She looked about as welcoming as the ghostly chatelaine, hung with skulls around her waist, of some Gothic novel or other, and her visage did not soften at the sight of myself. Rumour must have preceded me – of my foreign blood, my wicked city ways, or the like, for as I swept off my hat and bowed, she was fair twitching with anxiety.

'Lord Ambrose Malfine, madam, at your service. May I express my sorrow for Miss Lilian's misfortune, and offer my neighbourly assistance in any matter?'

The personage was murmuring, rather grudgingly, I thought: 'Oh, well . . . thank you kindly . . . your worship . . . that is, my lord . . .'

'And I would ask you to convey my compliments to the invalid. But how did the accident come to occur, may I ask?'

This question stirred things up. Mistress Jennet's eyes rounded brightly and she was opening and closing her

mouth like an anxious goldfish. I could see that there were
two warring instincts there: the desperate longing to impart
information natural to one of God's own gossips, and her
prudent nervousness of my own wicked reputation.

'Well, sir – I don't know nothing about horses . . .'

'Was Miss Lilian out riding on her own?'

'Oh no, sir! That would be real shocking, a young lady
out without a companion! What would people say? No,
Miss Lilian would not go gadding about the countryside
unaccompanied, I assure you!'

'No, no, of course not!' I soothed outraged respectability
till the hackles subsided. Genteel young ladies did not go
out all on their own, without even a servant in attendance.
They must be chaperoned at all times – even when going
about such ordinary rustic amusements as the shires might
afford. I doubted Miss Lilian could entertain any serious
hope of being corrupted hereabouts, at least, I had found
little enough opportunity when I was young, but Mistress
Jennet would not share my views. No, of course young Miss
Lilian was not unsupervised when the accident had struck
her down.

'Sir, the groom was with her.'

'Ah, yes, the groom. Well, perhaps, he observed how the
mischance came to happen. It may be, you know, that there
is a branch across the riding path that should be lopped, or
a molehill that needs digging out, or some such matter in
which I can offer my services.'

'Why, I don't think there was any such cause, sir –
it seems the horse stumbled and fell, and threw Miss
Lilian with it, just up at the top of the path through the
copper beeches – by that big clump to the right of the
track – and all seemed quite as usual. As for the groom,
well . . .'

Here an oddly fearful note came into the woman's voice. She suddenly seemed unconfident.

'He's been dismissed, sir.'

'Dismissed? Why, was he to blame for the accident? How could that have been?'

'Oh, I wouldn't like to say, sir. But Mr Overbury sent him away without a character straight after the accident. Dismissed him then and there, and without a testimonial. And Adams had been with the family these twenty years, sir, but then, he said he were doing it only for Miss Lilian's safety, that she were too precious to be set at risk . . .'

Her voice trailed off.

'Who is Mr Overbury?'

'Miss Lilian's uncle, sir . . . he's taken charge here . . .' she glanced nervously over her shoulder. 'I'm sure he means all for the best, sir. You must excuse me now . . . the doctor says she has some injury to her head.'

I felt an anxiety that I had not anticipated. I had expected to hear merely about an injury and an invalid: here I found the horse vanished, the groom dismissed and a stranger in charge. Still, the Westmorland estates had been in the hands of profligates, and although my sympathy is ever with the wastrels, I admit that a prudent hand on the reins might well be in Miss Lilian's real interests. Not all the world is willing to go to hell in my breakneck way. I almost took my leave at this point, but courtesy – or something more? – obliged me to inquire further. 'Is Miss Lilian well enough to receive visitors, may I ask?'

'I'm afraid Miss Lilian is asleep just now . . .'

A soft voice called out from somewhere upstairs: 'Oh, Jennet, Jennet!'

'Well, at any rate, she's not receiving visitors,' said Jennet, defensively.

'I quite understand, Mrs Jennet, pray do not let me interrupt you any more. Please give Miss Lilian my compliments.'

The door closed.

I turned away towards the grounds of Westmorland Park. It was an idyllic setting, the perfect subject for a painter's brush, the clear enamelled colours of a fine fresh morning in early September.

Looking back, I saw Westmorland Park from a distance, a Queen Anne house in soft reds, set in a bright-green parkland. There alongside the west wing, apricots trained by careful gardeners climbed up the walls, and against the soft rusty tones of the old bricks, espaliered fruit trees enjoyed gleams of autumnal sun. A little further along from the fruit trees, the sunlight winked in bright points of light on the glass of a newfangled conservatory, almost the only addition since the house was built a hundred years previously.

That morning, Westmorland Park was as mature and calm as the English country manor appears in a painting: a house set against a serene and perfect backdrop, an ideal image which an architect had conjured into life, into a solid reality in stout bricks and crafted plaster, and set down in lush green pastures dotted with old spreading trees.

I continued my prowl in the grounds.

A landscape painter, placing Westmorland Park amid emerald fields in the middle distance of his canvas, would note with professional observation that there is a charming detail which would, most effectively, draw the eye of the beholder into the picture: the little octagonal tower perched over the stables. Here, on this particular morning, a clock was striking its silvery notes through the freshness of the air. The stables are a short distance from the back of the house, for the owners here, unaffectedly horsy, have always liked to have their animals close at hand; the gentry at Westmorland Park were not used to waiting graciously at the front entrance for their mounts or their carriages to be brought round from the stables, but always had the habit of walking on their own two feet to the stalls and looseboxes at the back of the house, where they could inspect their equine charges, offer apples, chat with grooms and generally revivify themselves through breathing in the beloved familiar scents of hay, leather and prime horse-dung. I recalled my vanished friend, young Sam Westmorland, doing exactly that, on some hazy golden misremembered morning of our youth, which can never in truth have been such an idyll as it appears to me now.

I turned into the stable building. Rows of empty stalls, all neat and orderly. There was one occupied stall in the row, where the placid head of a once-dappled pony, a staid, elderly beast, whose coat was turning white with age, looked out at me with a modest display of interest. Out of habit, I rubbed the creature's nose, and peered into the other stalls as I passed along. In one, next to that of the pony, a length of dark tarry twine had been thrown in a disorderly sort of way, at odds with the general air of neatness which prevailed here.

Another stall appeared to have been but recently vacated by its equine occupant. The floor was wet, as if it had been recently washed; someone had forgotten to remove hay from the rock, and a fine set of harness hung against the whitewashed wall.

I peered down at the cobbled floor. Between the smooth stones, tiny rills of water still lay glistening, though the moisture was drying fast. All was orderly, silent save for the gentle shifting of the stout dapple in his stall.

Turning away to the park, I began to walk along the ride among the beeches and began to imagine my dead friend's daughter coming along here for her morning ride. That old grey fellow in the stables was likely the horse which the groom would have ridden. Miss Lilian Westmorland was noted as a bold young horsewoman – she had ridden a creature fit to whirl her along, as young riders love. I pictured her, with the red locks which she inherited from her father, flying out as she galloped along this very path towards the disaster which awaited horse and rider at the rise amid the beeches. Had I not heard she had a chestnut mare? A painter would have noted how the tints of the rider's hair and the colour of the horse's coat picked up the orpiment and saffron, the nut brown and tobacco tones, of the drying autumn leaves in the woods around.

I was walking uphill now, towards the clump of beeches. The path was smooth and clear, the going firm and dry. No overhanging branches, no inconvenient molehills . . . no trace of how the accident had come to happen here, unless one accepted that it had occurred through sheer chance, the irrational intervention of fate, or some fairytale about the workings of Divine Providence . . .

This must be where the fall had actually occurred, for the leaves and soil on one side of the path were scored and tracked, and marks crossed and trampled over, as presumably folk had come with a stretcher to carry the injured girl away. And to shoot the horse on the spot, put it out of its agony, and drag the wretched carcass away in a farmyard cart? There were no tracks of the kind that might be left by such a vehicle, nor which indicated a heavy load such as the dead body of a horse being pulled across the ground, but that signified little, for the ground was firm and solid, not apt to take impressions. There was no blood, neither, such as might have been caused by the pistol-shot that would have despatched the horse – again, that did not count for much;

31

there would have been but little blood and the traces might now be buried under falling leaves in any case – but there were some smallish dark smears on the smooth trunk of a tree, one of a pair of graceful birch trees, planted on either side of the path. Blackish, sticky stains, near a deep groove in the smooth bark.

I had now walked the terrain of the place where Miss Lilian Westmorland had suffered the accident, along the path which horse and rider had then followed, and made it my concern to note those signs which were accountable by subsequent events natural on the occurrence of such a disaster.

Turning back towards the house, I confess I forgot to admire the beauty of its setting, so deep in thought was I as I approached it. I did not again seek to enter by the front door, but swung round the house in an arc which took me to the stables once more, and to my friend the dapple-grey who looked hopefully in my direction. But I had nothing in my pocket, no lump-sugar or apples, for such a contingency, and instead stood peering into the stall next to his.

'What the devil are you doing here?'

The voice came from the end of the yard, and a good voice it was, too, ringing, dramatic, deep-throated. Belos would have said its owner would have performed well upon the stage, for my manservant, as a former actor, is a connoisseur of voices.

'I am Lord Ambrose Malfine! And who the hell are you?'

But I was somewhat modifying my greeting, even as he walked towards me, for I could see that there was something strange about this man's appearance: as he came closer, I looked into his face and it bore the marks of illness. Of a very severe illness, furthermore, for they were the scars of smallpox that disfigured his features. The poor devil had once been well-favoured enough, no doubt, but had fallen victim to a truly terrible illness, and one which he was fortunate to survive. I was reminded of my conversation with Sandys. Clearly, this fellow had not experienced the good fortune to have been vaccinated against the horrible infection.

'I own the Malfine estate,' said I – surely he would have heard the word Malfine, for it was not only the title which I bore but the name of the greatest mansion in the county – 'and have come out of a natural neighbourly concern for Miss Westmorland to see if there was aught I could do to assist here. I take a particular interest in livestock and came to see if you wanted me to send over a spare groom to the Westmorland stables. But who, sir are you?'

The man came up close. 'Lord Ambrose Malfine, I take it. My name is Casterman, your lordship – I am Mr Micah Overbury's man of affairs.'

'Mr Micah Overbury? I am not acquainted with the gentleman. I knew Miss Lilian's late father, but I believe Mr Overbury must be from the distaff side of the family. And I have not seen you in these parts before, Mr Casterman.'

'Mr Overbury has premises in Bristol, near the docks, and I assist him there – his business is concerned with imports and cargoes. Mr Overbury is the late Mrs Westmorland's brother – and now the trustee of this estate and Miss Lilian's guardian. As to the horses, I do not believe you will find anything to interest you, Lord Ambrose. Miss Lilian had a fine mare, but it had to be destroyed after the accident. In fact, there will be no horses kept here at all, except for such as Mr Overbury might require for his own use when he moves in here.'

'Oh, and what will happen to Miss Lilian?'

He stiffened. 'I understand Mr Overbury has made arrangements for her care. I am not at liberty to discuss his affairs.'

'Tight-lipped, aren't ye? But there, Mr Casterman, I intend you no insult, for the ability to keep silent is a valuable commodity in a man of business. In any case, I daresay the whole district will know all about it within hours – there's no point in being discreet in the countryside, man – why, the very turnips gabble in the fields! But' – here I turned back to the dapple-grey, standing patiently in his stall – 'what will happen to our friend here? I suppose he is the last denizen of the Westmorland Park stables? They were once renowned throughout the county, you know.'

'Yes, well, this animal will be sold off. Mr Overbury has his own carriage horses, of course, but this is just a common pony, kept for the groom, and the groom has . . .'

'Has been dismissed. Yes, I had heard.'

The pock-marked features produced a laugh. 'My lord, you are perfectly in the right of it! News does travel fast in the country! I dare say this pony will be destroyed as well – it's too old to fetch much, I should say, though I know nothing about horses.'

I peered round the yard. Casterman stood before me with a faintly challenging air, as if attempting to block my gaze. I had the strong impression he wanted me out of there.

'You know, I've taken a fancy to this creature,' said I, perversely, stroking the nose of the placid horse. 'D'you think Mr Overbury would consider an offer?'

'Why sir, you may try him on the subject if you wish, though why you wish to trouble yourself with such a useless old pony I could not say. There surely cannot be many more miles left in him!'

'He's slow, but he'll be steady,' I answered, again patting

the nose of the subject of the conversation, who tried to butt my arm in an unendearing way.

'Then if you seriously wish to make an offer, come into the house and speak to Mr Overbury on the subject now. The sooner the disposition is made the better, surely.'

The sooner we can get rid of you, is what I think he meant.

We walked across the cobbles in the direction of the house.

Mr Micah Overbury was standing in a room hung about with ornaments, baubles and filigree, a taste, I conjectured, not entirely in accordance with his own. 'Now I dare say that's a valuable vase . . .' he was saying to a young personage seated in an armchair, wrapped up tightly in a great shawl.

The young personage turned her face in my direction. I stood still with surprise.

Yet, no real cause for amazement, merely that the child was so like the father! Yes, that was the same dark-red colour hair, the lively eye, the visage of Sam Westmorland, my friend, the long-dead companion of my youth. For a moment or two I was startled, so close the imprint which the vanished parent had left upon the child resembled the remembrances in my brain. Yet this was a delicate, feminine, version, with a fragility that Sam Westmorland had never possessed, and the pale face of an invalid, to boot.

'Ambrose Malfine, at your service.'

I bowed over her hand. 'I had the honour of knowing your father, Miss Westmorland and if there is any service I can perform for you, you have but to command me.'

I turned to Micah Overbury, who did not look as though he would appreciate fancy conversation. Casterman bowed towards Miss Lilian, murmured something about urgent affairs to attend to and left the room. I decided a direct approach would be the most successful with Overbury. He did not look open to any sociable subtleties – and there was something I wanted.

'Sir, I will come straight to the point. There is a dappled pony in your stables – the sole remaining occupant thereof – and I have taken a fancy to it. The truth is, my manservant needs a reliable animal to carry him around my estate, and your man of affairs, Casterman, tells me that you may be willing to dispose of the beast. Would twenty guineas be an acceptable offer?'

Twenty guineas was an outrageously good price for the pony, but I had my own reasons for wishing to close the deal quickly. I could see that this most handsome tender was an unexpected pleasure for Mr Overbury, who could not avoid smiling, try as he might. He had probably not hoped to get anything but the price of the grey pony's hide from the knacker, and twenty guineas was in truth far too much, but I did not wish to argue upon the subject and Overbury was not suspicious. People who love money seldom are when offered an excess of it. That is how so many otherwise clever men come to be cheated. Still, meanness may be a virtue in a man entrusted with the guardianship of an orphan's estate.

I had not misjudged Overbury.

'Twenty guineas? Why, we can close upon that, I think!'

'Oh, Lord Ambrose, thank you!'

This was Lilian Westmorland. 'I will be so pleased if Dobbie goes to Malfine! You know, we have had him for years and years, and I would not have wanted him to go to strangers . . . or worse. I have already lost my splendid mare after the accident.'

'Lord Ambrose does not wish to hear your tales of woe, niece! Lord Ambrose, will you make the arrangements? I'd like to dispose of the horse as soon as possible. I am making arrangements for my niece to travel abroad for her health.'

'Yes, Lord Ambrose,' added Lilian. 'My uncle has been advised that the atmosphere of Egypt would be most beneficial for my health – but I confess, I do not wish to leave the Park!'

'Egypt!' I exclaimed. 'Why, the climate of Egypt is indeed recommended by many medical men, and besides, it is a most wondrous country – full of marvels! I believe it is quite the fashion for travellers to bring back some antiquity or other from the land of the Pyramids and the Sphinx. And you will get an opportunity to travel to that ancient world! I congratulate you upon your good fortune, Miss Lilian!'

She would have replied, I believe, but Micah intervened. He broke in, 'Yes, niece, now see how I care for your welfare – Egypt is an excellent plan, and besides, I believe that many expenses that must be incurred in this country would be met at a much lesser charge in those parts!'

This, as I knew, was quite true, and if there was actually little remaining in the Westmorland coffers, then indeed it might be a wise move to shut up part of the house and send its young occupant to a good climate where she might live at little expense. Micah seemed unprepossessing, but he would have a shrewd grasp of his niece's finances and perhaps he genuinely had her welfare at heart – her financial welfare, at any rate.

Micah went on, 'In any case, I have business with merchandise shipped from the Middle East, and Casterman can deal with my affairs when you reach Cairo. I can kill two birds with one stone, you might say, and my ambition is truly to get your inheritance in good heart, as well as to keep a check on my own business matters.'

If that were so, I reflected, the Westmorland estate would surely benefit from the Overbury hand in control, for my poor friend Sam had frittered away as much as he could in a short life, and his widow, by all reports, had been a woman with luxurious tastes. The girl would not, of course, wish to be parted from her home, but such a journey would provide mental stimulation as well as physical relief from the anticipated rigours of winter. Micah might be an unattractive personality, one who would be quite inimical to my own temperament, but I should not judge him too harshly on that account. If he was careful with the Westmorland money it would be so much the better for Miss Westmorland when she came of age.

Micah was now saying briskly, 'Come, Lord Ambrose, let's to business with the horse,' and I had little choice but to follow him to the door.

'Perhaps I should take another look at him,' said I, playing my fish to make sure he had swallowed the bait.

'Now, a bargain's a bargain, is it not?'

He was well and truly hooked.

'I fear I am a creature of whim, Mr Overbury!' said I. 'I'll take another look at the horse now!'

I had my own reasons for wishing to return to the stables.

Micah Overbury's hesitation was amusing. Clearly, he was torn: if I took the horse now, then the deal was closed and I owed him ten times what the old pony was truly worth. But he would have to rely on me to be true to my word and send over the guineas.

Either he let me have my way now, or he risked that I might lose my fancy altogether.

He made up his mind.

'Take a second look at the beast, then! Aye, do so!'

He led me through the back door and to the stables.

'Let's be done with it! The sooner I have dealt with everything here, the sooner we can get it all closed up!'

I walked along the row of stables with Overbury behind.

We halted beside the grey pony's stall. 'I'll have to have a bridle with him,' said I. 'I have my own mount tethered near the woods, so I'll ride back and send my man over in a day or two to fetch this fellow. Anything will do, Mr Overbury – did I not see a length of rope or twine or some such in the neighbouring stall . . . why no, I am mistaken!'

Overbury said, 'I care not what you take him with, my lord! Will this not serve?'

He indicated an old bridle hanging nearby, which I lifted down. There was a worn saddle, too. 'Will you throw these in for another guinea, Overbury?' I asked.

The man looked overjoyed. Here was a guinea in his hand for a bit of old harness worth a few shillings at most! He plainly took me for an extravagant fool.

I strolled along, tried the bridle on the grey and led him out for a turn, in the yard, his big feet clattering on the cobbles. 'I like him!' I exclaimed. 'Let's get the horse back in the stall and I'll send my man Belos for him.' I left saddle and bridle hanging up.

Micah walked back to the house and the door slammed as he entered it, calling out over his shoulder, 'You'll send the guineas over, then, Lord Ambrose?' as he turned on the step, and I raised a hand in acknowledgement.

I would ride on my Arab mare Zaraband; I could not lead the grey with me, for we would make but slow progress. Zaraband would kick up her heels crossly at being slowed down to the pace of this equine Chelsea Pensioner. Belos could go over to Westmorland Park with the twenty guineas

– no, twenty-one – and ride the grey horse back. The exercise would do both of them good.

On the way back to Malfine, I purposed to call in at Lute House, the residence of Dr and Mrs Sandys, which stood only a mile or two from the grounds of Westmorland Park.

They had been living there only a short time, for Murdoch Sandys had not been long in the district. Upon qualifying at Edinburgh he had, I understood, practised in one of the poorest districts of that city. I have the impression that he might be there yet, but Mrs Sandys desired to have their children brought up in more health-giving circumstances; when her elderly aunt left Lute House to them in her will, it seemed like a God-given opportunity to move to a balmier and healthier clime and furthermore the house was surrounded by sufficient grounds for Sandys to have a laboratory for his scientific investigations built on to the back.

Nevertheless, this removal from Edinburgh to Somerset did not seem to mean any diminution of Sandys' professional labours: he does not spare himself in his dedication to medicine, and, between attending on the country people and pursuing his own scientific labours, he sometimes appears quite exhausted. 'Do you write it up for me, my lord!' he exclaimed, when I recently asked him to make his own record of events to set with these papers. 'For I confess, I am often so weary of an evening that I fall asleep there in the parlour while Florence is pouring my tea! I should make a bad fist of any memoir I might engage to write, for I am dog-tired after my rounds! Do you think, by the way, that there is any chance of persuading the country people not to swaddle their babies up tight after the old tradition – their small limbs get no fresh air or exercise whatsoever?'

'Nay,' I answered, 'you must not apply to me for information concerning nurslings, but this I will tell you, that you will not get them to change their ways – it is the nature of the English to do as their ancestors have done from generation unto generation, no matter how plainly foolish the tradition – why, if there was a custom hereabouts to leap into a pit of blazing pitch on Lammas Day, they would all go a-leaping with cries of joy into the conflagration. What is Lammas Day, by the by?'

'Lord Ambrose, I am no more of an expert in these traditions than are you yourself!' says Sandys. 'In any event, I must beg to cry off the task of recording the medical events surrounding the Egyptian Coffin. If you need assistance, Florence will help you, I am sure, for she often acts as my amanuensis, and I keep nothing from her. You may apply to her for any details you need for your narrative.'

We had enjoyed many such lively conversations when he attended me at Malfine. I liked his talk more than his healing powers, for there is little enough philosophy amid the turnips, and Sandys is a reflective man, ready enough to relish a discussion of the ideas of Locke or Hume, with whom he is well acquainted. And I found him well informed about science and, wishing to be kept abreast of new discoveries, I offered Murdoch Sandys my highest accolade, the run of my library, the only part of this great house which is properly maintained, as is my pleasure. Wealth is to be valued for what the possessor of it is excused from doing, as much as for what he may do with his riches, for a poor tenant must struggle to keep his roof in repair, yet if I chose to let mine fall in, why there is no overweening landlord who can say me nay. My inner self alone can dictate my deeds.

I found as my wounds healed that I was becoming human in my convalescence, for I found myself wishing for a conversationalist, yet one who was no prating gossip nor portsodden boor such as dot the landscape hereabouts. There were only four persons living in Malfine, rattling round like so many peas in an enormous empty pod; the household consisted of myself, little Edmund Crawshay, Miss Elisabeth Anstruther, and my manservant, the aforesaid Belos. There was a groom who resided over the stables and a woman from the village who came in to do the cooking, also, but they did not sleep in the house. So I talked often and enough with Sandys, but there is nothing that tells one so much about a man as seeing him beside his own hearth, in the bosom of his family, which I had never yet done, for one may learn as much by observing how a person is treated by those closest to him as by questioning him openly – indeed, a great deal more sometimes, when the person concerned is shrewd and quick to know that their mind is being searched by another.

On that particular day when I rode from Westmorland Park to Lute House, Zaraband whinnied in an excitable fashion, wanting to gallop full out and protesting at being trotted sedately up the drive of Lute House, and thus no doubt alerting the occupants of our arrival well in advance.

Mrs Sandys was evidently fond of roses, for late-flowering damasks bloomed in the flower-beds.

I tethered Zaraband, who immediately, and just as the front door swung open, stretched out her excessively long glossy Arab neck and began to munch on a soft-pink bloom.

A pretty face peeped enquiringly out of the doorway, the blue eyes wide open with curiosity.

'Madam, Lord Ambrose Malfine at your service. I must beg to apologise for Zaraband! I am afraid she is dreadfully indulged, and this is the result – she is ruining the most delightful display of roses in England! Why, you must have an exquisite taste to grow these old damask varieties – may I compliment you upon your natural eye for beauty?'

I could see that the lady who had opened the door to me herself, not waiting for a servant, was attempting to take in all the details of my appearance, and I conjectured that she was asking herself whether this polite stranger (albeit he was dark-visaged with a long white scar running down the side of his cheek) and the flower-munching horse were indeed those staples of local legend, the hermit of Malfine and his demonic steed.

Politeness took over and won the battle with curiosity in the breast of Florence Sandys. And, try as she might to be proprietorially stern about the roses, she somehow curtseyed, invited me into the parlour, sat me down, hissed to a young person named Emmie to bring one of the best cups, and poured China tea in a thin smoky stream while her spouse, on the other side of the tea-table, woke unobtrusively from a nap.

'Ah, madam, what a charming house!'

'Yes, my lord, we are very fortunate, but I wish Murdoch would not drive himself too hard, for I fear he is too hard-working already – there are not enough hours in the day for him, I declare!'

'This is a social call, I assure you,' said I, hastily, in view of this heavy hint that they were to be undisturbed. 'I desired to ask about the condition of Miss Lilian Westmorland, who is the daughter of an old friend of mine. I understand her uncle purposes to take her to Egypt – do you really think her health will stand up to such an enterprise, Dr Sandys?'

'I have not been taken into Mr Overbury's confidence,' said Sandys, 'but I judge it would do Miss Lilian good to spend the winter in a warm dry climate. To tell you the truth, I am somewhat perturbed by her condition. Having to keep her strapped up and partly immobilised so that the fractures will heal has prevented her from taking exercise and from properly expanding her lungs – and besides, her appetite seems very poor. She is not recovering as she should! I wish she had half of your powers of recuperation, Lord Ambrose!'

'But it was not merely physically that poor Miss Lilian was suffering. She was, it seems, uncommonly distressed because her mare had to be shot after the accident,' said I.

'She can't seem to understand why,' said Murdoch Sandys. 'I told her it was best the poor beast should be put out of its suffering and that no one could hold her uncle to blame. But all she said was that I did not see Selene myself – but the girl was feverish, it must be acknowledged, and not entirely lucid. In any case, I shall be attending her no longer.'

It was obviously with mixed feelings that he then recounted his latest visit to Westmorland Park.

'Mr Overbury received me,' he said, 'and told me my services would no longer be required. He said that he thought his niece should travel abroad for her health, and that it had been determined that Egypt had the best climate to aid her recovery.'

Murdoch Sandys went on to say that he was quite pleased by this news, as far as the welfare of his patient went, for he had no doubt but that a change of scene and a warm winter would do the girl a power of good. But he was somewhat aggrieved, as I could see from the way he banged one of Mrs Sandys' best teacups into its saucer, by the arbitrary suddenness of the decision.

Murdoch looked weary, I thought; his hair was rumpled, his cravat awry.

'You work hard, Sandys, it is very true. I dare say all your time is taken up by your patients.'

Poor Murdoch ran his hand over his face, as if to wipe away his weariness with the gesture. 'It is true that I had ambitions, yes, as Florence could tell you. Could you not, my dear? But my aspirations lay elsewhere altogether – when I was studying at Edinburgh I had hoped perhaps to become a specialist in epidemic diseases – so much work was being done in that field! Think of the work of Dr Jenner of Berkeley, for example – and he was a mere country doctor such as myself, when all was said and done.'

'Well, Murdoch, I beg you,' said Mrs Sandys, 'do set aside some time for your own studies! It is so rare for us to be uninterrupted by demands for your attendance!'

'Oh, I must leave you in peace, Mrs Sandys! But one more question, if I may – do you happen to know what became of the groom at Westmorland Park? I understand he had a good reputation, and I myself am in need of another man – I have bought a pony from the Westmorland stables.'

'Why, no, I have no idea what became of the fellow. I believe Mr Overbury said Adams was greatly to blame for the young lady's accident, and sent him off without a penny piece of his wages. His sister lives near Malfine, in the village, I believe. You might make enquiries there, I suppose, but to my knowledge the man has not been seen since.'

'Yes,' put in Mrs Sandys, 'he has an unmarried sister; a very respectable personage, I understand, but there are just the two of them in the family – at least, so my maid tells me. She says that Miss Adams is a plain-speaking, ordinary sort of person, and not like to marry at her age . . . oh, I do beg your pardon, I am running on somewhat with mere gossip!'

I thought of the pock-faced man, Casterman, whom I had met in the stables. Had he been responsible for turning the groom away? I asked the Sandys if they knew aught of him, but they had not seen nor heard of him.

'Though I would like to hear the history of his illness,' added Murdoch, 'for it sounds as if he has been through a smallpox epidemic.'

Somehow I felt that Casterman would not welcome being questioned as to the terrible malady he had suffered, and who could blame him? It had left him bearing the mark of it for the rest of his life.

'Well, it's scarcely worth troubling further in the matter. Here's an end of the story, it seems! The horse has been shot, the groom – Adams – has been sent packing, and the young lady will be off to Egypt! I think my idle curiosity can prevail no longer. I shall leave the business there, and I am sorry to have taken up your time, Dr Sandys. Madam, my compliments. Pray, do not trouble yourself – oh, I see, I must make good the damage done to your roses!'

CHAPTER 4

On the following day, there was some business to be transacted at Callerton, and Belos went there on my behalf, so that it was fully forty-eight hours before I despatched him in the direction of Westmorland Park.

'I've got a horse for you, Belos, but you'll have to walk over to Westmorland Park, or get a lift with the carter, and then ride it back to Malfine. Aren't you Shakespearean troopers always calling for a horse? "A horse, a horse, my kingdom for a horse?" You can ride a horse, I take it?'

I suddenly realised I had never actually seen him on horseback.

'Yes, my lord!' he said, with considerable scorn. 'I had a splendid white stallion with a gilded bridle for *Henry V*. A magnificent beast. I rode through the streets of Bath at the head of the troupe and we were all in costume, to drum up custom for the theatre! They were fighting one another for tickets, after that! Oh, what a crush – and there was a glittering company in the boxes. It was a magnificent spectacle and the takings were the highest ever known! Ah, yes – now that horse was a *steed*!'

A guilty expression must have stolen over my face as I thought of the stout dappled pony over at Westmorland Park. Belos fixed me with a suspicious eye. I hastily added, 'Well, I am afraid this is not quite so splendid a creature – but on

47

the other hand you will be glad this animal is nothing like Zaraband, for I know you mistrust her temperament – this is a calm, steady, reliable beast!'

'Has the horse a name, my lord?'

'Why . . . I believe . . .' I cleared my throat. 'I believe it is called Dobbie.'

'Dobbie!'

Never have I heard such declamation, such clarion delivery, such utterly Thespian scorn concentrated upon the enunciation of a single word.

Belos repeated the name on a rising inflection of pained outrage. '*Dobbie*, my lord?'

'Of course, you can re-name the animal, Belos,' I added hastily. 'You can call it anything you like . . . call it Fancy . . . or Thunderboots . . .' I tailed off rather lamely, as Belos eyed me, suspecting some mockery.

'I shall call the horse Barbary,' he said, with great dignity. 'That was the name of the King's stallion in *Richard II*.'

'Barbary! Now there's a magnificent name. Yes, Barbary,' I heard him saying under his breath as he took his leave. He tried it over again on his tongue, and went off in the direction of Westmorland Park with his head held high. In kingly fashion, perhaps.

I strolled in the direction of the village that lies just outside the Malfine grounds. We have but one street here – and that you can hardly call a street, merely a muddy track, with two rows of tumbledown cottages, cob-built, out of the very earth itself. An ale-house at the end of the street is our one concession to social merriment, and Belos from time to time slips in there for a mug of porter; I suspect him of a taste for low life, though he insists that we keep up standards at Malfine, eating off plates and such mincing manners. But seriously, the truth is that he has a need for company from time to time, which I myself do not share. It is hard, after all, to have been an actor performing night after night in a crowded theatre, always to have been amongst jostling fellows and lively theatricals, and then to be buried in the depths of the countryside. His devotion to me entails sacrificing some aspects of his own nature. 'Belos,' I have said to him, 'My wounds are healed – if the life here makes you discontent, I beg you to leave and join a troupe of your Thespian comrades – why, I will ensure that you have sufficient means to set up as a – what d'you call it – an actor-manager, and then you can spout Shakespeare to your heart's content.'

But he will not leave me. Once, I saved his life, and now he bears the burden of that.

At any rate, on this occasion I did not purpose to take myself near the ale-house, for I did not wish to embarrass Belos who might have stopped there for some refreshment on his way to Westmorland Park. I walked therefore through the fields on the outskirts; there was a slight touch of frost in the air this morning. An urchin was idly throwing stones at a cat.

'Leave that off!'

The child dropped the pebble in his fist. The cat disappeared into the distance.

'Do you know where Miss Adams lives? Her brother was a groom over at Westmorland Park?'

The child gawped, recovered some of his wits, and pointed to the end of the row of cottages. There was one slightly larger than the rest, with a porch in which were signs of habitation such as a wet and muddy pair of pattens, but when I knocked on the door there was no response and after I had called and waited for a few minutes, I suspected that Miss Adams, if she were there, was not going to open her door.

49

The urchin had come running after me.

'He's gone away, mister. Ain't no one seen neither of them these two days.'

I gave it up.

A few days later the weather changed. An afternoon came that was cold and damp and there was an autumn mist swirling unpleasantly over the lake at Malfine. I was relieved that my charge, the boy Edmund, had left for his school in Hampshire before this saddest and gloomiest time of the year. And, though I grieved for myself that Elisabeth would be leaving shortly for her parents' house in Bristol, I pictured her and the boy both, safe and warm in their separate settings, with companions around them, and all that affection and friendship that Malfine, for all its splendour, never promised.

It must have been about three o'clock when I saw a horse and rider through the grey wisps of fog that had settled in the hedges and along the driveway. Belos, with his new charge. They had been out for a ride that afternoon.

Both of them were puffed and panting, hastening along as fast as the old grey could manage.

'My lord – oh curse this animal, I could not get him to go any faster – my lord, you are asked to come directly to Doctor Sandys!'

'Belos, what is it? Surely it is usually the other way around – Dr Sandys is sent for in great haste when the sick and suffering have need of him, but is he now summoning his patients? A novel way of drumming up business!'

'Do not jest, sir! There has been a dreadful tragedy. A young girl has been murdered and the body found near the lodge at Westmorland Park. Dr Sandys has been called to the spot, and desired me to make all the haste I could to fetch you over.'

The humour that the sight of Belos and his puffing
Barbary had evoked vanished in a second. 'What girl,
Belos? Tell me who it was?'

'My lord, I do not know – I did not see the body, which
I understand was found just outside the gates of the Park.
Dr Sandys chanced to meet me in the stables and sent me
over to fetch you with all haste.'

I had a sudden frightful vision: the body of Lilian
Westmorland trailing in the dirt, and all that dark red hair
bedabbled with mud to a rusty, blood-coloured tangle, wet,
dirty, matted with slimy greenery, as I had once seen the head
of her father. As I had last seen the head of her father, before
it finally disappeared beneath the waters of the river.

The failing light of an autumn evening was settling over the
countryside when I arrived. Murdoch Sandys was standing
over a dark shape huddled up on the ground, near the railings
that surrounded Westmorland Park.

He had been summoned to this spot by the lodge-keeper,
an old fellow who was in a high state of excitement. He was a
village ancient who had kept the gates of Westmorland Park
for many a year, and had been allowed to stay on by Micah
Overbury after the death of Mrs Westmorland.

The old man's aching joints would not let him sleep at
night, so he did not stay quietly within the rather dour, grey
lodge, but roamed around at night, walking for miles while
the rest of the world was in bed, and no doubt pondering
on the negligence of gardeners and landowners as he passed
along the heaps of leaves piling up round the railings at
Westmorland Park.

He had a dog, a well-trained animal, normally obedient
to his master's slow pace. This animal, yapping with a
frantic excitement, had suddenly began to pull the old

fellow closer to the railings. Between the railings, the dog got hold of something with his teeth which he was dragging and chewing with a slavering anxiety that seemed in itself to have been disturbing to behold. Said the old fellow to Murdoch Sandys; ' 'Twere more like a wild animal snatching at a piece of carrion that a tame critter on the end of a leash.'

Something, Murdoch conjectured, had been aroused in the dog, some deep instinct which humans fear to see surfacing from under the obedience which we enforce on other species.

'I told the beast to leave off,' said the lodge-keeper, 'but he had his teeth fast. "Stop worriting at it! Leave it alone!" That's what I were telling him, but the damn dog took no notice.'

The old man had been cruel, no doubt with frightened anticipation, and said he had struck the creature across the muzzle with his stick, but the creature would not let go of the thing it had in its jaws, which the old man still could not properly see, because it was hidden beneath a pile of leaves.

It seemed that the tugging movements of the dog had brought something into view, the first thing that the old man saw.

It was a hand. The dog had its teeth sunk into the wrist.

The hand was dabbled with something dark that might have been mud or blood. As the owner of the dog stared in a dawning realisation, a face came sideways into view from under the heap of leaves, jerking horribly, the dead eyes rolling as the dog tugged and an arm was pulled sideways.

Yet this was not the strangest nor the most horrible thing about this death.

In case this document may be read by eyes who are not

familiar with the persons and places I describe, I should explain that Westmorland Park has tall iron gates with handsome curlicues, and iron railings surround the expanse of its grounds, sweeping along to demarcate Westmorland territory and curving in a long swoop that leads towards the gates. It was just there, near a patch of shrubbery close to the lodge, that the body lay. Outside the railing leaves had piled up, blown by the west winds of autumn, unnoticed and untended by any gardeners. Indeed, I think that there were no more gardeners kept on, for I believe that horticulture was one of the expenses which Micah Overbury intended to cut down on. Here it was, outside the main gates, that the old man had come upon the body.

As I bent over this wretched victim and gently lifted the head a little the bonnet slipped to one side; I could see immediately that this was not Lilian Westmorland, even before I saw the face, for I had observed Lilian's hair had been cut short because of her fever whereas this girl had long locks that tumbled down as her bonnet tilted.

On this occasion, I confess that my immediate reaction, cruel though it may be thought, was relief, in so far as the death of a comparative stranger would inevitably mean less to me than that of the daughter of my boyhood friend, Sam Westmorland.

I did recognise this girl, however, though I had seen her on one occasion only.

'It is the housemaid from the Park,' I said to Sandys. 'I do not know her name, but she opened the door to me when I called on Lilian Westmorland.'

Without our actually discussing the matter, I realised why Sandys had sent for me, rather than for Sir Anderton Revers, who was actually the nearest magistrate. It was because I, Ambrose Malfine, am no respecter of the station of persons.

As Sandys sensed from the many conversations we had held during those visits he had paid to me when I was his patient, I may be regarded by my neighbours as an eccentric, and many would say that the most eccentric belief of all is this: I hold that one man, under all the flummery of wealth and titles, is no better than another – a view which is considered sedition even to utter in this besmirched country of ours – and therefore that one man's daughter is as good as another, and that this death of some wretched starveling skivvy did indeed merit investigation. Upon this point the stubbornly upright Scots doctor and the eccentric aristocratic recluse were in agreement.

'I'd like to take her back to Lute House,' said the doctor. It's too dark to see anything here, and the old man says he can't get an answer at Westmorland Park. I have my laboratory at Lute House, where I can try to find out what has happened to her.'

So I gave instructions. The body of the girl, little more than a child, was taken up and put on a rough-and-ready stretcher made out of a plank fetched from the Lodge and, covered by a blanket, carried to Lute House by two men called out from the village.

Sandys and I turned to walk behind, like a pair of mourners in a sad little funeral procession, and he said in a low voice, when the stretcher had gone a little way ahead so that the men carrying it could not overhear.

'There was something else. Something that means this is certainly murder – and perhaps after the most terrible sufferings.'

He was quite right to keep his voice low. If the country folk had known what he was about to tell me, they would have been all and every one in a cold sweat of fear.

Sandys told me what had happened when the lodge-keeper

summoned him from Lute House. 'I touched her cheek, doctor,' the old fellow said, when they arrived at the spot where the body lay. 'But it were cold. It were terrible cold.'

Murdoch had taken charge temporarily. He brushed aside a sweep of dry leaves, and uncovered part of a skirt, and then gently, little by little, the body of a young woman.

But this was not what proved to be most shocking.

Murdoch Sandys has practised medicine in the roughest areas of the city of Edinburgh, and in those narrow teeming tenements he has, I believe, seen every kind of injury that one human creature may inflict on another. No, it was not the poor child's dead body that horrified a seasoned medical man such as Murdoch.

It was something else altogether.

The cold chink of steel that slid onto the ground as her lifeless body was taken up. Murdoch stooped and took the metal in his hand.

Now, as we walked along side by side in the dusk, Murdoch held up something which glinted in the fast-fading light.

Two gleaming interlocked circles, like crude bracelets, but sharp-edged, and joined with a length of chain.

Manacles.

'Somebody has used the poor child grievously ill,' commented Sandys, 'and I care not whether she is a duke's daughter or a kitchen maid, I want to take some trouble to discover what has happened to her.'

With this, I concurred.

'The Park seems all shut up – there is a woman from the village there, a Mrs Martin, who says that Miss Lilian, her maid Jennet and the steward – or whatever he calls himself – the man Casterman – have departed for Southampton, where they are to take ship to Egypt! Micah Overbury has taken them to Southampton docks. The Martin woman was brought in only to spread the dustsheets on the furniture.'

'Good God, man!' I exclaimed. 'Have they left so soon?'

'Aye, apparently the *Great London* departs at six o'clock tonight with the evening tide – a vessel with both steam and sail; you know, there is a General Steam Navigation Company now which commissions passenger vessels for long journeys and I believe this is one of their ships. My wife heard that special rates were offered to encourage passengers to travel by steam, so I daresay that is why Overbury has decided his niece should travel by such a new-fangled means of transport! But I confess, I do not care for the idea of Lilian Westmorland travelling with that scar-faced fellow, Casterman, though I try to think that we must be generous and not allow ourselves to be prejudiced by the man's face. I wish she had someone to protect her – someone we could trust. Too late now, I fear!'

'Yes,' I answered, for there were but three hours to go before the vessel sailed, and no earthly way of reaching Southampton in that time. And yet, I suddenly bethought myself of a possibility, an outside chance.

'Do the ships out of Southampton not stop at Falmouth for mail? The last point at which they can pick up the packets and letters for Malta and Alexandria – surely that is when they anchor in Falmouth roads? The *Great London* will be there in twenty-four hours – and will take the evening tide from Falmouth tomorrow night!'

'Why, Lord Ambrose, you are in the right of it! But that's still no comfort to us – no creature alive could catch up with the *Great London* now – she is a steamship!'

'You are wrong, Sandys,' said I. 'There is a horse that can catch her! Zaraband can do it!'

CHAPTER 5

Elisabeth stepped out of the great portico at the front of Malfine. She was wrapped up against the autumn gales in a black cloak of wadded silk; her hood and long tendrils of escaping hair fluttered about her face.

I took her hands. I had found her in a perilous household, that murderous nest at Crawshay's Farm, where she had been forced to keep her own counsel, separated as she was from any family or friends who could protect or advise her, and had brought her to the safety of Malfine, where we two had shared a small kingdom for a brief time, now perhaps to end.

She is a brave spirit, and I did not flatter myself that she would be unable to stand the buffets of this world without me. Yet I had found her after so much suffering, and when least expected, so that her presence at Malfine was constantly surprising and marvellous to me and leaving her was now proportionately painful. And not only because we are of like mind and spirit, she and I.

The thought of her long white body under that fluttering silk pulled me back to her now, but she said: 'No, Ambrose, go you must; you have taken the protection of this girl upon yourself, for all you would deny the power of the world beyond. I have feared losing our life here – have dreaded it every night since you brought me here, if the truth be known, for we have led an enchanted existence at Malfine, as though this house were on a star. But I knew it could not long continue and the hubbub of the world must one day reach us with all its absurd and frantic cries.'

I released her and stroked a strand of that long soft hair which the wind was whipping about her face. Would she wait for me? That was in my mind, for the life that her parents could offer her if they wished for a reconciliation – a comfortable and respected life in a handsome establishment – how could my scarred body and my solitary existence and desires compete with that? It was not impossible that the loss of Elisabeth, the end of our hot and naked passions as well as of our cooler celebral intimacies, would be the price. The price, that is, of my redemption from a long-forgotten yet inescapable bond.

Her hands were cold.

'Do not stay here, I beg you, get back into the house and sit near the fire in the library till the carriage comes round.'

For we were bound to go our separate ways, at least for a while. She was leaving for her family home in Bristol, and I was to ride with desperation across a cold countryside in a last-minute effort to watch over the child of my old friend and to guard her from the harm that I sensed was closing in around her.

'I hate farewells!' said I to Elisabeth. 'I cannot delay this departure, I swear it, for I must get aboard the *Great London* when she anchors off the coast. It is just possible we can make Falmouth in time, and if I can travel on that ship, I may yet be able to protect the girl!'

'Is there nothing with which they can be charged?' said Elisabeth. 'Surely those two men – Casterman and Miss Westmorland's uncle – have they not transgressed any law? To shut up the house, to separate her from all her friends – does this not augur some great ill-will towards her?'

'There is nothing with which either of them can be charged,' I said. 'What would I be able to lay before a judge – that Micah Overbury has a tight fist? That Casterman has a pock-marked face? We have no evidence that points to their involvement with the murder of that poor child – yet I fear for Lilian Westmorland if she is travelling with Casterman, and away from her friends and neighbours here! One death has occurred already at the very gates of Westmorland Park, and I had the clearest impression that Casterman was determined to keep me away from the stables there. I cannot trust either of them, Casterman or his employer. You know there is a debt I must repay, and I am persuaded that this is my only means of doing it. God knows why I am such a fool as to be cursed with this damned sense of honour that jumps out now and again!'

'There is no gainsaying it! What can I do but wait till the fit passes! But, seriously, I fear for you, yet nothing will persuade you to a safer course of action, so I must turn my back and leave for Bristol, and make my peace with my mamma, for I will not wait for you here at Malfine and fret my life away in your absence. Write to me when you can, that is all I ask.' Elisabeth turned and walked towards the house, without looking back.

Had I lost her? Some women will wait and wail; others will stride away. It is not always those who sob and plead who are the most devoted, but those who will not wait are the ones we cannot forget.

Action, not thought, was my best course now.

I plunged with relief into the distraction of issuing orders. Belos, a fellow of modest appearance, a man who is almost unnoticeable to a fault as I often tell him, a person of average height, with nondescript brown hair and sober garments, stood calmly like the still centre of a hurricane as I whirled around him with last-minute commands. When I was in my hot youth, I would have leaped upon Zaraband's back straightaway and we should have dashed off into the storm with no thought or preparation whatsoever as I had done when fighting with the Greek guerillas, whose impetuousness knew no check. But I had learnt a little since then.

'Belos, if I make the rendezvous at Falmouth, I shall be travelling to Egypt. Will you arrange to have some necessaries despatched after me, into the care of the British Consul in Alexandria? And will you give it out that it is for my own health, and that I go to join my sister, who has hired a houseboat on the Nile for the winter?'

'Your lordship is surely taking a risk in exposing yourself to the rigours of such a climate. But, Lord Ambrose, is there not more to your sudden decision to embark for Egypt? Your sister, Miss Ariadne has been in Cairo for six months or more!'

'You are a shrewd fox, Belos! Well, there is something more – aye, that's true enough. Well, I think no one in these parts knows of that, so they should not find fault with the explanation that you give them. But look, will you not write to me and send the letters by the fast packet?' Here I had to issue more instructions, swinging my heavy riding cloak over my shoulders the while. Belos handed me a leather flask of brandy which I thrust into a pocket.

Even as we spoke, the groom, Pellers, came round the corner of the house, leading Zaraband. She was my only chance of getting across three counties, of covering moor and dale even in a bitter autumn, as it seemingly was turning out to become. If anything could get me to the port of Falmouth in time to meet the *Great London* as she started her long voyage to the east, if anything could dash between Lilian Westmorland and those who might desire to threaten her, it was this slender Arab mare, delicately boned, hard as steel, fast as the very winds of heaven.

'Fetch a horse-blanket. Roll it up and strap it on the saddle,' I said to Pellers. 'You are to follow by the stage coach to Falmouth, along the road through Newton Abbot and Buckfastleigh. I will leave Zaraband in the stables of the Royal Hotel at Falmouth – they have a man there who knows about horses. And then you can ride her home – in easy stages, mind! We have the devil's own task before us, Zaraband and I!'

Zaraband whinnied exultantly as I approached and set my foot in the stirrup. She longs for the challenge – that is her touch of greatness! And, like myself, she finds that challenge impossible to resist, and therein perhaps lies a fatal flaw which is common to our natures. We have saved each other time and again, Zaraband and I, from some idiocy or another – and we have landed ourselves in many a folly, too!

Well, there was enough of a challenge here to satisfy even the great Arab heart! It is, you know, a physical fact that their hearts are stronger than those of other breeds, as their minds are more intelligent and their courage higher.

The night lay before us. I counted that we had a little over twenty-four hours – perhaps about twenty-six – before the *Great London*, which had both steam and sail, winched up her mighty iron anchors and those massive steam-pistoned engines thrust her out towards the Atlantic, there to beat her thousand horse-power way round the Bay of Biscay regardless of wind or tide, her stokers like demons in hell shovelling coal into her furnaces, and so south till she anchored again in the calmer waters of the Mediterranean.

Against the immense strength of those engines, I could set only the frailty of flesh and blood – but it was the flesh and blood of an Arab mare. Zaraband is of the *asil* kind – that is, the purest of all the lines of descent, coming from the stock of the Five Mares beloved by the Prophet.

Pellers, the groom, I had employed after I caught him one day sneaking into the stables at Malfine: he was watching, a runty little fellow who had crept up from the village, his eyes as big as saucers, as Zaraband emerged from her stall. 'Beg pardon, sir – my lord – I have never seen anything like it – like this horse, my lord . . .' he was stuttering as I gripped him by his collar.

'What do you make of her?' I asked him.

Even as he struggled to answer me, and I felt his body shaking with fear, he still could not take his eyes off her. 'Describe the horse! Tell me what you see!' I shook him a little, just to persuade him.

He stumbled over his words, struggling hard to find them. 'Well, her head is very delicate – and she is quite small – much smaller than Squire Anderton's hunter. But she goes fast – fast as the wind – I saw you galloping through the woods one night – I've never seen such speed!'

'That's right,' I said. 'The Arabs are smaller than other horses. But they are also faster and stronger. They have more endurance, you see.'

I told him more about Arab horses: how they have immense intelligence, as is shown by the *jibbah,* or the great bulge of the forehead, so prized by the Arabs. How the muzzle is small, delicate and sensitive, yet the windpipe and the hind-quarters comparatively larger and more powerful than in any other breed. I told him the tale of Faris, the great Arab horseman who is credited with choosing the Five Mares from whom all Arab horses are descended. I told the gap-mouthed boy of the War Mares, the fearless creatures who share the Arab tents, are ridden into battle, and will defend their masters from all-comers.

'Can I touch the horse?' he said with awe when I had finished.

Zaraband courteously allowed him to place his hand timidly on her muzzle. This was unusual: she normally objected loudly to the approach of any of the heavy-handed local stableboys, none of whom I had thought of as remotely suitable to attend her.

'She does not mind you and I need a groom,' I said to young Pellers. (I had released his collar by this stage in our acquaintance.) 'Have you had any experience of horses?'

'Oh no, sir – your worship – none whatever!'

And he looked utterly woebegone and downcast, but he soon took heart.

'That is exactly what I want – someone who will learn to serve as groom for this particular creature. I would not want any village ostler or squire's stableboy, used to broken-spirited ill-fed hacks and worn-out ponies. I keep no other grooms but if you want to stay at Malfine, I will teach you your duties myself. But mind, you are to sleep over Zaraband's stable, and do not go near any other horse. You are for her alone, remember. It is not a question of training the horse, but of training you.'

That had been a year before, and I thanked Heaven for my foresight; I had now a well-versed groom whom I could trust to bring Zaraband back safely. But getting to Falmouth was the first consideration.

I have said that I did not dash off into the night like some young fool, without forethought or preparation – many a horse has been ruined by such idiocy, and I had worked out our route. The whole distance we must cover would be a good hundred and twenty miles, before we could come to Falmouth harbour. Young Pellers could take the coach which would follow the roads to the south of Dartmoor. But Zaraband and I must go the fastest way – and I confess that my heart sank when I stood in the library at Malfine, held a candle high over the maps spread out on the table, and saw the path we must follow. Through a gap in the Quantock Hills to Taunton – well, that presented no difficulty. Then keeping north of the Black Down Hills to Exeter. So far, so good; we could be well provisioned in such places. We would cross many small streams and water would be no problem.

But then I saw where we had to go. Right across the wilderness – straight over Dartmoor, that great expanse of emptiness, exposed to all the elements, between rocky tors and treacherous bogs, through the harshest moorland in England.

I did not doubt for a moment that Zaraband could do it. But it would be my part, if anything, to keep her in check, to prevent that mighty courage from driving itself to breaking-point. Another horse might have needed spurring on: Zaraband would, I knew, need no urging, for once she was galloping flat out without restraint, she would give every ounce of strength she possessed.

Now, on this cold wet evening, I swung myself up into the saddle. 'Belos, you will have thought this horse a spoiled and pampered creature,' I said. 'Oh yes, do not deny it – I have seen it in the way you look at her. But now you will know why I pamper her so. There is not another horse in England who could ride one hundred and twenty miles in four and twenty hours!'

He raised his hand in a salute, saying something. I heard not what he said, for Zaraband had already danced away into the night and the wind was rushing past as we galloped for the Quantock Hills. There was moonlight enough to see the road that lay ahead and the fresh winds of night blew out along our path; we were two creatures that longed for escape, for excitement, I realised. That was in both our natures, horse and man alike.

Our road lay through a part of Britain with ancient traditions, the West Country which had possessed its own kingdoms, its own legends, its own language, a part lying remote and isolated still, which had often rejected attempts to govern it from the remoteness of London. As we rode into the heart of this rebellious and stubborn land, I was aware that we were in some way moving deeper and deeper into England's past, a dark history that closed about like mist, and then was blown away again, so that it was forever wraith-like and uncaught.

I had not concerned myself much with this – the hot and sunlit history of my mother's land of Greece had captured my imagination in my youth, but now I felt myself for the first time conscious of those old curling vaporous ghosts that whirled and parted before us in our race for the coast. Through the gap in the Quantocks, we reached Taunton, and swept through the town, past the White Hart Inn, and I knew the spot – I had been told of it some time in that forgotten childhood – where West Country rebels who rose for the Duke of Monmouth had been hanged by the bloody and ruthless Colonel Kirke of infamous memory.

We had been fortunate, with moonlight to show us the road; the thickest part of the night was over and early in the wintry dawn we clattered into Exeter. I pulled into the livery stables, shook a surprised ostler by the shoulder, bade him bring fodder and water. For myself, I strode into the empty dining-room of the inn and carved myself a slice of beef, flinging a coin down on the table in my haste and taking a pull of wine. An hour's break here: I took mine lying in straw next to Zaraband's stall. When you have served in an army, even one as ragged and ill-disciplined as the band of guerrillas I had led in that hopeless raid upon the shores of Crete, you learn to take your rest when you can.

There was an orange glow of chilly sunshine as we rode out of Exeter and towards the wall of mist that lay beyond the town. I knew what that mist portended: the moor, the rugged hard heart of southern Britain, and the keeper of many old secrets of its history. We had to cover the forty miles between Exeter and Tavistock on the other side of Dartmoor along the rough track that lay across the very loneliest stretch of the moor; Dartmoor Forest would lie to the north of the road, the bright-green grass patches of treacherous swampland to the south.

It was bitterly cold out there in the mist, yet as the morning sun rose and the white clouds that hung so heavily over the land gradually lost themselves in shreds and wisps, like the intimations of a strange history which I had sensed during the previous night, I felt an exhilaration such as I had not experienced since my return from Greece – the excitement that came from straining every nerve, of feeling life pouring through every vein in my body. Zaraband was moving at a fine pace, yet I sensed that she still had strength in reserve and every ten miles or so we seemed to find a little stream where she could drink. We had a short stop at Two Bridges, the hamlet that marks the crossing-point of the two routes over the moor, where I flung the horse-blanket over her back to keep her muscles from chilling while we paused, and then we were off again to the south-west. And now the afternoon sun was sinking in the sky: the evening would soon begin, and then, if we could not make it in time, the powerful screws of the *Great London* would turn the ship out to sea, and Miss Lilian Westmorland would be committed to the mercy of Casterman, with no one to watch over her.

Not for the first time, I cursed my own selflessness in appointing myself unofficial guardian of my dead friend's daughter. Why could I not leave her to her fate? After all, there was doubtless nothing wrong with the man – why should her uncle desire to place her in the care of a villain? Sandys apparently thought we should give Casterman the benefit of the doubt. I was a fool, and a fool who would alienate the woman I loved and perhaps injure the horse which was my most precious possession – and all for the sake of a chimera, an enemy whose wicked shape I alone appeared to see, no more substantial than those wraiths of mist, or those ghosts of the past that haunted our route.

Well, we were committed now. Halfway across Dartmoor there is no turning back. There, to the south of our route, lay the long black shape of Dartmoor Prison. The autumnal sun was already beginning to set and in the distance I saw the twisted and stunted trees of Wistman's Wood, that old grove of oaks that has taken on gnarled and fantastic shapes with exposure to the terrible winds and storms that sweep across the moor. I feared that night should find us with no other option than to take shelter in that sinister patch of woodland, but we were fortunate – or rather, my good fortune and the horse's courage carried us on beyond it.

Not far now to get off Dartmoor and at least be able to seek shelter if need be, and yet we must continue if our race against time was to succeed. I slowed Zaraband's pace deliberately, though: the tussocks and potholes, the old clay workings and rocky outcrops could bring her down and kill us both.

It was dark when Zaraband ran down into Saltash, and I led her aboard the ferry across the Tamar. The ferryman looked strangely at us, as well he might, for we were spattered and weary, but Zaraband still breathed easily, which was my main concern. Arab horses have extraordinarily large and free windpipes. As we crossed the river, I sank against the gunwales of the ferryboat and tipped some brandy down my throat. The rain beat down.

On, on, deeper into the lost land, to Lostwithiel, the ancient capital of Cornwall, and there, high above the river, was Restormel, castle of the Earls of Cornwall, when this county had practically been an independent kingdom, beyond the reach of London. What was this journey, thought I to myself, but a voyage into a brave and vanished past, such a journey as I myself had made when I had returned to my mother's inheritance, her lands in Crete, that I had hoped in some quixotic way to reconquer for the present?

They moulder on, these old kingdoms, those that tower like ruined castles on the land around us, and those that arise within our minds, and we can neither rebuild them nor utterly abandon them.

Fuzzy black tree-shapes indistinctly crowded the sides of a valley: St Blazey, I conjectured, with Truro beyond.

Zaraband was flagging now, undoubtedly; even her great powers of endurance could not sustain this run for much longer. I took her beyond Carnon Downs, we splashed across a creek somehow, and I put her up the slope of a side valley: then the air changed, blowing salty, harsh, and there was the great mass of a fortress, outlined against the evening sky. Pendennis Castle at Falmouth, towering over the headland and facing stoutly out across the water. And in the great sweep of Falmouth harbour was a strange outline: a ship with tall black projections against the grey light: the funnel

68

and sails of such a ship as had never been seen there before, a vessel that carried both sails and steam, a ship supposedly unbeatable by any form of transport.

The ostler at the Royal Hotel gawped as I gave the reins into his hands.

'There's a groom on the way from Malfine in Somerset to collect this horse,' says I, 'and he'll have a purse of guineas for you if you treat her right – but mind, he'll know! She's covered nigh on a hundred miles now – so let her breathe up easy!'

With a last caress and whisper for Zaraband, I rushed on down to the harbour, and as I raced over the cobbled streets a sound drifted over the water. The rattle of anchor-chain, and the low throbbing of steam-pistons as brass, steel and iron began their unyielding work in the depths of the *Great London*. A fishing-smack lay in harbour. I flung myself down into it, pointing to the great vessel which lay further out to sea. The astonished skipper hauled on his ropes, his sails filled out, and we swept with the wind across the water towards the *Great London* where she was reprising her long and relentless journey to the East.

CHAPTER 6

The Narrative of Miss Lilian Westmorland

Lord Ambrose has asked me to set down my recollections of events following my accident at Westmorland Park, though I am afraid that I have but little elegance with my pen! I lack those literary touches that other young women seem to contrive. My spelling is not always correct, and, when I am in a hurry to write, I sometimes do not seem able to find even the proper grammar, at least so Miss Pallerton, my governess, used to tell me! I am afraid I was not the most attentive of pupils to poor Miss P. I teased her sometimes, and splashed my ink about quite often, though that was not done on purpose but because my nib always seemed to splutter!

But when I said to Lord Ambrose that I would prove an artless record-keeper, he did not seem alarmed. I confess, I did not know how to begin, but he told me just to set it down as naturally as if I were writing my diary! (only, he added, not so many exclamations!). Truly, that man knows things beyond human power, for how does he know about my diary and the exclamations? I always keep it locked up

71

safely and write it only when I am sure no one is about and have never told a soul about it (well, only my dearest S., since we met, and I have shown my dearest S. one or two entries relating to himself, but I am sure he would be far too embarrassed to confide such things in Lord A. So Lord A. must have guessed, but anyway, what he said was a great help in getting me started with my pen). So I will write down all the story of the Egyptian Coffin just as if I were telling it to the pages of my diary.

The only trouble is that I remember almost nothing of the accident which led to the strange and frightening events I must relate. I recall that morning, as I set off for a canter through the park around our house, on my mare, Selene.

I should here insert something about our home, Westmorland Park, where this accident took place. It is a Gentleman's Residence, so Jennet says, built in the reign of Queen Anne, of red brick which has gone a nice soft pinkish colour. There is an orchard close to the house, and a greenhouse against the south wall, but best of all are the stables at the back, with a chiming clock set over them.

On that autumn morning, I set out very early for my ride. I had been pent up in the house for days. I should explain here that my dear mother had died six months previously, of a lingering malady, and as my father had drowned even before my birth, I was left orphaned at the age of seventeen.

I had become accustomed to pleasing myself as to when I rode or walked or took exercise. On this particular morning, I felt that a ride out in the Park would best suit my spirits, and I longed to let Selene show her paces. I did not go out on my own, for sure, because that would not have been considered at all proper, and my Uncle Micah, who was staying in the house to attend to some business, would certainly have been very angry with me. He often lectured me on ladylike behaviour, and I have inscribed my reflexions on this in the pages of my diary many times before now, so I will desist from doing so yet again. Suffice it to say that Uncle Micah did not want me 'prancing round the grounds like a wild thing', as he put it.

In any case, I took the groom, Adams, on my ride that morning, but I had soon got ahead of him, on the stout little grey pony he always rode. Selene cantered, Selene galloped, and I let her have her head, which was as I know now a wayward and foolish thing to do.

It was most especially foolish, as I later thought, to let her gallop along the narrow path between the beech trees, although we had ridden along it so many times before that I would have said she knew every inch of the way, and I knew her every hoofbeat as she thundered along it. All seemed exactly as usual: we turned into the path from the direction of the house and everything along the way seemed the same as always. I recall the wind in my hair, the leaves of the beeches flashing past – and then almost nothing, save a great dazzling light. Well, I do remember one thing more, of that I am certain. But the next thing I knew was waking up in a quite different place.

I thought I was in hell. Black shapes, with red glowing embers around them and little yellow licking flames. And thick black bars – the bars must be to imprison the wretched creatures in their torment, so there would be no escape from this never-ending infernal torture. Truly, I thought this was an inferno . . .

'Is she awake?'

Who had said that? A voice from out of the burning depths? I thought hell itself had spoken to me, or at least the very Devil. Or was this a soul in bliss, far above in paradise, as the pictures in my mother's Bible showed?

I turned my head, and found I could turn it no more than a little, just a small way to one side. Hell was still near me: the black bars and the red fire that burned my face, burned my body.

'What have I done?' I cried, for I thought I had gone to the infernal place and was being punished for some wickedness. 'I never harmed anyone!'

Then I felt some water on my forehead. Water, in the midst of the fiery furnace. Cool drops of water. Surely I once saw a picture of a man surrounded by leaping flames and trying to drink water from a pitcher above his head. The stream from the mouth of the vessel flowed out beyond the reach of his blistered lips.

But, I reasoned, if I could feel water on my face, perhaps there was some remission allowed. Perhaps I would not be made to dwell in hell forever, then. Perhaps I was being released, or at any rate, allowed some mercy. I turned towards something cool that was being pressed against my cheek.

'Can you open your eyes, miss? Try now, try for me! Please, miss, if you can, speak a word to me!'

There was a burr in the voice – as comforting as a rough towel wrapped around me.

It was Jennet.

Jennet, my mother's maid, had nursed me since I was a baby, and would never leave off now that I was seventeen.

But I must confess I was deeply relieved to hear her voice. If Jennet was with me, then this could not be Hell, for Jennet could never have been sent to the Place of Everlasting Punishment. Why, she washes in cold water every single morning!

At any rate, the voice brought me back to the real world and I opened my eyes and almost laughed at Hell.

Hell was the fireplace in my bedroom, my own dear room at the Park, where coals glowed behind the black bars of the grate.

Jennet stood at the side of the bed, a silver basin in one hand, and in the other the cloth with which she had been wiping my hot face.

She put down the basin on the night table beside the bed, and came and supported my head, propping me up on pillows as I struggled to sit up. Yes, there were the Chinese scenes on the wallpaper, my childhood friends the painted Chinese ladies and gentlemen walking beneath hanging willow-branches. There were the white bed-hangings, embroidered with the Indian pattern of birds and flowers in bright colours. How I loved, when I was a child, to pull those curtains around me when I was safely tucked up in bed, and count the red blossoms and emerald-green parrots and the crested cockatoos that adorned my own private silk-stitched garden, till I fell asleep!

'You've been very ill, Miss Lilian,' Jennet was saying. 'You can't know how ill – the truth is, I never thought . . .'

'I do feel weak, Jennet. What's wrong with me?'

'That accident you had, miss. On the horse.'

'Oh, yes, on Selene. All my fault – shouldn't have ridden her so fast, I know that. I was such a fool this morning.'

''Tweren't this morning, miss.'

'No? Well, I must have been unconscious for a while. How long – how long have I been like this?'

'Two days, now. Oh, miss, I'm that glad to hear your own dear voice again!'

'Two days? Surely that's not possible! Since I fell from Selene?'

'Yes miss. And a longer time I've never known, for I've

been sick with worry about you. Dr Sandys, he's called here three or four times.'

I remember trying to turn in the bed, and feeling an agonising pain in my side. It made me gasp out loud.

'Don't try to move, miss. You've got several cracked ribs, the doctor do say. And a nasty bang you gave your head as well.'

But I managed to put my hand up to my head and felt my scalp with a shock of horror.

Instead of the long curls of which I had been quite proud, there was a rough stubble beneath my fingertips.

The red hair that had cascaded down so thickly, the hair that Jennet had brushed with a hundred strokes every morning, making me count them ten to each finger and ten to each thumb, had gone.

I cried aloud then, and Jennet hugged me.

'Don't take on so, my dearie. I had to cut it off for you. You were in a fever, such a fever, and it's much cooler for you like this. And Dr Sandys, he wanted to see if there was any injuries to your poor head, and he could not see anything for all your lovely thick hair, though praise God he found nothing but a great lump! Oh, I cried too, when I first saw it, truly I did. But it will mend, Miss, the hair will grow again, don't you fret – why 'tis coming through already! It'll be prettier than ever, I'll be bound!'

Of course, I know really she had done right to cut my hair off – it would make no difference after a while. That great copper mane – why it made my brow ache just to think of the weight of it, the weight that my poor head would have had to carry. And the combing and the brushing of it! And how hot and sticky it would have been! Jennet was quite right. Of course she was.

'Yes, I'm just being silly about it, aren't I? I must just

try to be brave and grown up. You are right, Jennet. And it will grow again – and thicker than before. I dare say it will be all the better for it!'

What a foolish thing to make a fuss about!

All the same, I instinctively looked around the room and saw that the big cheval mirror that used to stand near the windows had been taken away. And the triple looking-glass that used to stand on my dressing table – the mirror that had been a gift from my mother on my seventeenth birthday – that had gone too.

All I remember then is that Jennet held a little cup to my lips, and I was sipping a sweet, thick concoction, that somehow had a bitterness hidden under the sugar. One sip . . . two sips . . . my eyes were closing.

It was only as I dropped off to sleep that I realised that I had not asked Jennet about Selene. But I was sure the mare would be safe in her stable. She had surely not been hurt. I had a clear picture in her mind of the mare's graceful legs whirling round and round, rolling over at the edge of the lake until the great body rose up again and stood, shaking itself, on the bank. No, Selene was safe; I was sure that the horse had got up again, had even trotted a few steps towards me after the fall. Into my mind came a vision of Selene's long head with its white blaze, coming inquiringly down above me, as I lay there helpless on the ground. I was positive sure of it. It was the last thing I could remember before waking up in my bed. Selene had got up and moved after the accident – she might be a little bruised, but her limbs were sound; she would be safe.

When I woke again, the curtains at the windows were drawn and the oil-lamps were lit. The thick velvet of the curtains shut out any chink of light that might remain in the outside world, so I had no idea of the time: whether it were the middle of the night, or early in the morning. Outside the yellow circles of light cast by the lamps, the room was in utter darkness, and I somehow found this soothing.

There was a little silver bell on the table beside my bed, and I was just making the experiment of reaching for it to ask for a dish of tea or another hot drink, when the door opened and a small man with a stoop entered, followed by Jennet. As the man drew nearer to the bed, I recognised him; his face has the ruddy complexion that riding about in all weathers brings.

'Why, Dr Sandys!'

'I'm delighted that you recognise me, young lady. You must be feeling very considerably improved, is that not so?'

Dr Sandys attended my mother in the last days of her illness, when she had retreated from London and all those fashionable surgeons who could do nothing to save her, and only added to her pain.

'There is no sovereign cure for consumption, Mrs Westmorland, ma'am,' he had said bluntly, when first called to the house. 'No, I can make no promises – and any doctor that does so is a certain charlatan. I hope you will entrust yourself to my old-fashioned nostrums while you are in residence here at the manor. But, as I say, I will hold out no hope of a cure. That must be faced. But I hope to ease your pain – aye – that I can do. Not with blistering and cupping, though. Such treatments are not my way.'

Such treatments were not only too unreliable, they were too cruel, or so he had afterwards confided to Jennet.

So Dr Sandys had pursued his own course and built up her strength as much as he could, so that she was out in her beloved garden almost until the very day she died, and thanks to him, there was little pain at the end.

That had been only six months previously, and the loss of my mother was still a great grief to me, as I believe it will always be, but I was comforted to have Dr Sandys there, for he was so gentle with her and never troubled her unnecessarily. But I believe he has treated your wounds, Lord Ambrose, or at least, the wounds that they say you bore when you returned from Crete, for I have never seen aught but the thin white scar that runs from your forehead to near your mouth. That, I said to Jennet but lately, makes you look a more handsome gentleman than any smooth-cheeked young squire – save one, of course.

But I don't want to go off into past sorrows, and now must return to the record that I promised Lord A. I would make.

'You have had a high fever, young lady,' said Dr Sandys, when he next visited me after my accident. 'And some cracked ribs – but we have strapped you up, and your young bones will be healing already. But it's not the ribs that worry me.'

He had his stethoscope out, and listened to my breathing for a few moments.

I wondered why he was so concerned, and then, as I was sitting up in bed, I began a coughing fit, which lasted longer than I thought possible, till my breath was coming in painful spasms between gasping fits of coughing.

'Aye, that's what worries me, Miss Lilian. The fever has weakened your lungs. We shall have to take great care of that.'

'Oh, yes, most surely, I'll look after her.' Jennet was fussing round the other side of the bed.

'Please drink this, Miss Lilian.'

Jennet was holding a small glass containing a syrup. I

took it and sipped cautiously. A warm, soothing glow spread down my throat. It stopped the tickle which threatened another spasm of coughing.

'One of your country remedies, Jennet?'

I used to tease her about them. She is forever decocotting or whatever the word is – you will know it, Lord Ambrose, and mixing up potions from some smelly herb or other.

'Aye, but the doctor knows it, too.'

'Indeed I do. Oil of bergamot, and very effective it is. I never despise the old country herbals.' Dr Sandys was speaking from the other side of the bed. 'They often bring relief of the symptoms, you know. Though I cannot approve of Lord Ambrose's outlandish behaviour at Malfine – he is using some salve supplied by a gypsy woman upon his scars. Heaven knows what horrible concoction it contains – but it is having a sovereign effect upon his wounds, I must say. He thinks, of course, that I know nothing of the matter, but his man Belos found out about it and informed me, but what could I do in the matter? His lordship is a most determined man and if he will listen to the gypsy's counsel, who can gainsay him? I must say that he bears but a slender mark upon his face now, though the traces of his wounds will never disappear completely. I have advised him to take some foreign travel to complete his convalescence.'

'Well, doctor, 'tis mighty good to hear he's improving so well, for the truth is that he did fright the children terrible with those awful scars. They hid away whenever he pleased to ride outside his own grounds, though anyone with a tender heart must have had some pity for what the poor man had suffered in foreign parts. But he's a strange one, Lord Ambrose, living like a hermit in that great mansion of his. He's a deep one, if you like – he thinks too much, if you ask me!'

Here I must state that I am sorry, Lord Ambrose, to include these remarks concerning your character, but you did ask me to make my diary as complete as I could.

Dr Sandys' footsteps were retreating, but the ordeal of his patient was not over. I was dropping off back to sleep and my eyelids were already closed, when a stray thought drifted into my head, and I murmured to Jennet, 'Just tell me one thing, Jennet. How is Selene?'

'The horse, miss? Why . . .'

'Well?'

'Oh, miss . . . the horse is just fine, don't you fret . . .'

Dr Sandys' footsteps were suddenly returning and Lilian heard his voice, low but clear as he spoke to Jennet.

'You must tell her. It will do more harm if you tell her a lie now and she finds out the truth later. She will never trust you again.'

I sat up in bed and opened my eyes suddenly. My head ached, but I had a far worse feeling, a sick feeling, in my stomach. I think I knew what was coming. Jennet was flustered, her face flushed. She was twisting her hands unhappily in her white apron.

'Tell me what, Dr Sandys?'

'Your mare, Selene. I'm sorry, my dear.'

'What happened to her?'

'They had to shoot her. There, I'm sorry to have to tell you, but it's better that you should know the truth. It must be faced, my dear Miss Lilian.'

'Oh, doctor – she thought the world of that horse!' cried Jennet.

My head began to spin. Giddy, sick, I recollect crying out in protest, 'But I don't understand. Why was she shot?'

'Why? Well, it had to be done, my dear young lady. You would not have let her be left in agony – her leg was broken.

Your uncle gave orders for the groom to dispatch her. It was over very quickly, I am sure. They had to do it'.

I fell silent, slowly realising what had happened and feeling with a creeping horror the pain of losing that beautiful and gentle creature. It seemed like a heavy stone inside my chest.

And yet, I still had that picture in my head! I was sure I had seen the horse scrambling up after the fall – Selene had surely been standing, walking – so she could not have broken a leg! I had a stubborn vision in my mind of that last moment, before I had lapsed into unconsciousness, with the horse standing over me and the mist, the autumn colours of the trees, in the background.

'No, no . . .' I called out feebly now, 'No, it can't have been . . .'

'There, there, Miss Lilian,' said Jennet, 'don't upset yourself now – I'm sure there was nothing else they could have done for the poor creature. Try to get some rest now, my chick.'

'But you don't understand,' I remember protesting, weakly, 'She wasn't seriously injured! Her legs were sound – I'm sure of it! She was standing – she came over to me!'

By now, I was sitting up in bed, for anger was pouring into me, my bodily weakness momentarily overcome.

'Who shot her? Adams would never have let anyone hurt her, I know it! He was as devoted to Selene as I was!'

Dr Sandys was making soothing noises now, trying to calm his agitated patient.

'Send for Adams,' I continued frantically, turning from Jennet to Dr Sandys, and then back again, looking at their faces as if for signs of some secret hope. 'Send for the groom – he was with me that day. He'll tell you! He saw it all happen'.

'Oh, Miss Lilian,' begged Jennet, 'please calm yourself. No good will come of all this—'

'But why was it done, Jennet? Why was my poor Selene shot?'

'Oh, miss, it had to be done, and there's an end on it. And Adams – well, he's not here any more.'

'Not here? What do you mean? Adams has been the head groom here for years. What has happened to him? Has he gone away?'

'Dismissed, Miss.'

'Dismissed?'

'Yes, Miss. Your uncle turned him away. He said he would get another groom to . . . to see to your horse, and told Adams he was to leave the Park and go instantly. He went that very same day – none knows where. His sister in the village – she's not saying, not to a soul.'

'But why, Jennet, why?'

'Oh, it was your uncle, miss.' Jennet was in tears now. 'He gave orders for the horse to be shot and he sent Adams packing. Your uncle was carrying on about how Adams should have taken better care of you and not let such accidents happen – and we all knows how headstrong you are, miss, and poor Adams would stand no chance of stopping you if you had your heart set on doing something! But your uncle, he said he would have Adams out of doors that very day. So he went, miss, but not afore he'd told your uncle a thing or two – he never reckoned your uncle was treating you right, though 'twas not his place to say so. But he always took your part, did Adams – you and that horse of yours. Your uncle was just trying to protect you and save you from your own silly foolishness!'

I am not sure how long I lay in bed, drifting in and out of consciousness – several days, at any rate. I recall Dr Sandys saying I was mending, that perhaps I might soon be up and about, but the fever did not leave me, and then my coughing fits increased, and my ribs ached so I was near to crying with the pain. 'I fear her lungs may be affected,' Dr Sandys was saying over my head one morning. 'Let us hope that this does not end in a consumption, as is sometimes the case with invalids who lie abed and cannot well breathe and expand their lungs nor take exercise. We must take care, Mistress Jennet, we must take care!'

Well, my Uncle did take care, as I shall set down here!

My next clear recollection after that – and your lordship will pardon me, but my memories of this time are in fragments and little pieces on account of my fevers – my next recollection is that I was wrapped up by Jennet in fleecy white shawls against any possible draughts and sitting in a big armchair in the Blue Drawing-Room at the Park. A fire burned in the grate, although it was a sunny day outside. But autumn was here; the trees were bending in the wind. I could see them through the window, the branches and the scudding yellow leaves which the wind was carrying through the ground outside.

The Blue Drawing-Room speaks entirely of my dear mother's taste, and takes its name from the wall-hangings of sky-blue taffeta. The oval mirrors, wreathed in gilded bamboo patterns, reflect a watery sort of light, like the stones in my opal ring, and display my mother's collection of filigree ornaments and blue china, standing in sundry little niches and pilasters. Such a gleam of gold wires, of porcelain, glass and swagged ruches of powder-blue silk!

Standing masterfully against the fireplace, looking quite out of place and stroking his iron-grey beard, was my uncle, my mother's brother, Micah. I should explain that he had handled our affairs since my father had died seventeen years before, though whilst my mother was still alive he had not had full control.

I never liked my Uncle Micah, I must confess it. I was what is called 'prejudiced' against him, though Jennet had told me that he wanted only what was for my own good, and that he was a very respectable personage, which was the thing that Jennet admired most in anybody. While my mother was alive, I had never had much to do with him, so really I had but little cause for my dislike, as I must admit. There had been arguments between him and my mother, and I had once found her in floods of tears after one of Micah's visits to the Park. But, till now, he had not had much influence on myself, though he had made occasional attempts to interfere with my upbringing – wanting me to be sent away to a young ladies' seminary school, for example, where I might learn some restraint instead of running wild, which I believe was his constant complaint, and the idea of my going away was what had distressed my mother so on the occasion when I had found her weeping. She admitted that Uncle Micah had good sense on his side, but she could not bear to part with my company.

At that time, her will had prevailed. But now the case was altered, as I realised, sitting there in my armchair. Uncle Micah could interfere all he wanted. He was my legal guardian after the death of my mother, and my only near relative.

'I would never have permitted the expense of your keeping such a horse, in any case,' he was saying now. He had red, fleshy lips, buried deep in his grey moustaches, and his thick hair was still streaked with black. He had probably been a handsome man in his youth, I thought, but he had never married.

'We shall have to be very prudent as to your finances. I kept it from your mother, not wishing to burden her with these troubles, but I must tell you, Lilian, that Westmorland Park is very heavily mortgaged, and there are very few assets remaining. And there is not enough in your father's trust fund to keep you in this style to which you have quite inappropriately become accustomed. I shall have to be laying out expenses for you, do you understand that? You will be a burden on my pocket, young lady.'

I kept silent, not really listening to Uncle Micah's homily. On and on he ran: there was not so much left in my father's trust fund as I seemed to think – my parents had both been somewhat lax – well, careless, nay foolish, were the most appropriate words – foolish with money – and anything enjoyable in life, it seemed, also showed a want of proper respect for the precious lucre.

Uncle Micah gazed out of the window, and even the peaceful scene outside presented an object of grave offence. 'That tree!' he snorted, pointing at a luxuriant growth just outside the window, 'That absurd tree! Why, it must have cost all of fifty pounds!'

'That tree' was innocent of blossoms at the present season. It was a magnolia, obtained by my father for his young bride, when my parents were first married. Even then, my mother had a taste for the exotic: she pored over books of rare plants, over voyages of discovery to distant lands, and had heard of Lord Bute's famous gardens of rarities, where camellias, magnolias, and the Green Tea Tree bloomed, transplanted far from their distant homelands. My father had begged a specimen of magnolia from his lordship's head gardener, the redoubtable Archibald Thomson. As my mother loved to recount, it had, somewhat surprisingly, duly arrived, packed carefully in a crate, with instructions written in a rough countryman's hand. The tree had flourished on the south-facing lawn at Westmorland Park. Every June it burst into a magnificent scented spectacle, twenty feet in height, of great creamy flowers.

There seemed no point in telling Uncle Micah that the tree had cost nothing; it had been a graceful gesture from an old gardener. But there was more to my silence that that. It seemed pointless to say anything at all, for I truly believed that Uncle Micah disliked the magnolia for its beauty as much as for any possible cost. I do not know why I sensed this but I suddenly understood it as a part of his character, that is to say, I saw him as a grown-up would see him, yet understanding things that would not be voiced aloud.

I continued to listen, nodding when it seemed necessary. I found I could look out of the window at the same time, and watch a squirrel, scampering across the lawn to prepare its winter larder at the base of a tree. I found myself thinking how very interesting life at the Park always was, with these small creatures and the endless variety of activities that went on just outside the old house, where the birds and animals bustled about with their little lives. I much preferred to watch squirrels than to think about what my uncle was saying. In any case, I was drowsing in the sun that came through the small glass panes. Uncle Micah's voice was droning on and on.

'And there is really not sufficient money available to keep up an establishment such as the Park just for a miss of seventeen. Especially when that uppish miss has such stiffnecked and stubborn follies as you have displayed, young lady. Expensive horses, grooms, doctor's bills – all this adds up, you know. It adds up! Now, the Park cannot be sold, for it was entailed by your great-grandfather, and if you marry and have heirs, it must pass to them. But I intend to move here myself, to supervise the expenditure and ensure there is not the slightest waste! My house in Bristol can be sold, and I shall occupy the east wing.'

I began now to pay attention.

'And if we sent you abroad for your health, the savings would be very great, and I do not see why I should be at the expense of providing you with an establishment here,' he was saying. 'There is not enough interest coming into the fund to pay for the costs of running the Park. I shall have to assist out of my own pocket. And I do not see why it is at all necessary for a young woman to live in such a style.'

'Can't the man ever cut a sentence short?' I wondered at this point: I had lost track of my squirrel because of Uncle Micah's going on and on.

'I have made my decisions, which I will now proceed to communicate to you,' continued Micah, bearing out everything I had just been thinking. 'The west wing – that which you and Mrs Jennet occupy at present – is to be closed. The furniture will be sheeted up. As for the estate, I take no interest in that – the tenants can pay their rents, which do not amount to a row of beans – through an agent.'

'Oh no!' I gasped, realising at last the import of all this verbiage, though he still had not imparted his full array of plans for my disposition 'No, I beg you, Uncle, let me stay at the Park!'

'Why, niece, I have much more exciting plans for you – plans such as any young woman would delight in. You are to go abroad and I am determined to take control of your affairs myself; I am fully entitled to do so as your guardian, you know. Had I been managing things here of late, your unfortunate accident would never have occurred, for you would never have been permitted to have such an expensive and mettlesome horse. An old pony – yes, an old, safe cob, that would have been a perfectly adequate mount for a young woman. But careering all over the countryside on a thoroughbred!'

He turned and looked out of the window and a fresh cause for reproach met his vision.

'Come, come, dry your eyes, miss, for I see the thought of it upsets you – you are like your mother, too tender-hearted. And that conservatory of hers – that was another shocking expense that I would never have permitted! However, that is all now in the past, and I, as your legal guardian until or unless you marry – I will make the decisions now.

'You will leave the Park, but mind, it is for your own health, and I am acting with Dr Sandys' medical considerations in mind. He has told me that you need a milder climate for your lungs – you should not stay here throughout the winter. His advice is that your best convalescence will be travel to warmer and dryer climes, and I have made all due enquiries and been most conscientious in determining what will prove the most effectual in your case. I had considered that you might go to Italy, but the weather, I am told, is quite unreliable . . . (here Uncle Micah paused, turned up his eyes to the ceiling, as if in despair at the very thought of Italy's frightful unreliability in the respect of climate) and you might travel there only to find rain and mists as bad as any we might expect here.'

'Uncle—' I began, for I was going to beg him that I might be allowed some say in the choice of what part of the world was to receive me. But he carried straight on as though I had not spoken. 'Besides, I have made enquiries and Egypt is very inexpensive, I find – indeed, there will be a deal of saving if you spend the winter there, for it will be far cheaper than heating all the rooms at the Park . . . hmm, you may take Jennet as a maid – her wages are small. Besides, she saves the expense of having a nurse while you are still convalescing from your accident. But most of the other servants at the Park will have to go – I have already dismissed Adams, the groom – and I refused to give him a character, I may say, so he will not easily find other employment. I suppose the man may take to drink or crime for all I care. Incompetent, insolent – that's what he was, like all the other servants here. Your parents never took the trouble to teach them their place!'

'Oh, Uncle Micah, please – will you let me stay at the Park at least until spring?'

But even this stay of execution was not to be granted.

'No, miss, I will be at no more expense. The General Steam Navigation Company is advertising most advantageous rates for passengers embarking on its new steamship service, and I have already advised them I wish to make a booking. Jennet has been given instructions to pack such things as you and she will need. And I have already sent for workmen – they are already boarding up the windows of the west wing. Can you not hear them?'

And, indeed, I heard a distant thudding, as in some other room nails were driven into shutters.

The house will be like a blind thing, I thought. I hated the thought of those dark and silent windows, those sheeted sunless rooms.

The squirrel pursued his course across the lawn. Soon, the house would belong only to the small creatures that hid within its walls and ran heedless about the grounds.

PART II
The Great London

CHAPTER 7

The Further Narrative of Lord Ambrose Malfine

I write this record of events transpiring aboard the steamship *Great London* in Alexandria. Here I am preparing for a solitary crossing to Cairo. I do not wish to travel with the other passengers from the *Great London*; if Casterman is the dangerous fellow whom I suspect him to be, he will be forewarned by my presence on the ship. Let him believe that I have vanished into the sands; I have taken care to make arrangements that will, I trust, ensure Miss Lilian's safety in Alexandria.

It was extremely fortunate that I was taken aboard the *Great London* when she anchored at Falmouth to take on postal packets. This was discreetly accomplished as it was almost dark, so that the identity of the new passenger who now took occupancy of a vacant first-class cabin did not immediately become known. If anyone had been hanging over the rail of the great vessel when I went aboard, all they could have seen were lights flickering in a boat that drew up to the *Great London*'s side. A few minutes later, a cloaked figure made his way along the deck to the vacant cabin, and a sailing vessel drifted away into the night. All that anyone would have known about the interesting stranger, therefore, was that he was rich enough to secure a vacant first-class cabin, that he was secretive, and that he had damned long lanky legs.

We had a fearfully stormy passage, and in the Bay of Biscay the ship was tossed by such gales as I have never previously experienced. Almost all the passengers were horribly seasick, except for myself. I suppose that, having nigh killed me outright on several occasions, Neptune does not bother me with such petty torments as *mal-de-mer*. At any rate, I was immune from the general débâcle.

Miss Lilian Westmorland had embarked in extremely poor health. I had glimpsed her, once or twice, and she seemed increasingly pale and weak, and most distressingly uninterested in the world. It was ironic, therefore, that, a few days later, when the *Great London* headed valiantly into the storms of the Bay of Biscay, encountering forces that bucked her giant bulk as if she were a tin can, Miss Lilian was almost the only passenger apart from myself who was able to walk on deck.

Walking was perhaps an euphemism, for in reality it consisted largely of slithering about and hanging on to the ropes with which an anxious crew had surrounded the quarters of the first-class passengers, just in case any of their charges should possess stomachs of sufficient strength to enable their owners to crawl out of their cabins and on to the deck.

The steward had a theory that it was always the sickliest travellers that did best in such circumstances, so he commented that he was not surprised when we saw the slender red-haired figure of Miss Lilian emerging from her cabin. In fact, he wished he had taken a bet on it.

In spite of the wind, I could hear Mrs Jennet's little shrieks of anxiety as she called after her mistress with numerous injunctions against unnecessary risk-taking. The cries terminated in a pathetic whooping noise that indicated copious use was being made of the deep metal tray that the steamship company had so thoughtfully fitted into a special holder at the side of every cabin-bed. It was quite true that, as the brochure promised, no aspect of the passengers' needs was neglected.

From my cabin, I could observe that the first-class steward now made his way along the deck to where Lilian stood, holding on to the brass rail that surrounded the promenade deck.

I stepped out and started to make my way along the deck towards them. There was more than a hint of admiration in the steward's tone as he addressed her. Would she like him to bring a chair? One could be fastened to the deck for her, and she would be quite safe in such an arrangement. And oilskins were perhaps advisable.

Foam was flying all around them as he spoke, and his words needed little reinforcement from nature. Lilian thanked him, and he brought a folding chair which was lashed to stanchions on the deck, and oilskins which were arranged around her with fatherly care and pride.

'The sun'll be out, miss, just you watch! She's a-coming up on the port bow! Never you mind this storm!' The steward left her safely in her chair.

And presently, although the wind did not abate, the sun came out, and the heavy grey seas changed to a mass of opalescence under the pure and glimmering air.

It was not my intention to make myself known to her – or to any of her party. But I did not wish her to be left alone on deck, and therefore maintained my position some distance further along. I made no effort to approach my fellow passenger, and perhaps would not have spoken to her at all, if it had not been for an accident.

Lilian had around her throat a long, loose muffler of grey cashmere wool, and this was suddenly plucked from her as if by an invisible hand, and the gust of wind that had seized it carried the scarf along the deck in the direction of the stranger. Involuntarily, she rose from her chair, and suddenly, as the deck lurched under her feet, found herself propelled along with the speed of light as a mighty sea shook its back and heaved the vessel like a toy ship in a bathtub. She was therefore almost literally flung into my arms, to our mutual surprise.

'I applaud your courage, young lady. I see there are two of us who brave the elements today. But I am afraid you may experience a few mishaps before you are safely back in your cabin.'

'Lord Ambrose Malfine!'

'Why, you remember me? What good fortune! Then I need not introduce myself, though I must beg the pleasure of your acquaintance. I trust we may dispense with some of the formalities, meeting as we do in somewhat unusual circumstances!'

'Yes, I am Lilian Westmorland, of Westmorland Park. That is . . . I . . . it was my parents' home. And you were kind enough to visit after my accident, and you bought my poor old Dobbie! Oh, Lord Ambrose, that was such a generous act!'

'No, no, it was nothing! Dobbie is in fine fettle, I am glad to assure you, and gives excellent service to my man, Belos. But Miss Westmorland – what a delightful surprise this is, to be sure! Your father and I were companions in boyhood mischief, though I must confess I had not seen him for many a long year and if I judge correctly you have inherited his spirit, for he would have ventured forth exactly as you have done, storm or no storm!'

I had now got my arm under hers, of necessity, for the violence of the gale renewed, and she seemed too frail to press forward against it alone. 'But, my dear Miss Westmorland, let me assist you. The passengers' saloon is nearby, and I think there must be a member of the crew still upon his legs – if two landlubbers such as you and I can brave the storm, then surely we can be brought some restorative!'

The safe haven of the first-class saloon was but a few yards further, and I opened the doors with one hand and swung Lilian through them upon my arm, depositing her in the secure cushions of a plush-covered chair which appeared to be nailed safely to the uncertain floor.

In front of her was a small round mahogany table, its top surrounded with a little brass rail to provide for emergencies such as this. I sank into the chair opposite hers, and beckoned to an attendant, who came forward assiduously with the rapid lurches of one used to travelling in heavy seas. In no time, it seemed, Lilian had been helped off with her heavy oilskins and cloak, and a pot of tea was conjured out of the air and set before us.

Lilian sipped the hot liquid and seemed her strength appeared to be reviving. I contemplated her face: pale though it was, it had great attractions. Her eyes were great blue-green orbs, rendered more brilliant by contrast with the pallor of her face. Her hair, which had been cut short during her illness, strayed in red-gold tendrils across her temples. It would have been very easy for me to feel more than I should have felt in my role as old friend of the family.

'I congratulate you on your courage, Miss Westmorland, it is the quality I admire above all others. May I ask why you are on board this vessel?'

'I am going to Egypt, for my health. I believe that you know Dr Sandys, and he approved of my going recommending a warm climate; I have been very ill this last month, and it was thought a change of atmosphere would aid my recovery.'

'Yes, indeed, that warm dry air is held to be excellent for invalids. And there will be good riding there, when you are well enough – do I not recall that you are a very considerable horsewoman, Miss Lilian?'

I regretted that I had mentioned this, for there was a spurt of tears in her eyes, and she began dabbing at her face with her gloved hand.

'I believed so, Lord Ambrose, indeed, I foolishly thought I was a good horsewoman, but I learned otherwise, for I had an accident that cost me dearly.'

'That is why you have been so unwell?'

'No, not entirely. You see, at Westmorland Park, my mare, Selene—'

'Why, what a wonderful name! Goddess of the moon, Selene, who rides across the night sky in her chariot. Have you not seen that wonderful carved marble head of one of the horses of Selene – the sculpture that Lord Elgin brought back from the Parthenon in Greece? Is that why you gave such a name to your mare?'

'Yes – that is, I have not seen the sculpture, but my mother told me about it, and I called my horse after it. It was a fancy of mine – for my horse had a slender white blaze in the shape of a crescent moon.'

Lilian had to pause for a moment.

'The truth is that I took a foolish risk, and rode her too

fast, and my poor Selene is now dead – she broke a leg and had to be shot'.

She pressed her hand to her eyes.

I leaned forward intently, anxious not to miss a word. Her voice was faint, and I did not want to press her on this point. 'And how did that come to happen to an experienced rider such as yourself?'

'You are too kind in your estimation of me, my lord. I rode Selene along the path towards the clump of beeches in our grounds, not checking or slowing for a moment, and she must have stumbled'.

'An odd occurrence, on ground so familiar to horse and rider?'

'I did not see exactly what had occurred. I am not quite sure how it came to happen, but my Uncle Micah said that Selene had to be . . . had to be . . .'

'Do not distress yourself, I beg you, Miss Westmorland. I am sure your uncle was right to put an end to your horse's sufferings. You, and your safety, must have been his chief concern'.

'Oh yes, he was most perturbed. He dismissed the groom who had been accompanying me, and said it was the man's fault for not preventing me from riding so recklessly. So you see, Lord Ambrose, I have not only caused the death of my beautiful Selene, but poor Adams was turned away on account of my foolishness.'

'Miss Westmorland, I admire you!'

She stopped crying in surprise.

'Yes, indeed I do, for the hardest thing of all, the thing that takes the most courage in life, is to admit to our own follies. You have done so, and faced up to your actions, and that is a courageous step of self knowledge. Let me say to you, that accidents happen always and everywhere;

we cannot predict the workings of fate, and we must not blame ourselves for it. You have paid a terrible price for the loss of a moment's vigilance. I trust you will permit my speaking to you so deeply about the workings of our minds and feelings, for, as a friend of your father, I hope I may be of some support to you.'

'Indeed, sir, you have very probably stopped me from going overboard today, and if that is not real support, I do not know what is!'

We looked at each other, and burst out laughing.

'I did not mean to speak so literally, I assure you, Miss Westmorland! However, it was a great pleasure to be of service to you! Now, I beg you, allow me to assist you back to your cabin. The gale still blows across that treacherous deck!'

We resumed the paraphernalia of cloaks, scarves, gloves, then rose to our feet. Lilian was pinning her cloak against the wind with a brooch her mother had given her, a gold pin in the form of a horse standing within the silver crescent of a moon. She saw that I noticed it.

'A gift from my mother, on the day when I got Selene.' She held the brooch out to me, so that I could see the inscription engraved on the silver surface of the moon: 'To my darling Lilian, from her loving mother. Many happy moons!'

'A beautiful gift, and most imaginative!'

I handed it back to her, and she was re-pinning it when the ship took a sudden lurch and she involuntarily grasped my arm.

It was at this moment that the doors in front of us burst open, as if with the force of the hurricane, and a figure erupted into the saloon. It was old Overbury's major-domo, Casterman.

'Miss Lilian, come with me at once! What do you think you are doing here! And you, whoever you think you are, take your hands off her!'

Casterman moved threateningly, head lowered like an angry bull, to confront us. For a moment, he and I stood opposite each other; he was a solidly made man, but a good six inches below my height. Before he was quite aware of what was happening, I stretched out my arm and had the luck to grasp him firmly by the throat, my thumb sinking snugly into the carotid artery. This is an old Thuggee stranglehold, the knack of which I have acquired somewhere in my reprobate life. I maintained it for a few moments whilst we conversed – although the conversation was somewhat one-sided, I must admit.

'I will tell you who I am! I am this young lady's neighbour; I had the honour to be a friend of her father. I am, sir, as you may perceive, a gentleman, but that does not disqualify me from being able to kill men with my own hands if I perceive the desirability of so doing! And I do not take kindly to threats and insults, I assure you!'

Casterman was choking satisfactorily now, and I dropped him into a convenient chair where he slumped gasping like a stranded fish.

Lilian rushed forward, exclaiming, 'Oh, pray, Lord Ambrose, do not kill him! Perhaps you do not recall that Mr Casterman is my uncle's man of business – I do not think he can have meant to insult you intentionally.'

'Yes, we have met on a previous occasion. I beg pardon, Miss Lilian. I did not wish to alarm you. I shall overlook this flunkey's behaviour. You are, I take it, entrusted to his care by your legal guardian, but I hope you also have friends who will assist you. If you wish at any time to turn to me, I trust that you will do so.'

I left them; it was unfortunate that my presence on board had been revealed to Casterman, but as long as I travelled separately once we had disembarked, he need not be suspicious of me.

And, outwardly, he could not be said to be in the wrong. He had encountered his young mistress arm in arm with myself, a man of doubtful repute who might be threatening her virtue – or at any rate, compromising her good name – and he had acted accordingly, exactly as befitted a good steward of his master's property.

Besides, there might be some truth in his fears for Miss Westmorland's virtue. In my juvenile days, I might well have laid siege to it. Yes, in my young days – and perhaps not so young!

I loathed the fellow, but he might be in the right.

CHAPTER 8

The Further Narrative of Miss Lilian Westmorland

Here, before I get any further with my recollections, I must make a confession. I had seen Lord Ambrose once before – from a distance – and yes, I had written it into my diary!

I was out taking a country walk with Jennet one day, in that happy time before all the unhappiness and disaster befell us, when we saw a rider approaching in the distance; he seemed to halt and watch us.

'But, Jennet,' I whispered, as I was tugged protestingly along the path, 'do you not think that gentleman was taking some particular interest in us?'

'Come away this instant!' hissed Jennet, dragging me along.

'That is not a suitable gentleman for you to meet – no, not at all! That is Lord Ambrose Malfine! He who owns that mansion, the great house that is also called Malfine, near Westmorland Park!'

'But then he is a neighbour, of sorts. Should we not stop and speak to him? After all, we are met here by chance, yet

103

we live within ten miles of each other. Would it not be mere politeness to greet him?'

'No, it would not! The man has a most strange reputation!'

'Oh, tell me, tell me, Jennet!'

'He lives all alone, apart from some governess, a boy who's not his and a manservant, in that great house, with half its rooms boarded up. And what's more, the governess is French – or leastways, brought up in France! And they say he never receives company – does not show his face in public, since he was nigh half killed in some war or other – he ran away from home when he was seventeen!'

'Exactly my age!'

'Yes, Miss Lilian, and would have been given up for dead, only that valet of his, Mr Belos or whatever he calls himself, he brought his lordship home, covered in wounds, a year or two back. Dr Sandys says it was a miracle he survived. But now he's recovered, he doesn't see a Christian soul for months on end – he never goes out in society, though they say he's the richest catch for hundreds of miles, for Malfine is the biggest estate in the county, and his grandfather left a fortune in the stocks and shares, as well. But he's a strange one, Lord Ambrose – why, he never goes hunting even, won't have the hunt on his land! D'you know what he told the Master of Hounds? "I'll not have the Malfine foxes disturbed, and if they need culling, I'll shoot them myself!" Shoot foxes! Old Sir Anderton near died of apoplexy when he heard that! And the parson's given up trying to call at Malfine – it's always, "His lordship is not at home today", when parson says he can look through the doorway and see his lordship's boots steaming on the chimneypiece, and his lordship's long lanky legs inside them!'

'He sounds the most interesting man in the world!'

'Oh, don't you give him a second thought, Miss Lilian! Why, he's all mixed up with foreigners! He lets them thieving gypsies take their caravans on to his land and camp on Malfine ground for all the world as if it belonged to them! And his own mother was a foreigner – Greek, or some such! So you see, Miss Lilian, the man is very probably close kin to the devil himself, and no fit creature for the company of a young lady such as yourself. And now I'm going to take you home, for you are getting far too interested in the gentleman, it seems to me, and we had best try and get back as soon as we may.'

Until that glimpse in the drawing-room at Westmorland Park, when I was so ill, this was all I knew of Lord Ambrose, and of course I was dying to meet him after all the terrible things that Jennet had said. So you may imagine how excited I was to encounter him again on board the steamship that was carrying me, with Jennet and Mr Casterman, to Egypt.

The first day I ventured out of the cabin was when the ship was ploughing through rough seas in the Bay of Biscay. I had not felt anything as invigorating as that scudding air since I had galloped on Selene's back through the fields of home. The white crested waves swooped up and down, like great hills in perpetual motion, but I sensed no fear. As a matter of fact, I felt better than I had done for weeks.

I had improved from the first day on board. The pain and nausea had stopped, and my fevers and night sweats evaporated. I slept well, rocked on the sea, trusting to it even when it grew rough and ready.

On that morning, I had eaten the invalid food Jennet had ordered (the devotion Jennet had displayed in giving the menu to the steward, when her own face was a delicate shade of green, could not be underestimated). I had partaken of ('partaken' is the ladylike word, is it not? – should it be partook?) – anyway, I had eaten, that is what I mean to say, neat's foot jelly, chicken cream and eggs beaten with sherry, but I was still hungry, and was planning to order a substantial dinner for myself upon my return to the cabin.

But then, a most unladylike thing happened! I literally fell into the arms of Lord Ambrose!

I had no idea even that he was on board, but he seemed to have sprung out of nowhere, and saved me from falling headlong along the deck as it tilted with the waves. All was confused while he propped me up and made some polite remarks, and the next thing I knew was that we were taking tea and I had a chance to contemplate him in more detail.

Long, long legs! They were clad in snuff-coloured twill trousers, and their owner was also wearing a plain black dress-coat with a white cravat. Above the cravat, a dark, lean jaw, with the traces of a scar that did not detract from his visage. I hope he will forgive me for mentioning that his mouth had a nice amused smile, as he gazed across the table at me. And those eyes, yes, those were the eyes, and that the penetrating gaze, which I remembered from his visit to Westmorland Park. We had a conversation, which was sorrowful for me as we talked about dear Selene (though I felt better afterwards), so I will not put it down here as it would start me weeping again and I would spoil the paper.

And then, after Lord Ambrose and I had finished our tea, we stood up to leave and to don our cloaks and scarves and gloves, when who should come rushing in but Casterman!

He was threatening and shouting, but then something happened, and seemed to happen fast – very fast indeed.

Casterman is not a small man, by any means, but Lord Ambrose Malfine, without appearing to move at all, was suddenly towering over him, and a long black-gauntletted fist had grasped Casterman's throat, and just lifted him up and *threw him into a chair*! Just like that – I must put in some exclamation marks!!!

Then Lord Ambrose said something nasty to Mr Casterman and something nice to me – I can't remember exactly what, except that he said that he would help me if ever I needed it and I must be sure not to forget that – and off he stalked!

Mr Casterman seemed very shaken by the incident, and somehow it had *altered* him. He seemed a different sort of man, somehow, as he apologised to me, which is something he had never done before and I would never have believed he would do to anybody.

'I beg your pardon, Miss Lilian – I was afraid that a stranger might have tried to detain you in conversation for evil purposes. I was concerned only with your safety, and I had no wish to offend you – or Lord Ambrose.'

His speech was very polite and civil. I confess that I cannot like him, however, though I do pity him for the marks of the smallpox that he carries on his face, and for the suffering he must have undergone.

Anyway, let us forget about him for a little while. I had put it all out of mind, and was in high spirits as I looked upon the wondrous shores of Egypt! The *Great London* steamed majestically into the harbour of Alexandria. It was an afternoon of golden sun, and we on board had a sense of achievement. We had outrun the grip of winter. That was how Mrs Cornwallis, another first-class passenger with whom we had become acquainted, put it, in rather a poetical way, she being quite a literary lady.

Passengers and crew had now enjoyed a week of calm voyaging, so that most of us had recovered from bouts of 'landlubberly' *mal-de-mer*, and were sufficiently interested in the world again to crowd to the ship's side and watch the process of navigation into the great harbour. Aches and pains, slights and squabbles, seemed all to have been forgotten in the excitement.

I had continued in the improvement in health which the voyage seemed to have brought me, and I am sure that my walks on deck, breathing in the healthful salt air, had greatly contributed to this. There I was with the other passengers, hanging over the rail and gazing at the ancient harbour of Alexandria, the home of the lighthouse that had once been one of the Seven Wonders of the World. Piles of ancient, golden stones surrounded the harbour: what had they once been, I wondered. I saw ancient columns here and there, a fortress in the distance.

'Will we have the chance to do a little sightseeing?' I asked Mrs Cornwallis, who stood beside me at the rail. Mrs Cornwallis, as all the passengers knew by now, was an experienced traveller, voyaging to see her son who was a high-ranking civil servant in India. But I must not say anything to the detritus of Mrs Cornwallis – she is truly the kindest of ladies and had pressed many remedies for *mal-de-mer* upon poor Jennet. None of them had worked, but that does not detract from Mrs C.'s generosity, does it?

'Why, yes, I believe so. We will disembark and then spend the night at an hotel here in Alexandria before we depart again on our way to Cairo,' she said as we watched the bustle in the harbour.

I confess, I had been hoping that I might see Lord Ambrose upon deck to view the harbour of Alexandria with the other passengers, but he kept to his quarters, or so it seemed. There had been no repetition of our previous encounter and I had always been accompanied by the friendly Mrs Cornwallis or by Jennet, as I took a turn about the deck, with Mr Casterman following behind. His behaviour had been beyond reproach since that incident in the first-class saloon. Perhaps Lord Ambrose had frightened him into good behaviour; I was delighted at the thought that there was someone in the world who might be capable of putting a fright into the seemingly imporous Casterman.

Considering that Lord Ambrose's cabin was next to mine, I might have fairly expected to see him in the ordinary course of the voyage, but he appeared to keep his quarters much of the time. At night, I could see the light from his neighbouring porthole shining out upon the sea, as I gazed out of my own cabin. 'He must be studying late into the night,' I told myself, and derived some comfort from the gleam from his cabin as it flickered out over the waves, like a friendly night light that promised me safety. I expect he always uses a dictionary when he is not sure which word to use: I confess that it is a very bad habit of mine to guess with difficult words.

'Why do you think he insisted on having that cabin?' I asked Jennet.

'Oh, he's a strange one – it'll be some whim or other, believe you me!' said Jennet, brushing my hair. 'You don't want to take any notice of that!'

But I could not stop myself from thinking of my neighbour, sitting there reading alone, late into the night.

I had myself collected up some books on Egypt, which Uncle Micah had approved of, and had set myself to do a little study of the exotic country to which they were bound. I had pondered a few pages of Mr Wilkinson's advice to travellers.

'Many persons ask if bathing in the Nile is advisable. Nothing can be more conducive to health and comfort . . . the crocodile is not so much dreaded by bathers as might be expected . . .'

'No one can visit the harems and courts of the private dwellings of the Cairenes without recalling the impressions he received on reading *The Arabian Nights* . . .'

'Passing through the court of the hotel the traveller sees the various preparations for a journey across the desert . . .'

I recalled Casterman saying to Jennet, 'Why, Mrs Jennet, please to remember we are not going to an uninhabited wilderness. Cairo is a great city, with hotels and merchants and bankers. But do not forget you will need a good woollen cloak.'

'Mr Casterman, shall we not be broiled like lobsters in the heat?'

'No, no. The nights in the desert can be very cold. There is a night sky of unimaginable brightness and glittering stars – but cold, cold!'

As we prepared to disembark, all these fragments whirled round in my head like gleaming flashes from a prism, promising delights and excitements ahead.

PART III
Egypt

CHAPTER 9

The Further Narrative of Miss Lilian Westmorland

We were to spend two nights in Alexandria before travelling to Cairo along the Mahmoudiyah Canal, and Mrs Cornwallis, who was resident at the same hotel, had proposed that a little sightseeing party be made up. This needed little encouragement, and four persons, Jennet, Mrs Cornwallis, Mr Casterman and myself had hired a carriage and a guide for the day. Dislike Casterman though I might, I could not but admit that he was extremely useful on an expedition such as this, fixing a price in advance after much negotiation, and pointing out the sights of the place, which was evidently well known to him.

Thus aided, we had viewed Pompey's Pillar, had marvelled at the obelisks called Cleopatra's Needles, had driven through the Christian quarter and seen the Coptic church. It was then late afternoon, and the party was all somewhat hot and dusty: but I, with the recovery of my usual high spirits, wanted to continue our expedition and feared that the weariness of Mrs Cornwallis and Jennet might put a stop to it just as I was getting a taste for the exotic colours, the date palms, the noise and bustle of the streets.

I was, therefore, both pleased and surprised when Casterman proposed further sightseeing.

'Do you see the old fort out there, at the end of the promontory? We could drive out to it, if you wish. That fort was built by the great Sultan, Qait Bey, over three centuries ago on the site of the Pharaohs of the ancients, the lighthouse that was one of the seven wonders of the world. Qait Bey started his career as a slave who was bought in the market place, and intrigued and murdered his way up to the throne. But he was a great warrior. Very few Europeans visit that fort: it would be quite an unusual thing for you ladies to have seen it.'

Jennet, as might be predicted, exclaimed that she was too weary and dusty even to set one foot in front of another, but I was intrigued and excited by the prospect, and Mrs Cornwallis said that she would be quite agreeable, provided that she might be allowed to stay behind in the carriage and rest while the others explored the place – it would be something to write to her son in India about, after all.

We all finally set off, accompanied by Casterman and a guide from the hotel.

The towered fortress looked like a mere speck at this distance, but within half an hour we were close to it. As we drew near, I was suddenly aware of how high those towers were, how dark and forbidding seemed the entrance.

The carriage came to a halt.

Mrs Cornwallis remained in the comparative cool of the conveyance. There was a burst of Arabic between Casterman and their guide, and the driver and the turbaned dragoman both settled down in the shade of the ancient walls. 'There is no point in their accompanying us,' said Casterman. 'I know the place and can show you ladies the way. And it will be better if they stay with Mrs Cornwallis, in case she is in need of anything.'

The entrance seemed suddenly cold as we passed beneath it. In the courtyard, various pieces of lumber seemed to be lying about, dusty and neglected. There was no sound from the outside world, except for the occasional cries of birds and the occasional sight of a wing over the edge of a parapet: perhaps they were nesting in the great crinolines. A corner of the yard was still in direct sunlight: otherwise, the shadow of evening seemed to be descending. But, looking up, I could see the golden stone of the towers still outlined against a brilliant blue sky, and my enthusiasm for exploration was not checked. 'There must be a wonderful view from there,' I exclaimed, my head bent backwards as I peered up.

'Miss Lilian, I beg you, it doesn't look at all safe to me!'

'Why, Jennet, there's a staircase in this archway!'

The door was open.

'Oh, Mr Casterman, I beg you, don't let her go up it! I'm sure there'll be some mischance or other!'

'Mrs Jennet, the staircase is safe, I do assure you. Miss Lilian, I will lead the way, to make sure there is no insecure footing, and you follow. Mrs Jennet, you may stay here and wait for us, in the shade of the wall, if you desire.' And Casterman stepped through a doorway at the bottom of a tower.

Jennet, already breathless on account of the heat, would not bring herself to tackle the winding stone stairs. She remained at the bottom, where there was a bench cut into the stone, but she was irresolute and anxious. I stayed with her for a few minutes, trying to persuade her she might safely ascend. But when it became clear that I would not prevail upon my companion, I turned towards the stairs, and followed where Casterman had led.

The stairs were firm and secure underfoot, though ancient and worn, for the stones had been so closely fitted by the old builders that I was sure they could be trusted still.

The cool, dim interior of the tower was a relief after the heat outside. There was a slit window at each turn of the stairs, and I could see quite well enough to climb.

After a few minutes, I found Casterman was waiting for me. He was sitting on a window-seat at one of the turns in the tower.

'I waited to see you were quite safe, Miss Lilian. Do you know, the Sultan who built this fort, Qait Bey, put out the eyes and tore out the tongue of an alchemist who failed to change lead into gold?'

At that, I must confess I suddenly felt quite dizzy. Why did Casterman have to tell me that?

I remember that his face seemed very pale. There were drops of sweat upon it, yet it seemed to me that it was not that natural perspiration that comes from some exertion in the heat.

'There's a wonderful view from the top,' he continued. 'You can see the ships out in the bay, with all the people looking like so many ants.'

Is that what human beings truly are to you, ants? The thought crossed my mind as we confronted each other upon the stairs.

'I want to go all the way to the top, Mr Casterman, but is it very far?'

'No, Miss, not very far. Follow me.'

We continued to climb and I followed Casterman's footsteps as they echoed round and round the winding stair, tramping endlessly just out of sight and just beyond. Steadily, the ground glimpsed through the window slits fell away. Now Jennet was a tiny black doll, sitting on a toy bench far below.

Birds flew past our tower: Casterman and I were in a different kingdom now, the kingdom of the air.

I glimpsed sheets of blue water through the slits in the stone. The bay was spread out before them, as Casterman had promised.

The footsteps above me seemed to be going faster and faster: I was having difficulty now in keeping up. Perhaps I was beginning to feel a little giddy again; perhaps I had overtaxed my strength. But I would not give in; I would not call out to Casterman to stop or even to slow down. I had set out to get to the top of this tower, and get to the top of it I would.

Suddenly, the echoing footsteps ahead of me ceased, and I emerged through an archway into blazing sunlight, so that I had to stand still for a few moments and rub my eyes till they adjusted to the appalling brightness.

Then I saw that I was on a little roof, with a parapet on the side overlooking the sea. And there, as Casterman had promised, was the great sweep of the harbour, with tiny creatures moving across toy ships, their sails like shreds of white and their masts like matchsticks. Delighted, I watched the scene for a few minutes before I wondered what had become of Casterman, who must have come out ahead of me on to this roof but was not visible.

Then I saw, a few yards away from her, a door in a low wall, and, a little further away, Casterman's head and shoulders appearing above a wall that divided my section of the parapet from a stretch beyond. As I looked, he turned and smiled at me, and opened his mouth, calling something out, but I could not hear what it was, for a gust of wind swept it away with the cries of the gulls that circled around them. But he was surely beckoning me, smiling, urging me on. There was a little door in the parapet between us. I walked towards it.

The door was of weathered oak, with an iron latch, the handle smooth and worn, I suppose from the fingers of the innumerable sentries who had paced these ramparts and walked through this doorway.

I was just about to set my hand upon it when there was a shout, and a figure dashed in front of me.

'No! Not that door!'

It was a young man who must have fairly hurled himself across the roof of the tower to get between myself and the door. I could not take it in for a few moments, so astonished was I, and it was a minute or two before it dawned on me that he had shouted in English.

'I'm sorry to have alarmed you, but truly, it is not safe up here! You should not have ventured up this far!'

There was a gust of wind, and the door now seemed to slowly swing open of its own accord. And through it gradually appeared the sight of a great chasm, a black, yawning void in which a bird fluttered with alarm. Broken rafters jutted out over the depths. Over the depths in which I could see a glimpse of the ground, hundreds of feet below.

'Please, stay still for a few moments, till you recover.'

The stranger had taken my elbow, was turning me away from that terrible little door and towards the safety of the stairs. I stood with my eyes closed till the world steadied down.

Then I stared at the man who had come between me and my death. He was young, dressed in riding-clothes, with large, open, grey-blue eyes and light-coloured hair. There was a pause: I somehow had the impression that we were both trying to get our breath.

'Sholto Lawrence, Miss Lilian, at your service.'

How did he know my name?

He seemed to read my mind, and became rather flustered.

'Oh, forgive me, I fell into conversation with the lady waiting for you at the floor of the tower – Mrs Jennet, is it not? She expressed much alarm about your safety, so I volunteered to hasten up the staircase to ensure that all was well with you . . .'

His voice trailed away. We both looked at the doorway.

'I see that I was only just in time!'

I realised now that in the other direction was an archway, and through it there was a covered gallery leading round the tower, a safe walkway.

I watched with a kind of immobile fascination as Casterman came hurrying, his black figure moving between pillars and columns, running towards us. He was shouting something.

'Miss Lilian, thank God you are safe . . . I had no idea . . .'

My rescuer did not wait for Casterman. With a gentle pressure, he impelled me safely to the top of the staircase that wound down to the ground, back to Jennet and safety. I moved obediently, still numbed with shock and only half aware of what Casterman was saying as he joined them at the top of the stairs.

'Miss Lilian, Miss Lilian, thank God! I thought you were . . . I saw you going towards that door . . . I curse myself for leaving you alone . . . I tried to warn you, but I fear you could not hear me. Those timbers have decayed since I last was here.'

What was it Casterman had shouted as I went towards that little door that led to an abyss? Had he truly called out a warning? Perhaps. It could have been so.

In fact, was I at all certain about what I heard?

I had to admit that I was not.

Gradually, we descended. Mr Lawrence was between myself and Casterman on the way down.

At last, we emerged into the sunshine at the bottom of the stairwell, and Jennet flung her arms around me.

'Why, miss, I've been that alarmed! This young gentleman here, he offered to go and find you out and make sure you was safe – oh, sir thank you! Miss Lilian, the young gentleman is from Cornwall, only think of that!'

'A fellow West Countryman, indeed,' I exclaimed. 'Well, sir, this is a fine chance that brought you here, as it has proven, for my sake! let me thank you with all my heart!'

Casterman was following on behind, and emerged from the tower. Should I accuse him? But of what? Of leading me carelessly into a spot that might prove dangerous? I had no evidence at all that he had acted maliciously, as I believe lawyers say, for there was no testimony apart from my own fleeting impression of his face as I moved towards the gap in the roof, a mere glimpse of an expression – why, no one would believe me, surely! I would be dismissed as a silly girl who had got herself into danger and tried to blame it on another. And my impression of Casterman – I knew that was not 'evidence'. People would say that was just a matter of the feelings of a young and inexperienced female who had been thrown into a state of panic by her near escape from a frightful danger. Nobody had listened to me after my riding accident, when I had tried to tell them about Selene. Nobody but Lord Ambrose – I recalled the serious way he had spoken to me, as if I were a real grown-up person whose word could be accepted, during our conversation in the first-class passengers' saloon.

We made our way back to the carriage.

Suddenly, my spirits were raised. There was an unexpected sight, a fine horse tethered close by, in the shade of the walls. Mr Lawrence knew something about horses, then.

Sholto Lawrence untied his mount, and prepared to ride along behind the carriage, asking as he did so, 'May I escort you back to the town?'

Casterman suddenly interspersed, with an edge of indignation in his voice, 'Thank you, I can look after the ladies!'

I spoke out determinedly. 'Mr Lawrence, I am sure we should be glad of your companionship.'

And, fortunately, Mrs Cornwallis added her agreement.

'Yes, to meet a British gentleman in such a spot as this – how could we reject your offer, sir? I am sure that my son in the Ministry would think it quite appropriate in such circumstances, and he is a stickler for etiquette, I assure you!'

It was settled, and when we reached the town, it was even agreed that the young man should come and take dinner in our hotel. Casterman glowered throughout the meal, but could do nothing in view of the politeness which we were all determined to show to the stranger.

'But, Mr Lawrence, where do you travel from Alexandria? Shall we not see you in Cairo?' enquired Mrs Cornwallis when Sholto expressed his regrets that his stay at our dinner table could be but a brief one, as his imminent departure was planned and could not be delayed.

'Alas, madam, I am taking the steamship for Marseilles in the morning. I am returning to England, you see – my mission in the East is accomplished.'

'And may we enquire what it was?'

'Indeed, ma'am. I am interested in horse breeding, and I have been studying the Arab methods – and I have purchased some fine Arab specimens of horse-flesh, which I hope to have at stud on my estates near Newquay. But I do not wish to bore you ladies into stupefaction with the tedious details of my passion for those animals!'

'You could not have said anything that would interest me more!' I exclaimed. But our conversation could not be prolonged: young Lawrence was waited for at the livery stables where his charges were to pass their last night upon Egyptian soil before embarking for the green pastures of England.

And now I must confess that I thought about Mr Lawrence for some time after he had ridden off down the dusty street and I made a very long entry in my diary, but I will not put it down here, for it consists of my private reflexions. Suffice it to say that Sholto Lawrence had quite put Lord Ambrose out of my mind.

Lord Ambrose has said that it is most important that I should continue with my narration (and also he has lent me a dictionary; he just put it into my hands without saying anything!). Even though some of what I saw in Cairo was very frightening and still troubles me greatly, I will set it down as well as I can, though it is about the wickedness of a man who must have brought misery and despair to many. How anyone could be so cruel is beyond my mind to understand, but that it was so, that it happened, I am a witness and must make my record.

So I am going on with my history of what occurred, although nothing of any interest at all seemed to happen for some days after the departure of Mr Sholto Lawrence from Alexandria. At least, nothing that I took any notice of, though Jennet was forever telling me to stop daydreaming and regard the scenery, etc, as we travelled from Alexandria to Cairo. But I will not set my daydreams down here, only what really happened to me after we had got to Cairo, where we arrived late one afternoon.

That first view over the city is so clear in my mind that I can see it yet. In my room at Hill's Hotel there was a finely carved screen of dark wood inlaid with mother-of-pearl which sheltered the room from the heat of the Egyptian sun, and in this screen was a door. When I stepped out through that door on to the balcony of my room, Cairo lay before me in the early sunset: a golden and pink flush over a city of pencil-thin towers.

There was still a hustle in the streets below. I had already become accustomed to some aspects of Egyptian life, even from our very short stay in Alexandria: the shouts and calls of water-sellers, perfumers, food vendors with their wares set out on trays slung from their necks. The cries of women sitting by the roadside with mountains of fresh fruit for sale, great weeping strawberries and melons like small suns, mingled with the shouted commands of some wealthy merchants pushing their silk-clad way through the crowd. To all the human cries that echo through the city are added the exotic animal noises, the shrieks of pet parakeets, the braying of donkeys ringing through the narrow alleys.

I could identify the angry groaning noises of a camel train: Mr Casterman had explained to us that camels always make that terrible noise when their heads are turned away from the river and out towards the deserts they must cross. He knew about fear, I think, in animals and in humans.

I was getting used, too, to the apparent chaos that always seemed to prevail, yet always resolved itself into orderliness in some unexplainable way. This city of Cairo, through which we had journeyed on the previous day, did not seem to me to merit what some of the British people on the ship had said about it. It was certainly no dirtier than Bristol or Southampton, the biggest English cities I had seen, and by all accounts Cairo was no worse than London, which my poor mother had always said was the grimiest place in the world! To my country-bred eye, the filth and mud churned up by the wheels of carriages is one of the most striking features of our great cities, though I daresay many of our countrymen and women would prefer me to keep quiet about it, but I am like the child in the fable, who would blurt out that the emperor had no clothes! And I was much shocked on my first visit to Bristol by the ragged creatures who made a precarious living by sweeping a path for the rich through the muck of the streets. Cairo seemed to be kept much cleaner. Little carts drawn by donkeys were continually collecting up rubbish and the dust was laid by men who sprinkled water regularly in the streets.

We had taken rooms in Hill's Hotel, as I have mentioned, where I believe most British travellers stay when in Cairo – most *respectable* British travellers, anyway, said Mrs Cornwallis, who had attached herself to our party. Jennet was very grateful for her company.

Mrs Cornwallis said there was an area of the city called the Frankish quarter where some Europeans had taken up residence, but the only Britishers there were eccentric and unreliable – artists and so forth, and a young girl such as I had no need of such raffish company! Of course, I longed to go there, but it was Quite Impossible!

On this first afternoon, just after our arrival in Cairo, Jennet was still asleep. She had spent the previous days packing and unpacking in agitation and was constantly asking me questions that I could not answer. Had we brought enough clothes . . . were they the right garments . . . what would the washerwomen do with our fine lawn underwear . . . would we be cool enough . . . warm enough . . . ?

Jennet had finally retreated to bed for a nap in a state of acute exhaustion and had not yet arisen. For the moment, as I looked out from my balcony, I could enjoy Cairo undisturbed.

And enjoy it I did! As I gazed out over the city, I actually felt for a moment the inclination to bless Uncle Micah for sending me there after all, so exciting was the prospect before me. His decision about my future had led me to this view. Just below my window, some men were working on a cart which was tilted up with its wheels spinning, as yet turning idly in the empty air. It suggested to me strange journeys that were yet to come, across rocky wastes and through enchanted streets. Just beyond the cart was a row of chairs of an old-fashioned type, rather like sedan chairs, which I had seen only in illustrations but never in use. Those chairs, I knew from Mrs Cornwallis, were for European women to travel in if they wished to venture to certain parts of the city which were unaccustomed to women who did not wear the veil, the covering garment of all respectable Mahometan ladies. And the closed chairs were also a protection against the sun of Egypt. Casterman had warned me against it. 'I know that you love the outdoors, Miss Lilian, but I beg you to revise your ideas for the time that you are in Egypt. You will find that the sun, though it may not seem so sharp and fierce as you imagined it, can even on a cloudy day pierce the clothing and burn the skin. Sunstroke is common in those who have recently arrived and do not take proper precautions against the dangers of the heat. When you are in Cairo, you must take care never to go out without a veil and a sunbonnet, and then you should travel in a closed chair, the kind that has a screen or gauze through which you may see the sights, yet pass through the crowds quite unobserved yourself.'

Did I really want to be cut off from the world by a veil of gauze?

I was pondering this when I remember that suddenly on that afternoon there came an extraordinary noise, like the screeching and spiting of an enormous cat. I saw with a shock where the sound emanated from, a creature like something in a fairytale: a huge and beautiful spotted cat, with white-frosted whiskery face and ruff of cream and gold speckles, long tufts of fur at the tips of the ears and eyes of a devilish green. This poor beast was imprisoned in a long and narrow cage; scarcely able to turn, it writhed its slim body against the iron bars. Using long hooks on poles, a group of men were cautiously trying to load the cage on to a cart. The prisoner shrieked with anger and tried to bite the bars.

I winced as its teeth clashed against the cruel metal. Was it a lynx? I thought I recognised it from a picture in a book. No doubt it was bound for one of the zoos of Europe where it would be put on display and prodded at by children with sticks.

Saddened by the sight I turned my head away, and yet I breathed in still the inescapable strange scents of Cairo. There was at that instant an odour which I will always associate with that city, full of a heavy sweetness, yet underlying it something sharp and wild, a strong catlike stench from the cage in which the lynx was still fighting its useless battle. A city of powerful scents and colours, intense heat, extremes of pain and pleasure.

I confess that I was, if truth be told, rather hurt that Lord

Ambrose had not said farewell at Alexandria, when the passengers had disembarked from the ship. I had expected to see him thereafter on the way to Cairo, but there had been no sign of him till now.

'Well, if he wants to pop up like the devil in a pantomime and give everyone a nasty shock, I've no doubt we'll see more of him,' had been Jennet's comment when I ventured to ask her if Lord Ambrose had been seen in Alexandria by any of our party. (Lord Ambrose, you did ask me to set it *all* down – and I do possess some tact – I did not mention your name to Mr Casterman!)

There were two ladies who arrived later, the Misses Harvey, who occupied the room adjacent to my own, and introduced themselves almost as soon as they got into the hotel. They had news and it was all quite exciting, what with the Ostrich. We were drinking lemon water from little gilt-rimmed glasses on the terrace of the hotel when the great excitement occurred.

'Oh, sister, is that not an Ostrich?' shrieked out Miss Harvey, staring over the terrace and dropping her glass of lemon water in alarm.

I am sorry to say that, much to the alarm of the Misses Harvey, it was indeed an Ostrich! It stalked round and round the courtyard of the hotel on its great long legs, pursued by its keeper and a gang of small boys. The Misses Harvey stood up nervously as it approached the terrace and the monstrous turkey-head peered at them sideways on.

They fled indoors, dragging me with them, so alas here the Ostrich part of my story draws to a close!

CHAPTER 10

Letter from Lord Ambrose Malfine to Sholto Lawrence, Esquire

To be despatched from Cairo with all haste.

After your departure from Alexandria it was my plan to watch the disembarkation of my fellow pasengers, and their transit to Cairo, from a distance. I preferred to keep my self-appointed watch over Miss Westmorland unobtrusive – a stratagem which did not succeed in keeping her safe. I had given instructions that luggage despatched after me by Belos should be conveyed directly from the slow packet which brought it, pitching along a few days later in the swift wake of the *Great London*, to the *Zubeida*, my sister's houseboat, moored upon the Nile. But the damn fools loaded it for Hill's Hotel, as was usually the custom, and I caught up just as it was being taken off the coach outside the hotel. I watched from a small shop across the road.

The coach was heavily laden with trunks and boxes and I was forced to sit through the lengthy unloading which was accomplished by porters clad in the magnificent livery which the hotel provided. The uniform was lavish with red and gold and a tall major-domo, his shoulders adorned with swashbuckling epaulettes, was supervising procedures. An encouraging crowd of onlookers rapidly formed; jeering children and friendly advisers shouted various cries of help and encouragement from the sidelines. Suddenly, I caught sight of the name stencilled on one of the trunks waiting to be carried into the hotel: MALFINE. And there was the crest, the wolf's head surmounted by a golden 'M' adorned with all manner of twirls and curlicues.

Nevertheless, I hoped still to avoid discovery of my presence in Cairo, and not just to keep watch over Miss Lilian from afar like some pantomime wizard, but because I ardently desired to avoid the idle gossips of the English residents in Cairo, a tedious brigade for whom discerning the faults of the native inhabitants is the major pleasure of the day.

Unfortunately, there were two ladies who arrived in this coach, the Misses Harvey, who were to occupy rooms in the hotel.

'Lord Ambrose was to have travelled with us,' said Miss Harvey whose voice I could hear from the other side of the street. 'But he made only the briefest of appearances, did he not, Jane?'

Miss Jane Harvey, who is somewhat younger than her sister and has a still-beautiful face marred by a squinting eye and a habit of putting her hand up in front of it as if to hide the defect from the world, gave a smile at the memory.

'Oh, indeed, it was most dramatic. We were all seated in the coach at Alexandria, with the one vacant space – we understood a gentleman was to arrive at any minute to travel with us. And then, just as it was time to leave and the coachman was fretting to be off – you could hear the bridles of the horses clinking as they chaffed their heads

with the delay – there came a man riding up on a mount –
Oh, I assure you it was a fine animal – was it not, sister?
I rode often in my youth, you know, Miss Lilian – now
where was I?'

'Lord Ambrose came riding up and Jane, I think, will
never get over it!' said Miss Harvey tartly.

'Yes, that animal was as fine, compared with the
coach horses, as is my best muslin compared with the
coarse cotton on that beggar's back. And Lord Ambrose
called up to the coachman and said that he would not
be accompanying us – that he had been lent that horse
by a friend with whom he had met unexpectedly. And
Mr Wilkinson . . . that was one of the gentlemen in the
coach . . . Mr Wilkinson said that he would warrant the
friend . . .'

Here I withdrew into the back of the premises, from
which I sent a messenger desiring that my luggage should
be sent on to the *Zubeida*, so I cannot vouch for the details
of Mr Wilkinson's warranties, but you will gather the
general gist, and why I so desire my presence in Cairo to
remain unknown to ladies such as the Misses Harvey.

But, I confess, I love this country! In spite of all the
trials presented by my fellow countrymen and women,
nothing can prevent me from the delight of a gallop at
dawn across these vast sands, once teeming with life and
activity, that surround the city at so short a distance, nor
from explorations among the caves and rocks, the ruined
coffins and the bones of the dead. The heat of Egypt is a
delight to me, I love even the dust of this city flying in my
face as I ride through the streets. More and more, I seek out
Arab society and study their language, and draw further and
further away from the west in spirit as well as in body.

But, in two respects, there are ties which I cannot

131

sever. One is that of offering some protection to Miss Westmorland. The other is that I cannot forget a pale English face, long flowing hair, eyes filled with intelligent fire, last seen upon the steps of Malfine. Will you go to see Elisabeth Anstruther for me, Sholto, if this reaches you, and tell her how you found me? I am, of course, far too proud to beg that you should do so.

I shall write again as soon as there is anything to report affecting Miss Westmorland's well-being. There are many ways of meeting death in this city and I hope that she will never come to any of them.

CHAPTER 11

The Further Narrative of Miss Lilian Westmorland

There were, I believe, no long-term residents at Hill's Hotel. The whole place seemed in a constant state of turmoil, for travellers were arriving and departing (and some contrived to do both operations at once) at every hour of the day and night. As well as those who were setting off for overland journeys, and preparing to cross the desert to Suez, to take ship for India, there were travellers journeying further up the Nile. These were engaged in fitting out boats and filling them with supplies, and included the Misses Harvey, who intended to travel to Luxor, where the climate would be especially beneficial for the consumption from which the elder lady suffered, and which was the reason why they, escorted by Mr Wilkinson, had travelled to Egypt.

'We are going to spend the winter in southern Egypt, where the air is so dry and still that the doctors say my sister's lungs will stand a chance of healing,' said Miss Jane to Lilian. 'Why do you not consider coming to Luxor – it is said to be a far healthier place than Cairo?'

'Yes, indeed,' said Mr Wilkinson, who had joined us one

day on the terrace for tea. 'I do not wish to alarm you, Miss Lilian, but there are sometimes infections in Cairo. The place is so populous and the streets so close and narrow that it cannot well be otherwise. Whereas at Luxor there is very little danger and everything to be gained from the climate.'

My cough, and the feebleness from which I suffered as a result of my accident, had already undergone a dramatic improvement. The rise to good health which had commenced on the *Great London* seemed to be continuing here, for I did not appear to suffer from the fevers that assailed so many of my travelling companions. The weakness of my lungs that had so troubled Dr Sandys seemed very nearly to have disappeared. So I saw no great reason to remove to Luxor.

But I did mention to Mr Casterman the advice which I had been given by Mr Wilkinson.

Casterman's answer came very quickly and smoothly.

'Well, Miss Lilian, I would not suggest that we quit Cairo now,' he said. 'For one thing, it would be desirable to rent a house here even if we wish to travel about the country, for nothing is as tiresome as having all one's luggage transported everywhere, as if we were so many snails having to carry our homes upon our backs! And then, besides that, I have some business to perform on behalf of your uncle. There are merchants here in Cairo whom he wishes me to see, and bankers' drafts he will send to settle our expenses, which will be addressed to me here in Cairo. So you see, there are good reasons why we should not quit the city. But perhaps if you should wish to make a visit to Luxor later on, to look at the temple and so forth, I am sure there need be no difficulty about that.'

This did sound reasonable enough and I decided to raise

the subject again with him later, when we were more settled from the upheavals of the voyage. The opportunity arose sooner than I expected.

Two days later the Misses Harvey invited me, with Jennet and Mrs Cornwallis, to join their party in the *dahabeeyah*, that is, a kind of houseboat, in which they intended to travel to Aswan. It was all ready for the journey sooner that had been expected.

When this invitation was reported to Mr Casterman, he was adamantly against it.

'No indeed, Miss Lilian, I cannot think your uncle would wish you to travel in the company of perfect strangers! Why, we know nothing of such people. I could not countenance such a step.'

It was on the tip of my tongue to reply that Casterman was after all but a servant; he had no right to decide whether I should accompany the Harveys or not. But I bit it back! It was in any case impractical to go without my uncle's man of business, for, whatever Casterman's social status, he was irreplaceable here in Egypt; he knew the ways of the Orient, he spoke fluent Arabic, he had been entrusted with our financial arrangements. I was powerless to argue with him.

Besides, there was a deeper reason. Once before, when a servant entrusted with my safety had begged me to show discretion, I had refused. Poor Adams, the groom, had counselled caution, and I had ignored him. The result had been the death of my beloved Selene. I was much sadder and wiser than I had been at Westmorland Park, and I think I had been partly helped and comforted by Lord Ambrose, for our conversation on the ship had given me much cause for reflection.

So I accepted Casterman's insistence that we should stay in Cairo. What else, in truth, could I have done?

The first few days in Cairo passed agreeably enough, however, after our friends had left for Luxor. There was a trip out to see the Pyramids, when our small group of Europeans stood in the tides of sand, brown like the fur of an animal, that drifted round those almost-fabulous structures. Clothes clinging with sweat and dust, we even ventured some way into the Great Pyramid, where we crept along in stifling darkness lit by the candle of our guide. Flickering shadows jumped from wall to wall of the narrow passage-way. I wanted to continue to the centre of the great tomb, but Jennet was gasping and fainting and we had to take her outside.

But we just stood there in the desert and gazed for a while. I felt so tiny; we were so out of place, upright dolls in our stiff Western dress as we walked a little way down and stared at the massive head of the Sphinx protruding in the sand. Casterman remained with us (he had not entered the pyramid, having done so in the company of Mr Belzoni the great explorer, or so he informed us), looking upwards at the Sphinx and beating off the small boys who ran round offering us necklets or drinks of sherbet. I wished the man would go away, but told myself it was because his face perturbed me. I wished to think only of the tremendous prospect before us and not to be agitated by thoughts of petty human wrongs.

So there we stood, unsuitably dark-clad, uncomfortable, dwarfed by the grandeur around us. I had brought my sketching-pad and, seated on some fragment of an ancient building, tried to record that moment. Casterman's black stovepipe hat and tight trousers and Jennet's swathed heavy skirts were outlined sharply against the desert sands. I had again discarded my bonnet; my hair was blowing in the dry wind, in trailing curls, for it was not yet long enough to pin up and it flew in front of my eyes as I tried to sketch. This desert was far from being empty, as I had imagined it; it was full of the relics of human existence, of carved and chiselled stones and ancient rubbish silted up here and there in the sand.

Back in the hotel I recalled that scene. I fancied that I could still smell on my clothes that curious acrid ancient odour, carried from drifting heaps of dried-up waste, of twigs and shreds of ancient cloth, coarse and brown and torn like paper, of bones in fragments, of a nest of dead baby bats, blind and hairless, that a thin yellow dog was nosing from the debris. I felt the smell of it had penetrated my clothing and sunk into my skin; that it was in my lungs and in my hair, that it had seeped down through my very pores. In the marble-floored bathroom at Hill's Hotel I took off my heavy dress and clinging petticoats with relief. The layers of fine cotton were soaked into a heavy wadding by the running sweat and fine sandy dust that had sifted through all my clothing. The great marble tub had been filled by the servants with cool water and it was with relief that I stepped in and took up my sponge.

By this time, I was wishing that Casterman would make faster progress with his search for a house. Jennet was already loud in complaints; she could not unpack, there was not enough space for our things, the hotel laundry regularly lost buttons and handkerchiefs. The privy, in the inmost depths of our suite of rooms at the hotel, though it was emptied daily, was perfumed with some flowery jasmine scent that Jennet complained of bitterly, saying that it was quite indecent (though I secretly thought it was delicious). And as for me, there was a limit to the entertainment I could derive from taking tea with the crew of comparatively elderly ladies who were my usual companions at the hotel tea-table, for the Misses Harvey had been followed by quite a succession of similar travellers who came, hired their houseboats, and departed along the Nile.

Mr Casterman regularly set off from the hotel and was gone long hours on business affairs, he told me. He promised that he was negotiating for a suitable lease on a dwelling in the Frankish quarter, a house that had until recently been occupied by a French merchant and thus was adapted to Western tastes, but that it was still not ready. He could not tell me when the time would come when we might move thereto from Hill's Hotel.

I think it was on the third or fourth day of our stay at Hill's Hotel that Mr Casterman took us on a visit to the Khan el-Khalili, the great souk or bazaar of Cairo. We (that is, Mrs Cornwallis and myself – Jennet was not so anxious) had been begging him to take us on a shopping expedition, where we might have an opportunity to make some purchases of the goods for which the city is famous – the fine silks, the damasks brought from Syria, the muslins of India, the riches of all corners of the east which are heaped up in the souks by the merchants of Cairo.

Mr Wilkinson had said that there were sometimes infections raging in the city, and Mr Casterman himself attributed our delay to his concern for our safety. He wished to make quite certain, he said, that rumours of an outbreak of that terrible disease, the small-pox, were false. He finally pronounced that he was satisfied there was no cause for alarm.

And here I must explain that the Khan el-Khalili is not an open market such is usually found in English cities, but a great covered hall, or rather, series of halls, roofed over, swept and cleanly, so that one may roam free from the incursions of sand and dust. Mr Casterman told us that it was very old indeed, having been founded some five centuries previously, and some of the old buildings still lay at the very heart of the souk, but that it would take a long time to penetrate that far!

He spoke the truth in that regard, for there were not just a few stalls but whole areas given over to some particular merchandise – to sweetmeats, to jewels, to shawls, to ribbons – every kind of luxury for which one might desire.

The scents of musk and jasmine floated out from the perfumery shops, mingling with the odours of coffee and mint tea, which we were offered everywhere, to try and persuade us to linger and to buy. I never saw nor imagined such fine things. The most delicate organdie you can imagine, almost transparent, violet-tinted, and smelling of violets as well! Cashmere shawls from India, the furs of strange creatures, long and silky, pantaloons of scarlet satin for women – one could never imagine such things, even in dreams, as were for sale in that great bazaar!

We plunged in deeper and deeper. Casterman had aided us in purchasing some lengths of silk and muslin (Jennet turned her head aside from the scarlet trousers, with many exclamations of shocked modesty, but I confess I rather longed for a pair!) and our party was now rather weary; Casterman himself seemed rather bored, as well he might be by all this female flim-flammery.

But we reached another part of the souk, one where there was furniture for sale – all kinds of little brass tables and inlaid cupboards – and then came upon a section where the vitrines were full of curios. Some were quite ordinary, such as cameos or wooden statuettes, but some were exotic things, like little figurines of bright blue that Mrs Cornwallis said she believed had come out of tombs, or necklaces of gold and beads of blue and red, which she thought had been taken from mummies, which was a very disagreeable thought, for I had read about this way the ancient Egyptians had of preserving their dead forever, embalming them and wrapping them in bandages so that they could be taken even now from the sands and one could see here a bony hand, there a jaw with all the teeth still in it, gaping at a person from between the wrappings. I hoped we were not going to see any mummies on this expedition, and we did not, so I was fortunate. But we saw something else.

We saw an Egyptian coffin.

It was right at the back of the shop, which stretched much farther back from the street than one might have thought. We entered because the window had a pretty display of antique necklaces, and saw a sign in English, 'Antiquities and curios – consignments expedited anywhere in the world', and as Mrs Cornwallis claimed, 'Well, at least if they speak English, that gives one some confidence!'

Mr Casterman entered first and I followed. I brushed past all kinds of dusty relics, crowded together: I remember such things as a small stuffed crocodile, a tall lamp supported by the carved figure of a turbaned servant, a gilded Chinese screen. The general effect was of the lumber room of the world.

I did not understand at first what the long, low object at the back might be, for as I began to see better in the dim light I beheld that one end of it was carved into the shape of a human head with a great gold and blue wig, and there was a human face painted upon it. Wings enfolded the shoulders, and painted necklets and jewels adorned the breast. It seemed more a strange kind of human-shaped statue that was lying upon its back.

Mrs Cornwallis and Jennet were some way behind me, still at the entrance, and I desired very suddenly to leave the shop altogether and return to the sunlight and crowds outside. In fact, I turned about and hastened towards my companions, trying to avoid numerous little tables crammed with dusty glass decanters, china statuettes and the like.

But it was too late! A shopkeeper had emerged, not, as we expected, an Egyptian in traditional garb, but a man wearing European dress topped by a fez, who bowed courteously and indicated some little gilt chairs. As if by magic, a small boy bearing a brass tray with tiny tea-glasses appeared, and Mrs Cornwallis and Jennet sunk irresistibly on to the velvet seats of the chairs and gave little sighs of relief. Another moment, and tea-glasses, to which even Jennet had now become grudgingly accustomed, were placed in their hands.

After a hard day's shopping, it requires a superhuman effort to resist tea and a comfortable chair. It was very plain that Jennet and Mrs Cornwallis would not budge for some while, so I, who was not feeling quite yet in such a state of exhaustion, began again to cast about the shop out of idle curiosity, and found myself wandering back again, ending up confronting the strange object at the rear of the shop.

To my surprise, Mr Casterman seemed interested in it. He was peering down at it, and paced its length a couple of times.

The proprietor of the shop hurried back towards us.

They seemed to know each other. 'Ah, Mr Casterman!' exclaimed the shop owner. 'It is good to see you again!' He turned to me enquiringly.

'This is Miss Lilian Westmorland, and Miss Lilian, this is Signor Morino, an Italian acquaintance who has helped me occasionally on business matters. Miss Westmorland is the niece of Mr Micah Overbury.'

'Oh yes, of course, the name of Mr Overbury is well known to me! He has many business affairs here!'

'But I had not thought Uncle Micah had any interest in antiquities!' I exclaimed. 'He has never mentioned any such thing.'

'No, I do not mean in connection with the business I carry on here,' said Mr Morino. 'Mr Overbury deals with letters of credit, business loans, and so forth.'

There was a slight pause. Then the Italian resumed the conversation very smoothly, as if there had been no little hiccup, if I may so call it.

'This is a fine specimen of the antique we have before us – I was most fortunate to secure it. It is a coffin, from the Pharaonic age, a rarity now, for these things rarely appear complete on the market.'

'Where does it come from?' asked Casterman, eyeing the long shape.

'Oh, it was found in some tomb or other, at Saqqara, near the pyramids – but the local Arabs would never tell me where exactly! If they have found a tomb, they keep it to themselves, and bring the best things to us, the connoisseurs, without revealing where they come from!'

He bent down as he spoke, and, placing his hands on either side of the headdress, slowly raised the top.

I half expected some mummified figure to lie inside, some skull-like features to peer out at me, and I confess to shrinking away as the lid came up, but the inside was empty, save from a little dust and a few dried leaves. I could see now that the whole top of the coffin simply lifted off, like the lid of a box.

'It is made of wood,' said Mr Morino. 'Most of the ancient

sarcophagi are made of stone, and weigh a ton or more, but this is very light. It would be quite easily shipped, if you were interested in purchasing it.'

'Well, I think it rather morbid!' said I. 'I would not care to have such a thing lying round at Westmorland Park!'

The Italian gentleman seemed rather amused at this and we laughed together for a few moments. I thought he laughed rather excessively and did not quite care for this.

Then he turned to Mr Casterman, and they began to talk business matters, and I returned to Mrs Cornwallis and Jennet, and sat with them on the little gilt and velvet chairs. I believe Mrs Cornwallis made some trifling purchase of a cornelian necklace for her daughter.

It was a quite unexceptional occasion, in many ways.

CHAPTER 12

The fast-falling Egyptian dusk was coming down just as Mr Casterman hurried downstairs one evening into the lobby of the hotel. It was a few days after the shopping expedition, and I had been invited to take tea in Rodah Gardens with the latest consignment of elderly ladies to arrive via the Alexandria coach. I was just entering the lobby and bidding farewell to my companions as Mr Casterman spoke.

'Miss Lilian, you will find that I have already given orders for our removal to a house in the old part of the city – I assure you, it is most suitable for your accommodation.'

I was taken completely aback and protested accordingly.

'But Mr Casterman, I have but this moment come back – I have been to visit the gardens on Rodah Island! I am not at all ready to pack and shift off to some other place at a moment's notice!'

'You will find that your things have already been placed into trunks, Miss Lilian. I gave Mistress Jennet the necessary instructions whilst you were out.'

'But this is intolerable! Am I never to be consulted?'

'I am afraid you must tolerate it, Miss Lilian, for we shall surely lose our chance of getting this house if we do not establish ourselves in it immediately. The French merchant who had it has just vacated it and there are plenty more who would make good offers to lease it, I assure you. Mr

145

Morino has been good enough to use his influence with the owner and persuade him that we would make the most reliable tenants – but we cannot afford to delay!'

What could I say? I whirled away in anger and ran upstairs to my room, where I found Jennet in a positive tornado of packing, all the while issuing instructions to two porters who were collecting up baggage and piling it up on the landing. Occasionally she would signal to them to retrieve some trunk or case and dive within it, to emerge with a cloak or a pair of shoes or some mysterious mis-wrapped parcel tied up with string.

'Oh, Miss Lilian, why, whatever shall we do? Here's old poxy-face has told me to get us packed, bag and baggage, and be ready to move to some heathen household where we'll not have another Christian soul to speak to, I'll be bound!'

All was hubbub and chaos. No one would listen to our questions. The porters were moving the luggage downstairs and I had found I had no choice but to follow my baggage, which contained everything I possessed in this alien land. Every traveller will know the disturbing experience of seeing one's entire little store of possessions moving away from one strapped up in suitcases – and besides, I had not even any money to speak of – only a few piastres in my purse which I carried for *baksheesh*.

Outside the hotel, I was ushered straightaway into a shuttered conveyance, with tiny screens through which it was possible to see scraps of the vitality of the city as I was carried alone through the streets. Here was a *mamlouk*, a mounted horseman, one of those soldiers who had started their careers as slaves. He was clad in magnificent scarlet and golden silk finery, and was brandishing the flat of his sword as he forced a way through the crowded streets. There was a lady hidden within flowing veils, mounted on a white mule and preceded by a servant who ran ahead on foot to clear a way through the throng. Now came a man wearing a strange rough-looking cloak of animal skins and wearing a tall hat decorated with a moon and stars. The crowd parted before him as if by some unspoken command, though he had no sign of wealth – indeed, his face looked thin to the point of beggary – and he carried no weapon.

All these were glimpsed briefly as we jostled along, bobbing and weaving through the crowds, along with great piles of oranges, gold-embroidered robes hanging on high racks, models of fairy-tale castles stuck all over with bits of mirror, dishes of porcelain so fine you could see your hand through them, adorned the shop-fronts in narrow alleys. It was evening now and torches were lit against the coming darkness, so that the whole glittering spectacle appeared as if against a back-drop of violet-blue velvet. I was, in spite of my fears, still mesmerised by the sights and excitements of Cairo, the lively expressions of the people, who laughed and called out as they bartered and chaffed and thrust their way along.

We were climbing up a slope now, and moving steadily away from the direction of the Nile. Once or twice, above us, I glimpsed the great towers of the Citadel, the fortress built by Saladin to crown the city, and real fear arose that we might be making for its rough dark walls. Once inside the Citadel and nothing more might be heard of me ever again. Was there not a well which Crusader prisoners had been forced to dig till they dropped of exhaustion? Was that not the place where centuries ago the young Sultan Faraj, attacking his wife in a fit of insane jealousy, had chopped her to pieces, pursuing her as she fled from room to room? Or were these old travellers' tales, told to frighten the innocent?

We did not seem, after all, to be ascending to the Citadel. I could no longer see the occasional European face, red and sweaty in among the gold and brown complexions of Egypt, nor the red fez that betokened an Egyptian official. There were no more shops and stalls; the alleys grew ever narrower and we passed between tall houses, hidden from the world by elaborately carved window screens, from which an occasional patchwork of faint lamplight was cast into the street. There might be invisible eyes behind those screens: it was impossible to tell for sure, but I sensed that our little procession of porters, mules and baggage was being carefully scrutinised.

It had become utterly dark, and still we were making our way into the very heart of the old city, twisting and turning through streets that grew ever tighter. The leaders of our party now carried flaming torches mounted on iron poles, and the wayward jumping of the flames made an unstable reddish illumination of the high walls on either side of the alleys, which seemed to seal us in as if we were winding our way through a maze. We had left the crowds behind, and the narrow ways along which we passed were now almost empty; here and there a dog lay sleeping in the street and was roused with kicks that a mule might pass.

As suddenly as we had left Hill's Hotel, we turned into our new destination.

We were in a courtyard, surrounded by several storeys of rooms on all sides. In the centre of the courtyard was a fountain, whose water ran in a silvery sheet over a carved marble slab. I could sense the cool moisture in the air around it, and by the flickering lights of torches which were supported in rings around the walls, I saw arched galleries which ran around the first floor, and on the level above were latticed and shuttered projecting windows, remote and silent.

We had created some bustle in the courtyard. The baggage animals were being unloaded and taken to stabling. Looking round, I could see that the entrance through which we had come was a great timbered door barred with heavy iron, and with only a tiny wicker opening in it through which anything of the street might be espied. On a bench beside the doorway sat a large and powerful-looking turbaned figure, dressed in a long blue robe, and with a scimitar tucked into his belt.

Casterman was suddenly there, directing operations. I slid wearily out of the carrying-chair and made my way up a flight of steps which Casterman indicated. I paused and looked round for Jennet, but could not see her. I wanted to go and ask Casterman about it, but all initiative seemed to have deserted me; I felt disoriented and helpless, a stranger in an utterly strange land.

Entering a door at the top of the steps I found myself in a long room, inside those shuttered windows which overlooked the courtyard from a great height. It was a long, narrow room, lit by hanging lamps swinging gently in a tiny draught, casting moving and revolving shadows which increased my sense of confusion. Two women were moving towards me and gentle hands were plucking off my cloak. A tiny glass of hot scented tea was put between my fingers and as I drank my eyelids closed with a weariness which must have come from my exhausted feelings rather than from any physical weakness. The sights and sounds of the city, the strangeness of the place in which I found myself and an overwhelming and unaccustomed feeling of helplessness had so tired me that I drifted off to sleep as I half sat, half lay on a couch which seemed softer by the moment.

There was a sharp sunlight filtering through the tiny apertures of the screen over the window; within the screen itself, a small opening allowed a patch of bright-yellow light to fall in a pool upon the floor.

I was in a long gallery, the room overlooking the court-yard. I had been brought coffee, eggs, bread and a bowl of scented water to wash in, and my brief exploration suggested that these living quarters were luxurious. Looking round the room, I saw that the walls and ceilings were delicately painted with a faded design of roses and tulips. The soft carpets beneath my feet were of a thick and lustrous pile, with blue and red lozenges of jewel-like colour woven into dense patterns. The doors and window-screens were of some dark wood, intricately carved with starry inlay of mother-of-pearl and ivory. Low divans heaped with cushions and small brass tables stood about; there seemed to be no richness lacking.

But, after taking in my surroundings, my first reaction had been to go to the door at the end of the gallery and fling it open. Where was Casterman? And where was my dear Jennet? I felt a terrible anxiety about her welfare and about my own, I must confess!

As I stepped forward to cross the threshold, a bulky turbaned figure rose up ro bar the way. He did not say anything: indeed, words were not necessary.

I was not going to be allowed to pass.

There was a soft plucking at my dress and I turned to see one of the two women who had been in the room on the previous evening, a slender girl with enormous dark-brown eyes beneath arched brows and a gentle expression on her face. Shaking her head sadly, as if to say, 'It is useless', the girl drew me away from the door.

As I turned to look fully at my new companion, I saw the most exotic being I had ever encountered. She was tall, with gleaming black skin; her hair was braided with silk cords and threaded with gold coins and ornaments, and upon her cheeks and arms were tattoos of blue stars. She wore a chemise of white and long trousers of crimson silk, with a loose flowing garment of crimson damask silk thrown over all. Her fingers were tipped with henna and her feet were thrust into velvet slippers intricately embroidered with gold.

She pointed to herself and said 'Rahaba' several times over. I understood that to be her name, but could make out nothing of her speech.

Who was she? She was richly dressed and yet she did not appear to be part of the household, for over the next few days I realised that Rahaba and I were alike prisoners here. We could not leave these luxurious rooms, and like myself Rahaba saw no one but the other girl, she who had given me the little glass of tea upon my arrival and was plainly a servant here, or the scimitared keepers always on duty at the door, one by day and another by night.

And I knew something else: Rahaba was plainly unhappy. She spent much of the time peering down at the courtyard through the tiny lattices of the windows, as if watching and waiting for something or someone and from time to time she wept, softly.

It did not take long to understand that there was no means of escape for us. Beyond the gallery lay only some smaller chambers, furnished with necessities for making coffee and so forth, and a small cool hall with an exquisite sunken marble fountain. From these apartments in which Rahaba and I were confined there was no way out. I began to understand where we were. We were in the harem of the house and it was well-guarded.

I saw nothing of Casterman for the first two days of our imprisonment, as I gradually came to know our situation.

Our captivity took on a certain routine, delightful enough if freedom had been among the luxuries we enjoyed. At noon and again at evening dishes were brought to the woman's quarters by the servant girl, who remained always silent. She carried in trays of food: soup with rice and lemon, pilaws of lamb, handfuls of raisins. The food was good but our appetites were poor and when she returned a while later, the trays were still heaped with food. From time to time we heard other occupants of the women's quarters: the sounds of children's voices, occasionally of a baby crying, filtered through from somewhere close at hand.

A number of times I stood at the windows, calling out Jennet's name, hoping that there was some part of the house where my faithful friend was kept, but there came no response, save the occasional barking of a dog in the courtyard. When I broke down in tears at last, after all my cries had gone unanswered, Rahaba drew me gently back into the room, shaking her head as if to say, 'Do not waste your breath! It is hopeless!'

We tried to speak to the girl who brought the food, but she would not reply, keeping absolutely silent all the time. She seemed timid and too frightened to respond to the Arabic which Rahaba sometimes poured out when she appeared. But I felt that the servant was looking somehow in a pitying way at Rahaba. The thought came into my head that she seemed to be seeing a future victim, a prisoner who would not long remain in this comfortable captivity.

But she did not look at me in the same way. She avoided looking at me whenever possible. I wondered if she thought I had the 'evil eye'.

Casterman eventually appeared. He strode into our quarters, ignoring the terror of Rahaba. Making towards me along the length of the room, he ignored my plans for information and release, embarking immediately on a long tirade.

'Miss Lilian, you are here for your own safety, I assure you. There are rumours of all kinds about riots in the city – feeling against Europeans is running very high and little is needed to spark off trouble. It is even dangerous for any European face to appear in the streets. You run much less risk here than you would in Hill's Hotel, where Franks, as they call us, are known to be gathered together – that makes it an obvious target for a mob attack. This is the old quarter of the city and you are well hidden, but you must really remain within these walls till the danger is past! Believe me, I am thinking of nothing but your own security from any insult or violence! And as for this young lady, Mademoiselle Rahaba, she, too, is sheltering here from danger, for her father is a very highly placed official suspected of bribery who likewise would be the target of a mob should he as much as venture into the streets of his own city of Cairo! He has asked me to find safe accommodation for his favourite daughter until the storm should blow over and his family can be safely re-united, so you see, Miss Lilian, that this is no tyranny on my part, as you seem to imagine.'

I was genuinely alarmed by this speech. What might become of me should I succeed in my efforts to venture outside this strange household? I was almost prepared to accept Casterman's assessment of the situation. The man was so powerful a presence and put forward his arguments so eloquently with that mellifluous voice that I felt myself almost seduced into trusting him, though I observed that Rahaba still wept and cried as if she would never be comforted.

'But why I may not have Jennet here and communicate with my friends?' asked I. 'With Mrs Cornwallis, or the Hays? Could I not write to them and let them know where I am?'

Casterman smiled quite pleasantly. 'But of course, my dear Miss Lilian! Mrs Jennet returned to the hotel on the night of your arrival to fetch some more items which she believed you needed – I believe the good lady mentioned some medicines which she thought would not be obtainable in our somewhat Oriental household here – and of course I have been reluctant to convey her through the streets these last few days for fear of the crowds. But I will see that she is got out of danger as soon as possible and brought here to join you. And as for writing to your friends and letting them know your whereabouts, I must tell you that houses here do not have such neat directions and addresses as in the West End of London, but you may certainly write to your friends and I will undertake to have the letters delivered to them, I promise you. I will have pen and paper sent up to you and you may give me the letters directly, as soon as they are written! There, does that not make you feel a good deal happier – come, you must not be downcast, for you are in perfect safety, and I trust, quite comfortable! Is this not an *Arabian Nights* palace? I have rented it from a wealthy gold merchant, complete with his servants and his furniture!'

'It is a beautiful house,' I said, and meant it, but I knew it was also a golden cage.

Casterman sounded plausible enough, however. But still I held back from trusting him, for two reasons.

One was fairly straightforward and not difficult to explain. It was impossible not to think that he had led me into danger at the fort near Alexandria. I went over that incident time and time again in my mind and could not banish the thought of Casterman's outstretched hand beckoning me on. Beckoning me until I would have stepped into an abyss.

Had he known it was there? How could he not have done so – he had visited that fort on previous occasions. That much was clear from the evident familiarity with the tower which he had displayed. And if he had known about the missing beams, then quite deliberately he had taken me into a death-trap.

The second reason for my mistrust was more difficult to pinpoint. It was somehow in the way Casterman looked at Rahaba. Forced as I was in my present surroundings to try and communicate with gesture and expression, I had become more sensitive, I believe, to the language of look and movement, in a way in which our free and easy ways at Westmorland Park had never constrained. I had been a lively, thoughtless young person – I had to confess this – but I had also been open and confident in my nature. Now I was forced to study my surroundings and my companions as never before, for I realised that those trusting days were gone: I had to become thoughtful, wily, subtle in my dealings with the world.

So I observed, with my eyes downcast, the glance which Casterman gave to Rahaba, who now held an organza scarf up to her face as her sobs subsided into a kind of hopelessness. I tried to think of how the look on Casterman's face might be described and a strange word sprung into my mind. Miserly. That was it. Like a man staring at his wealth.

Why did I think that? I cast my mind back and suddenly recalled an incident that had occurred when I was about thirteen years of age and had been passing through Callerton town on market day, with my mother. We were in the carriage which was pressing its way through the town square and I observed through the window an exchange which I only partly understood. An old man with a beard was pushing a woman forward with one hand and with the other was taking a gold coin from the outstretched palm of a farmer. The farmer's face was red and a stench of ale reached me on the breeze which blew through the open carriage window. The old man's face was fixed, not upon the woman, but upon the coin and had stamped upon the features the expression which I now saw upon Casterman's as he gazed at Rahaba. Most men would have been transfixed by her beauty.

Casterman was like a miser staring at his gold.

I turned the thought over, watching them and another word came to mind. Covetous, that was it. I had heard it in church. I repeated the word to myself, trying it out as a description of his face. It fitted exactly. Covetous.

I no longer trusted Casterman because I had learned to observe. No, I thought, he was not to be believed, not for myself, not for Rahaba, yet, as I had learned wisdom and caution in my captivity and to restrain the impulses on which I had always previously acted, I said nothing then. I thanked him as if I were in my mother's drawing room and there was nothing in the slightest degree amiss. He bowed and took his leave and left us to our captivity.

And as for his promise of conveying my letters to my friends, that was all very fine but writing materials were never sent up to me as he had promised, so how was I to write without pen, ink or paper? None was brought and though I ransacked all the fragile pretty cupboards and caskets in the harem I found nothing to serve my purpose of trying to find some saviour in the outside world. Piles of silks, tinted muslins that fluttered as I opened the ivory-inlaid doors of a press, jars of perfume, boxes of sandalwood – but not a single object of any practical use.

On the second day after Casterman's visit I determined to try something. Racking my brains for some means of communication with the outside world, I followed after the girl who brought the trays of food.

'Please, I need your help!'

The face was concerned but uncomprehending. The two of us had not a word of any language in common.

I made writing gestures with one hand, and this the girl evidently understood but a look of fear came into her eyes and she shook her head vehemently. No, she would not help me to obtain any writing implements, that was obvious.

In despair, I clung now to the name of the one person in Cairo whom I believed could help me. Mr Sholto Lawrence had left for England and I could not count upon his aid. And Jennet loved me dearly, of that I was sure, yet danger was obliging me to think like an adult and not like the child who had clung to Jennet's skirts; she had advised me to the best of her abilities, and that well-intentioned advice had been that my Uncle Micah doubtless had my welfare at heart! Devotion, I understood suddenly, is not always more desirable than judgement. No, Jennet would not see through the traps that had been laid by cunning hands; she would no doubt be more fearful and anxious than was I myself. I was troubled sorely for her, but under no illusions that she could assist me. Yet one person still remained in Egypt who would surely come to my assistance, if he could but be alerted to my plight; had he not said that he would act as my protector if I should ever need him?

'Lord Ambrose Malfine,' I said to the girl. 'Please go to Lord Ambrose.'

Surely he would be well known in Cairo – he was such a distinctive creature! At any rate, anyone in the European community would certainly know of him.

'Lord Ambrose,' I said again, and then suddenly, on an impulse, I unfastened my gold and silver brooch, the galloping horse within the crescent moon and pinned it to the girl's garment.

'Help me! Please!'

The girl was gone.

Several tedious days and nights followed, during which we continued to lead our lives of outer luxury and inner despair. The monotony seemed unbroken, though I tried to pass the time by learning a little Arabic from Rahaba, but was unable to make sufficient progress to discover anything about her situation, or whether she in her turn had learned aught about this strange household. Somehow, I could not find it in myself to enjoy the delights of the exquisite food with which we were served, the girl who brought them being as impassive as ever, though after two or three days her place was taken by another, so that even a familiar face was denied to us. These delicacies that were sent up from unseen regions of the house as if in a magician's feast, orange sherbet, dried raisins soaked in anise, apricots, dates stuffed with marchpane – all these dishes seemed to taste of dust. Trays of food were taken away scarcely touched from our sad and silent rooms behind the high window-screens. Rahaba divided her time between pacing up and down or peering hopefully out of the windows at any slight disturbance in the half-perceived world below.

One day at last there came an excitement into our routine. There was a bustle in the courtyard beneath our windows and, peering out, I saw the figure of Casterman, attended by several other men, one of whom appeared to be arguing violently with him. The situation was maddeningly frustrating, for Rahaba was clearly alarmed by what she had heard but although she turned towards me and was trying to convey something urgently, it was impossible to make anything of what was passing in the courtyard below.

Suddenly the door of our apartments flew open and two men, not in robes and turbans but in Western dress, seized Rahaba. Casterman followed them into the room and did nothing to prevent them from dragging the girl away, screaming piteously though she was.

And then something changed. I was puzzled utterly. Rahaba was at first resisting her tormentors, but a few words were exchanged which seemed to alter the case completely. A word which I could not catch recurred several times and Rahaba repeated it in a low voice, with the most fearful tone I thought I had ever heard issuing from a human throat.

'*Aywa*,' said one of the men very gravely, and again, '*aywa*.' I knew this meant 'yes' in the Arabic of Cairo.

What Rahaba plainly feared was being confirmed, but, whatever it was, the enemy was elsewhere and not in this room, for to my astonishment the girl stopped her struggles and began to accompany her captors willingly. She was given a long cloak and a kind of hood to throw over herself, which completely concealed her distinctive dress and features.

When she saw that I was not to accompany her, however, for the guards made no attempt to take me along with them, Rahaba turned back towards me, beckoning and calling my name, but I was not to be permitted to go with them. Casterman barred my way.

'No, Miss Lilian, you are not to accompany them. Oh, no harm will come to her – she is merely being taken home, I assure you, and she will be delighted to see her family once more. We are acting entirely in her own interests and she understands that now. And if you will be patient but for a few more days, you too will join your friends again, I promise you, for my arrangements in Cairo are now complete and my business is nearly done.'

Before I had the opportunity to say anything more, Casterman vanished through the door at the end of the women's rooms. I heard their voices all growing fainter, Casterman's deep baritone among them, as they descended the staircase.

Through the shutters, in the fragmented mosaic that was my view of the outside world, I saw Rahaba being helped on to a mule that was standing in the courtyard; her guards climbed on to their mounts also and with a sharp clatter of hooves the whole little procession swept out of the gate and beyond my sight.

I struck the shutters with the palms of my hands, in frustration at being deprived of the only human society which had been permitted to me, but the sound echoed round and round the walls and there was no response: only silence and dreary emptiness.

I passed a fearful and solitary night, barely realising that no food had been brought in the evening, and still the next day no one appeared.

At length I went to the door that led to the stairs, where usually sat the turbaned and scimitared figure who was on guard. I cautiously tried the handle of the door.

It did not move. The door would not yield. It was locked fast. I was a prisoner with absolutely no means of communication with the outside world.

I longed at first to give way to despair and wanted no more than to lie on my bed and weep, but I forced myself to try and make sense of my situation. Why was I locked in here alone like this? And how long would this solitary captivity last?

To none of these questions could I arrive at any sensible answer, but I comforted myself with the thought that, however frightful my entrapment might be, relief must come before long. Casterman could not go too far in mistreating me, nor could he utterly neglect me, for so many people knew that I was in his charge and he must ultimately answer for my safety. Why, all the guests at Hill's Hotel must have heard about my precipitate departure in Casterman's wake, and somewhere out there was Jennet, who would surely never abandon the search for me, come what may!

Thus I tried to buoy up my hopes. I sat on the soft couches of the harem and pictured the scenes in my mind's eye. The hunt for me – the bustle, the alarm! Jennet would surely alert the British Consul in Alexandria if her young mistress did not appear.

A noise in the courtyard beneath intruded into this pointless revery of escape and safety. There were still servants in this strange household, it seemed, for suddenly a woman dressed in dusty black erupted into the courtyard. Four men in robes and turbans emerged after her and they were carrying what looked like a makeshift stretcher upon which lay a long and motionless shape covered by a white cloth.

The woman began that strange sound that I had heard once before, and that Casterman had told me was called ululation: it was broken with sobs and weeping. In a display of the greatest grief she tore her face with her nails and flung herself forward to the stretcher, but the turbaned men would not suffer her to touch it and another woman emerged from the doorway and caught the first mourner in her arms.

I suddenly took in the garb of the bearers; swathes of veiling were thrown around their mouths. Not only that: their hands were gloved.

I shuddered, not stopping to analyse my sensation of extreme fear.

The strange little procession disappeared below, but I could still hear weeping in some part of the building.

It was a long, hot afternoon in the palace-prison. A yellowish dust hung in the air; waves of heat swept over me like washes of warm water. From time to time I turned to an ewer, poured a little of the perfumed water out into a silver basin and splashed it on my face and arms, yet it seemed to bring me no relief. Every few minutes the cries of women broke out, now from one side of the walls, now from another, and they seemed to echo in all the alleyways around.

Finally, as the afternoon at last grew a little cooler, I heard a new commotion beneath the window and, looking out into the courtyard, saw now a number of stretchers – perhaps five or six – were lying on the dusty ground and on each there was a recumbent form. Some seemed alive, judging by their feeble movements; with others, a white shawl or cloth laid over the whole form, including the face, indicated that the end of this world's torments had at last arrived for the poor wretch beneath the shroud.

I shrank back into the room, too horrified to continue watching.

Shortly after, I heard a sound at the door, as of the key being turned in the lock. I rushed forward, and heard footsteps retreating down the stairs, and I was almost sure that I recognised Casterman's step. Had I perhaps misjudged him? Was he releasing me at last from my captivity?

The door that had so long kept me prisoner was standing open.

*   *   *

Yet I hesitated, on the very threshold of freedom. From the depths below there came only silence.

I longed for freedom – of course I did! But something whispered that this was a trap: that I was being offered a delusion of liberty for some other, sinister, purpose, as a man may release an animal from a trap, not in mercy, but because he wishes to bait it further.

But there was little choice.

I set my foot on the first stair and began the descent.

Suddenly, there was a scream from below, a man's scream, deep in the throat.

Should I after all prefer safety above, in that gorgeous desolation? If something terrible was happening in this house, was not the safest thing to pretend that I knew nothing about it, to stay up in those luxurious quarters as if unaware of what threats and torments lay below?

I found myself continuing down the stairs with a part of my brain telling me that I was a fool and yet my feet seemingly carrying me on into a display of idiot courage. Lord Ambrose told me later that was how men are in battles: every ounce of intelligence counsels flight and yet something drives the body on towards its own destruction.

The scream did not come again. All the way down, the only sound I could hear was a low weeping. At the bottom of the staircase room opened out to the left closed off only by a curtain. I pushed the heavy folds aside.

There was a mattress on the floor and on it lay a man with his face turned away from the door. But as I entered he seemed to roll towards me in some great spasm, though I saw that he could not be seeing me, for he was blind. Must be blind, because his eyes were covered by great festering sores, which massed likewise over his face and throat. He gave a sudden convulsion and watery blood gushed from his mouth and nose.

With fresh horror, I saw that as if the torments of his malady were not enough, other cruelties had been inflicted. His hands were tied down to his sides, making it impossible for him to aid himself in any way, impossible to reach the cup and ewer that stood at his side, like the tortures that afflicted Tantalus. But a woman appeared from the shadows across the room. It was the same woman I had seen weeping in the courtyard, her cheeks bearing the long gashes inflicted by her own nails. She pulled my away, and moved towards the man. Then she lifted the ewer and poured a stream of water into the cup and then, cradling the poor diseased head in her arm, gently dropped a little liquid between the scabbed and blistered lips.

With an instinctive start of sympathy – it was not bravery for whatever courage my animal spirits had possessed upon the staircase they failed me now – I moved towards them.

CHAPTER 13

The Further Narrative of Lord Ambrose Malfine

I arrived in Cairo without mishap and went straightaway to join my sister Ariadne and her husband, Charles, on board their houseboat the *Zubeida*, which was moored on the bank of the Nile near Rodah Island. I had sent word ahead from Alexandria so that they would be forewarned of my coming.

It was my purpose to keep my movements unknown to the chattering British society centred at Hill's Hotel, for, as far as Casterman was concerned, I desired to be the watcher rather than the watched. I could best serve Miss Lilian by remaining concealed from her and those around her.

As I neared the bank of the Nile I could see Ariadne leaning back in her chair and contemplating the magnificent view beyond the polished deck of the boat, where she was sitting beneath a white canvas awning lined with blue. On one side, the minarets and domes of the city of Cairo reached up into the purplish haze above. On the other, across a narrow stretch of water, was a fringe of brilliant-green vegetation and the lush gardens of Rodah. The heat hung all around, like a warm veil.

I recognised her straight away, though I had not seen her for a decade and a half at least, and then she had been a plump child about ten years old, running about at Malfine on a visit home one summer. She was not happy there, I sensed it, deprived as she was of the playmates to whom she had grown accustomed in London, and I could still remember the beaming happiness on her small face as she departed with her nurse.

My father was dead by then. He had never desired to have Ariadne under his roof, believing that her birth had caused the death of our mother; I think the aunts who were caring for Ariadne in some corner of Belgravia thought that the child should become acquainted with her ancestral home, but the visit was not a success. Ariadne did not return, though a room was kept for her at Malfine, and our mother's clothes and jewels were at her disposal should she ever wish for them. All the time when I was running wild at Malfine or starving and fighting in Greece, Ariadne was growing up in London with those respectable old aunts, learning to be a proper young lady at Miss Primmish's Academy, or some such institution. (My sister laughs now as I recall this – 'Nay, brother, it was no such name! Miss *Pintish*!')

She did not, in fact resemble our mother at all, having inherited my father's blond English looks, while I have inherited my mother's Greek dark eyes and black hair. We are not the least alike, neither in appearance nor, as I thought, in character, though one or two similarities were to emerge.

We did not correspond directly all through the years of my Greek adventures, though after I had reached my majority I went to the British Consulate in Patras and affixed my signature to various documents which would allow my sister a gentlewoman's education and dress allowance from the estates which I had inherited. I expressed my opinion that she should have a proper education and learn to speak some languages and do some figuring instead of receiving the usual young lady's training in idle tittle-tattle, but this must have been dismissed as youthful eccentricity and I think had no effect whatsoever upon the choice of school for my sister. It was as well therefore that she turned out to possess a great fund of common sense, which made up for the deficiencies in her schooling.

The lady on the houseboat was a grown woman, wrapped in veils against the mosquitoes, yet I recognised her instantly: there was that fair hair springing from her temples in lively curls, as our father's had done; there were the large blue-grey eyes impressing with their candour; there was that beaming smile that I remembered the child Ariadne turning upon the object of her pleasure.

Which was now myself; she rose and moved to greet me and I hastened on to the deck of the boat, where my sister flung her arms around me.

'Why, Ambrose, this is such good news! I have been in correspondence with your manservant Belos, you know – he wrote through our lawyers to tell me how terribly wounded you had been – and I was intending to come to England and cheer your convalescence! So it is doubly a delight to see you here – and looking so well. Charles – my husband – will be back very shortly – he is longing to see you.'

It was but a few moments before I was seated next to her and a glass of lemon water was poured out for me.

I felt my spirits relax in that enchanted setting, and yet the desert was close, though beyond our view as we sat on the deck of the *Zubeida*.

As travellers to Egypt know, the desert is somehow omni-present. Even in the crowded streets of Cairo a sudden flurry of wind-born sand will remind the wayfarer of the wider world. Cairo is surrounded by desert which continually presses in upon it; if it were not for the human army ceaselessly brushing and sweeping away the drifting grains of sand, in streets, in courtyards, in palaces and hovels, constantly repelling the invasions of sand, the city would eventually vanish beneath the dunes, swallowed up like the lost cities of the ancients. As I write this, grains of sand are drifting on to the very pages and I have to pause and shake them off.

So we were conscious, even though we could not see them, of the vast deserts that stretch away beyond the thin green fringe of the river, and of the massive creamy white bulks of the pyramids of Egypt and the great silent head that broods there, a presence felt far beyond its purviews.

I think that Ariadne has now accepted that her life with Charles is destined to be, as mine has been, a traveller in distant lands. She told me about her husband and his interests and profession in that first occasion as we sat side by side, looking at the exquisite view. Charles is a geologist, engaged in a search for new knowledge beyond the boundaries of Europe. Ariadne is caught up in his restlessness, with ceaseless exploration which brought him to Egypt to study the rock formations out of which arise towering desert cliffs, and from which the very Sphinx itself was hewed.

The *Zubeida* is not only their houseboat but their home while they are resident in Egypt. It was Charles' idea to stay so pleasantly on a boat moored to the riverbank, said Ariadne, while he consulted with men of science as to the geological formations which surrounded them. There was,

I understand, a particularly clever engineer with whom he had been preparing a map.

I was well disposed to my brother-in-law for this charming idea of houseboat living, which appealed to me as somewhat more imaginative than one might have thought to find, but after I had met him I realised that it was also a very prudent course of action, for Charles is nothing if not careful. He took the view that it was much healthier to stay on the river. 'It will be so much safer here,' he said that evening when we enjoying a *pilaw* in the dining room below deck. 'In case there is any epidemic in the city we can isolate ourselves so easily from infection – just pull up the gangway and sail southwards down the river to healthier places such as Luxor or Aswan. And what more beautiful spot than here?'

It is indeed a glorious place, where the blue waters of the Nile flow around the flowery stretches of Rodah Island. From the deck of the *Zubeida*, we could see tall tulip trees and the brilliant colours of bougainvillaea. This houseboat life in Egypt was handsomely pleasant: the *Zubeida* had cabins fitted out in brass and mahogany, a sitting room on deck, and awnings sheltering the passengers from the fiery heat of the Egyptian sun. It became our custom to sit on the deck every evening and watch the magnificent blaze of the sunset.

The *Zubeida* was one of the larger *dahabeyahs*, or passenger boats, that cruise the waters of the Nile. It seemed that Charles had followed the usual precautions taken by travellers in Egypt who desire to live on a boat to keep infection at a distance and had watched as the *Zubeida*, stripped of all her old furnishings, was deliberately sunk into the waters of the Nile to rid her of all rats and insects. The boat was then hauled out of the water and set afloat again and once her cabins and decks had dried out they were redecorated and the whole ship furnished with new chairs, beds and hangings, so that it was certain that she could not harbour the slightest thing that might spread disease.

The *Zubeida* in fact offered very considerable creature comforts, which I have never affected to despise. When we fought in the mountains and crossed the high trails and passes of Crete, I went often without food, and our small band of soldiers thought themselves well enough fed with a few loaves of hard bread, a handful of black olives and a pitcher of rough wine or spring water. So, as a battle-scarred traveller who has had to tighten his belt often enough in the past, I now congratulate myself on my good fortune whenever any of the delights of life are placed before me.

To return to the *Zubeida*, she had a crew of some eight men, headed by the *rais*, Ahmed, and including a cook who could provide all meals required by passengers and crew. The boat had a kitchen built in the forequarters with its own iron ovens, their walls sealed with gypsum plaster as a protection against the spread of fire. The stores of oil, flour, beans and cheese were carried aboard in great Ballas pottery jars, well stoppered and proof against insect invasion. Sweet well water was brought on board regularly, and I may say the houseboat was virtually self-sufficient in almost all departments: if need arose, we could lift the gangplank, cut ourselves of from the shore, and survive for a month or more.

The crew included Faridun, the ship's cat, whose task it was to prevent any re-infestation by small rodents. Charles toyed with the idea of getting a mongoose, for they are said to be very effective hunters of snakes as well as of rats and mice, but a mongoose would always remain a wild animal and when we were at anchor would have to be tied up to keep it on board. Whereas Faridun's loyalty could be bought with titbits of fish, though I cannot say he repaid them with the vigilance of a hunter and was usually to be found beneath Ariadne's chair, as indeed cats are depicted in some of the paintings I have seen in the ancient tombs of Egypt.

That first evening, as we sat side by side on the deck, there was remarkably little conversation; we fell somehow into an easy exchange of silences and casual talk. Charles returned from a visit to the city, where he had been speaking to some mining engineers who hoped to open up the shafts in the Eastern desert where the ancients had once mined gemstones, and we spoke a little of the treasures of the past which lie concealed in the deserts beyond the Nile.

'I hope to amuse myself with some study of the ancient monuments,' said I. 'Do you know of the studies of hieroglyphs which M. Champollion has undertaken in France? I feel I myself must make an attempt to recover something of these mysteries.'

'If anyone can do it, you can, brother-in-law,' said Charles. 'I am sure of that, for Ariadne has told me that you have the damned quickest brain ever encountered.'

'Charles, don't swear!' said Ariadne. 'But we may thank Heaven that at least Ambrose does not seem to be engaged in any such venture as that in which he suffered such dreadful wounds.'

'Some might think him very courageous, to have joined the Greek uprising in fighting for their liberties against the Turks. It was a high-minded and noble enterprise which he was engaged in – you may be proud of him, Ariadne. Though courage seems out of fashion in these feeble days.'

High-minded and noble! God, if Charles but knew! He has never seen a battle – the reeking filth of the dead, the blood and mud and tumbled guts of the wounded, the gibbering fear of the living who will kill anything and anybody, who will maim and torture and stab other men in the back that they themselves may survive – and as for me, I was no better than the rest when it came to battle, for all my youthful talk of liberty.

But Ariadne was as innocent of cynicism as her spouse.

'Proud of Ambrose – yes, I am. But I am also frightened for you,' turning towards me, 'frightened for you because of your impetuous nature!'

I interrupted this account of my glowing merits.

'Have no fear, for I have learnt some wisdom, I assure you. I was a young man when I went to Greece. I will risk my life less readily now, I can tell you! I no longer burn with the ideals of eighteen.'

'Well, if you should find you want to burn again, brother, you may truly do so in the desert, if you do not take care. But I hope you are grown more circumspect.'

'I am a good deal older and wiser, you may be certain of that. I intend to pass my time quietly studying the monuments, and I wish also to explore the city, of course.'

I did not wish to present the complicated history of Miss Lilian Westmorland at this point, lest my sister's fear of my impulsive nature should seem justified. At a later date, I resolved, I would tell her of the young woman who might at some time have need of protection. I now changed the subject. 'Can you recommend a guide to Cairo for me – I mean someone who really knows the city from the inside – all its nooks and crannies and alleyways!'

'As a matter of fact, I believe I know just the fellow for you,' said Charles. 'He cuts a somewhat unusual figure, not in the ordinary run of guides, but you won't mind that, I imagine. It's a sheikh, a very learned man, who studies learned histories; he has helped us with the knowledge of the old Arabic geographers, who knew the routes across the deserts and the places where gems and metals were mined. But I warn you, he wears tatter-demalion animal skins, and looks half-starved, for I believe he abstains from food for days at a time. They say, however, that he has connections in all parts of the city, for it is whispered he is the sheikh of all the *harafish*, the beggars of Cairo! He can tell you anything you want to know about any quarter of the city – I'll ask the *rais* to send for him if you like. My love, was that not a mosquito?' Charles turned to Ariadne anxiously. 'Have you got your veils with you? I will ask Ahmed to bring them, if not. Let us all sit up on deck and watch the sunset. We can dine later and exchange our news when Ambrose is fed and rested after his travels. Does that suit your inclinations, Ambrose?'

Of course, I assented. The sunsets of Egypt are splendid beyond anything, short and fierce, so that night seems to fall with tremendous rapidity, like a dark velvet curtain. On that evening the great blazing disc of gold and orange filled the sky to the west and slowly sank, as we watched, beneath the black rim of the land, and as it sank I thought of Elisabeth, as I do every night at sunset and at every dawn.

Whatever was to come, whether our future lay together or apart, mad or rational, I knew I loved her to the deepest dregs of my heart. But my heart has been through many adventures: it is older and wiser than once it was!

The old sheikh, he who dresses in animal skins and lives with the poorest, the beggars, the conjurers, the *harafish* of the streets of Cairo, came to me on board the *Zubeida* a few days later.

It was early in the morning, that fresh and cool hour when anticipation of the day is still a pleasure, when birds and jackals rule the desert and fishermen stretch their nets in the pearly morning light that is reflected in the waters of the Nile.

He called softly from the bank, a gentle whistling sound which we had pre-arranged, for I had already sought out in Cairo the Arab guide to the city whom Charles had recommended. He was a learned man, with a tumble-down house near the great mosque of Shaykhu, where poor scholar have studied and been housed for many centuries, and his cell-like room was crammed with parchment manuscripts. He was known to have contacts everywhere among the beggars, the eyes and ears of the poorest of the poor. Barely a donkey moved or even a mouse stirred but one of his *harafish* knew of it, and the tale would eventually find its way to him.

Yet, poor though he was, he would not act for money alone. He hated the thing that I hated, the relentless piece of cruelty that was in train. He could exist on a daily crust of bread and a bowl of water and he had his sacred texts and the companions of his mind and soul: what did he need of foreign money?

On this morning, he said nothing, but plucked at my sleeve and guided me through the sleepy streets till we came to the banks of the canal which flows alongside the old city. It is choked in many places with weeds and sometimes with refuse, but there are still fishermen in some clear stretches, and this morning something had been caught in the nets. As we drew near I asked him what had taken place in my stumbling Arabic, for I had a still imperfect command of that language, but he shook his head and was silent, looking grave and distressed as we made our way along the canal bank.

There was a small group of men on a rough and narrow wooden quay and their catch lay motionless in the water.

The long net had trapped her, along with brownish-green water-plants and small silvery creatures, and her young body was held fast in its knots. The fishermen still looked shocked, appalled at what they had netted at first light.

I leaned down into the water and drew the net closer to the shore amongst the brown swirls of the canal. On either bank of this narrow cut, tall houses peered down at us, their occupants invisible behind the wooden lattices, but I thought I heard prayers being murmured from somewhere nearby. In this city, nothing is ignored: everything that happens is seen by eyes which may be behind a screen or a veil.

The fishermen were muttering blessings and prayers as I lifted the girl up out of the water. The face turned towards me with the swirl of the current as I pulled her to the land and as the body moved I saw the flash of gold and silver pinned to her garments clearly visible beneath the surface. A brooch made in the European style, fashioned to a special design. A gold horse's head within the crescent of a silver moon.

It was on account of this clue to a Western connection that my old guide had fetched me, hoping that I might be able to shed some light on the matter. Alas, there were other traces that were tragically familiar to me.

Around the throat were deep-purple-red marks, exactly as I had seen on the body of that poor girl two continents away, on a wet evening in England.

It is true, then. The evil of which I had suspected this creature – it is proved beyond any doubt. To do this to a young and entirely innocent human being who has scarcely begun to live – how right I was to fear him and to pursue him like a very hell-hound. Only I had not followed him close enough, for if I had I might have prevented this death of an innocent, another young life caught and crushed in his net of cruelty, like that poor servant girl at Westmorland Park whose lifeless body I had gazed upon less than a month ago. That had been some warning of what was to come, and I bitterly reproached myself that I had not anticipated this terrible crime which I was not in time to prevent.

This killer possessed a deliberate and careful mentality; he adapted his methods according to his needs: for some victims, a careful and elaborate plot. For others, a hasty dispatch where it best suited his purpose, in the deserted grounds of an English mansion or in an alley-way of Cairo.

Slowly, I unpinned the jewel from the sodden garments and held it up to the light.

'Can you take me to the house?' I asked the sheikh, showing him the brooch.

He nodded and turned away to lead me up a narrow flight of steps cut in the very rock of the city, towards the heart of old Cairo.

Rage was burning in my throat as I set after him; the pin of the brooch drove into the palm of my hand, but I scarcely noticed it.

CHAPTER 14

Thank God I was in time! I burst in to that dreadful household like an avenging angel, yet, for all my bravado, there was no human enemy with whom I could grapple.

He had gone, of course, and left his filthy deeds behind him.

This was a cunning man, the most skilful strategist I have ever countered, who had devised a scheme so subtle and so wicked that it was almost perfect.

Yet, for every stratagem there is a counter-stratagem. I had my own armour against his attack, had already summoned it long ago in England, in the quiet house of an obscure country doctor. I did not, I admit, have prescience of the full extent of Casterman's malice; that, I think, would lie beyond the ken of all but demons. No, my armour was literally to protect myself: it was donned for purely selfish motives, viz., to protect my skin, literally. The preservation of one's own hide is one of the greatest steps a man may take in order to add to the general sum of human well-being and happiness and I shall never allow any cant about sacrifice to persuade me otherwise.

So it was that as I rushed into that room I would not allow Miss Lilian Westmorland to exhibit any signs of merciful charity towards the sick. I flung myself towards her and pulled her away from that bedside as she was in the very act of stretching out her hands towards the sufferer; I pulled at her as if I were dragging her from a fire, as if hot coals were touching at the hem of her dress, tugging her back and out of the door just as she reached out towards the poor wretch lying on his palliasse.

'Come away! Come out of this pestilent air!'

We stumbled to the other side of the room and through a doorway beyond which there lay a flight of stone steps leading down to the canal. There was a small skiff lying empty, which I conjectured belonged to the doomed household from which we had emerged and I drew a dagger from my belt and cut through the mooring rope. Leaping into the boat, I pulled Lilian down after me with an outstretched hand and then seized the oars and propelled us away.

'Do you know what it is?'

'I . . . I think so. Smallpox?'

There seemed no need for an answer.

'Is that why – is that why the man's hands were bound, Lord Ambrose? To prevent him from tearing at his scabs?'

'Yes, for pulling off the crusts ensures the most severe disfigurement – that is, if the poor wretch survives at all, of course. The flesh that comes away with the scabs of the pustules leaves deep craters behind that mark a man for life – but that poor fellow was not likely to live, Miss Lilian. We are in the very midst of an epidemic of one of the most vile and virulent diseases known. You saw the blood coming from his lips and mouth? This type of the disease, where the sufferer haemorrhages, is the most savage. There is little hope for any of them in that household, save one man alone.'

'What do you mean?'

'Do you not know, Miss Lilian? No, I see by your face that you have not guessed and who could blame you for not understanding such a twisted labyrinthine web of evil? This is how it was. Our friend Casterman has had his beauty spoilt, has he not? Upon his face the marks of smallpox are entrenched and there they will be till the day he dies. But there is one great compensation for the suffering he endured when he caught the contagion, for they say that those who catch the smallpox and live will never catch it again. No, Casterman is immune to it – he may walk freely through a household where the fever rages, he may breathe the pestilent air, touch the sufferers, even feel upon his own skin the ghastly effluents of their disease, and yet he himself will not take it. He is safe!'

By this time our little skiff was moving down to the point where the canal joined the Nile, which rushed in to scour it in the time of inundation and then subsided tranquilly, as was at that present time the case. Our small boat slipped without incident into the smooth stream of the great river: the sun shone dully upon it so that its waters had the lustre of molten lead.

Lilian Westmorland's troubled face evidently reflected the thoughts which were flashing pell-mell through her mind.

'But, Lord Ambrose, you – you will be liable to . . .'

'To catch the smallpox? No, I will not – I confess, I did not break into that plague-stricken household to rescue you at the risk of losing my life from the pestilence! I am afraid I must disillusion you of any notion about my heroic qualities, for an honest Scottish sawbones, a mere country physician, has like a good angel protected me from evil. You remember Dr Sandys?'

'Oh, very well, for he treated me after my accident – and he was my mother's physician also.'

'And if you had stayed long enough under his care, instead

179

of being whisked so precipitately aboard the *Great London*, I doubt not that he would have vaccinated you also, when he knew that you were being sent to Egypt. But your uncle allowed no time for any such precautions.'

'Why, that is true! We scarcely had time to pack before Uncle Micah sent us away! Vaccinated, you say?'

'Aye, Sandys is a humble follower of the great Doctor Jenner, who supposed that infecting a patient with cowpox, that disease to which dairymaids are prone, would protect him against the worse evil of catching the smallpox, or at any rate, against having it in any form which should prove mortally dangerous. So one fine day when Sandys was pleading for a patient upon whom to experiment, and myself contemplating travel at that time, I took myself to Sandys' small laboratorium, where he cut my shoulder and inserted into the wound some matter from Sally Harker's cowpox pustules – poor Sally being the latest person in the district to have fallen victim to the cowpox. I am therefore reasonably certain that I cannot or at any rate cannot dangerously become infected with that dreadful disease, the smallpox.'

'But I have had no such treatment!'

There was a look of dawning horror on the girl's pale features, as she realised the implications of the strange and terrible scenes which she had witnessed in that household where disease was raging.

'You may well escape infection, for you were shut off from the world. But the servants took the disease and the very food which was brought to you was prepared by them, although I saw no such tokens upon the face of the poor girl who was found in the river.'

'Oh, Lord Ambrose, how dreadful! Who was she?'

For answer, I produced the brooch: the little gold horse

within the crescent moon, in the protection of the moon-goddess, Selene, which Lilian Westmorland's mother had commissioned for her daughter.

'The girl to whom you gave this token – they found her before she could reach me – but they did not notice this brooch pinned to her robes – or did not realise what it signified. At any rate, the old sheikh who is my eyes and ears in the city heard that a girl from a strange household had escaped and died – and the brooch told me the rest of the story.'

I spared Lilian the full details of the girl's death: the same dark-reddish bruised marks of a hand which had seized her throat in a powerful grip and throttled the very life away, as it had done to another girl in another country, to that poor Maggie Dermott, the skivvy of Westmorland Park.

'I would say that your uncle quite possibly failed to have you vaccinated on Casterman's advice, for they are men of the world who would have known of the risk and it was known even before your passage was booked that a serious smallpox epidemic was gripping the Middle East – word was in the London papers not two months ago.'

'Do you mean that my uncle deliberately sent me into danger?'

'I am not sure whose idea it was to lead you into such dangers as you have endured, your Uncle Micah's or Casterman's. It was Casterman, was it not, who placed you in such peril in the tower at Alexandria?'

'Lord Ambrose, however did you hear of that episode?'

'Ah well, let us merely say for the moment that I have my means of knowing things! But after that attempt had failed, there was another easier route – all that was needed was to get you to Cairo – or any other Oriental port – and into a house where you were beyond the reach of help. Then Casterman, who can walk into chambers ravaged by the smallpox with impunity, had only to keep you there till the contagion struck. He could even have encouraged it – perhaps he offered to have some sufferers nursed in his own household, out of his great magnanimity, and then he opened the door of your quarters and turned you loose – into the very cock-pit of infection! Think, then, how plausible their case would be – 'Miss Lilian Westmorland tragically passed away during an epidemic of smallpox' – why, we see such reports daily in the newspapers! Such deaths happen frequently to Europeans travelling in the East – you may see their tombstones in the graveyards here! Some of the better-informed would think 'Well, foolish girl, she should have had a vaccination!' but no one would consider your death in the slightest degree suspicious!'

'But Casterman virtually kidnapped me and took me away from Hill's Hotel! There were many people who must have known of that – Jennet, for instance.'

'All that he would have had to say was that he was protecting you to the best of his ability by taking away from the crowded and busy centre of the city so as to lessen the risk of infection. As for anything Mrs Jennet might say, he could easily say that she had misunderstood his intentions and foolishly returned to Hill's Hotel of her own accord; in any case, most Europeans are fleeing from the city, some south to Aswan and Luxor, some north to Alexandria to leave the country altogether, and Hill's Hotel is deserted, for word of the pestilence has spread about. Mrs Jennet, I understand, has gone to Alexandria to raise the alarm and ask the British Consul to launch a search for you. But if Casterman had announced that you had fallen a victim to the smallpox, what could the Consul have done? Your death would have been accomplished and with no evidence whatsoever to point towards him.'

Lilian Westmorland looked down at the swirling waters of the ancient river. 'He would have killed me? In that horrible way! To let me die of that disease!'

'Oh, yes, almost certainly you would have died. He survived, but he was a strong man and must have good nursing when he himself contracted the smallpox, but you would probably have received no medical attention and would surely have succumbed. He could have ensured that you were left unattended in your illness. The sufferer will die of dehydration in such circumstances, if not from the fever and haemorrhaging.'

'But my uncle would he truly have committed me to such a death? After all, I am his own flesh and blood!'

'Your uncle may not have understood what Casterman intended. As to their motive, you are the heiress of Westmorland Park; either your uncle may wish to obtain absolute control of the estate, or Casterman, as his man of business, may have a financial interest in the affairs of the Westmorland family.'

'But I have never done him any harm!'

It is a terrible thing when you are young to understand the abyss of malevolence which another human being may feel towards you. I saw by Lilian's horrified face that she was even then struggling to grasp the depths of Casterman's malice. Why should he hate her so? How could he contrive such a cruel end?

I knew what she felt. When I was a young man, I sensed it myself – that innocent strain that protests at the back of one's mind. 'But I have done nothing,' it sings. 'Why should I be hated so? – What has provoked this? – I deserve it not! Why should another human being encompass my death?'

There is ultimately no point in even asking such a question. Creatures such as Casterman hate and kill, not because they are provoked, but for reasons of their own, inexplicable to the common run of humankind. That cool and calculating mind had contrived the most excruciating death for an innocent young woman as dispassionately as others would crush a fly.

The skiff pulled up on the opposite bank of the river and the bulk of the *Zubeida* loomed up, moored next to the shore.

I hailed the houseboat from the land.

The figure of Charles appeared on deck.

'Will you not come aboard, brother-in-law? And that young lady who accompanies you? Dear me, Ambrose, you undertook to keep out of trouble here!'

'Charles, don't be facetious! Listen, seriously, there's something terrible happening in the city – an epidemic of smallpox has broken out. For God's sake, pull up the gangplank and let no one aboard! I'll return in a couple of weeks – until then, I advise you to make a fortress out of the *Zubeida*.'

Some rumours had already reached them, it seemed, for Charles was willing to follow my advice. I explained our dreadful situation, and though Ariadne, who by this time had appeared at Charles' side, pressed me warmly to come aboard, saying freely that they would share our risks and expressing the utmost anxiety for the plight of poor Miss Westmorland, I would not do so. To put the *Zubeida*, her crew and her passengers, in danger of a most horrible death was unthinkable.

I made some arrangements for communicating with the houseboat eventually, if we should once again be able to face humankind. Then I turned away from the friendly bulk of the boat and all the safety and comfort which it promised. I knew suddenly how it must felt to those afflicted with leprosy, doomed to remain beyond the reach of the common kindness and companionship of their fellow men.

I joined Lilian Westmorland where she waited near the little skiff. We left the river and began walking across sands which shifted in soft creaks under our footsteps. The scorching heat of day had now begun, and struck up from the ground as well as down from the heavens. But we had several miles to trudge through the sand before we reached our destination and safe hiding place.

Those great distinctive shapes suddenly loomed up on the horizon.

'The Pyramids!' Lilian exclaimed.

'Yes, we are in the desert. We shall have to live for a while in their shadow, for I must ask you to remain patient for a while longer. You have borne your captivity in the midst of the city – now I must ask you if you can withstand the isolation of the desert – that is, with my company alone, for some time, I am afraid.'

'Cannot we go to find Jennet in Alexandria? Oh, I do long to see Jennet again!'

How to answer this innocent plea?

'Miss Lilian, I have to tell you this: you are not yet out of danger.'

But Lilian was fast understanding the full implications of her plight.

'Oh no, of course! I may have taken the infection though it does not yet show upon my skin! I was in that house, where the sick were being nursed. That woman I saw cradling the man in her arms – she may probably have taken the disease from him – and I perhaps have anywhere touched something that was infected! And if I have caught the disease then . . .'

'Then you may pass it to others. Yes, but in any case Mistress Jennet is not in Cairo at present, for she went to Alexandria to speak to the British Consul and persuade him to launch a search for you. And I know that your generous spirit will be patient a little while longer; I am afraid that we must consider the possibility that you are infected with the smallpox. We must watch your state of health carefully over the next ten days or so, but from my understanding of medical matters if you have no symptoms after two weeks have elapsed then you may be pronounced clear of infection. Until then, Miss Lilian, I must ask you to lead the desert life with me! We shall shelter here in the tomb of an old Egyptian, which will provide us with roomy chambers and I will account myself your cook and physician until such time as we can be sure you are clear of the disease. My sister's houseboat is moored not far from here and we may have some supplies from thence.'

By this time we had reached a stony cliff amid the desert sands, which had a flight of steps cut into the living rock. The dark entrance to the tomb as almost imperceptible at a distance; I myself had discovered it quite by chance and cleared away some of the dune that partly blocked the entrance, and had brought some planks and palm-branches to bridge the mouth of a pit which lay a short distance inside the mouth of the tomb, a deep hole dug by the ancient builders of the tomb in order to entrap any thieves who should attempt to raid that solemn burial chamber. The chances of anyone else apprehending this God-given hiding place were remote, especially as the smallpox meant that fewer travellers than before were likely to come visiting the area.

Lilian paused and looked up before she moved down the steps after me, and saw the great shadow that stretched over her head, almost as if protecting her. Strangely enough, the

Sphinx which loomed so close to where we tiny mortals were standing seemed to promise security and strength, an ancient benediction held out high above us. The girl clearly did not fear the ancient monolith, nor the desert tomb into which we now descended. They were clean and innocent compared with the entrapments of Casterman.

The weeks that followed were desperately uneasy, for it is much harder to prudently wait out the course taken by an invisible enemy than to launch an attack upon a dozen fighting men, and all the time the poor girl was aware that at any moment sentence of death might be passed upon her. Day by day she begged me to recount the symptoms of infection and day by day I reassured her and pronounced her still free – yet we both knew that the next morning she might awake with the tell-tale signs upon her.

Daily I tried to recall the Arab physicians' accounts of the course of the fever and watched my young charge for signs of the appearance of the sickness, the shivering and backache, the influenza-like symptoms which precede the onset of the smallpox.

So the days passed slowly and painfully. Some of the time she spent on exploring the tomb which had become her temporary residence and perhaps her last, with its wall-carvings of gods and men, of a goddess with great wings of midnight blue, of jackal-headed creatures bending over a corpse, of a mighty boat that filled the starry heavens. These I endeavoured to explain to her, with as much as I had understood of their ancient learning.

'Who was buried here?'

'I do not know. His body has disappeared without trace and so has the sarcophagus which contained it. He was some great man, that is all I can tell.'

We penetrated as far inside the tomb as we could, to where a fall of rubble blocked the way, and I sketched for her the various tunnels and chambers, and showed her where the robber-trap lay at the entrance, the pit over which I had laid some planks, and where we must take care always with our footing, lest we stumble and the flimsy bridge should shift and tumble away. I had at that time no means of making it more substantial: this was the best that could be managed for the time being.

At night I slept outside in a tent where a yellow oil-lamp hung through the small hours as I wrote or studied, for I had books and papers with me, carefully stored in boxes just outside the entrance to the tomb. It had been my intention as I had told Ariadne and Charles to live here alone for some weeks and devote myself to recording these antique inscriptions upon the walls, but as it chanced this seclusion now made the perfect retreat for the ordeal which Miss Westmorland now had to undergo. The tomb which should have been my study had become a quarantine or *lazaretto*.

And yet, I must confess it, even in these circumstances, I did not entirely experience the virtuous and monk-like existence of some Desert Father, for I was at close quarters with a young woman who intrigued me and not only with her courage and determination. Lilian Westmorland's large blue-green eyes, her tall slim figure, the charm of her brow and hair – all these had a powerful attraction, and my feelings for her threatened to move from the category of the safely paternal to that of a lover. Elisabeth, perhaps, would wish no more of me, would not be waiting when I returned to England. Should I not, thrown together with this beautiful young woman, follow my natural inclinations?

I cannot give thanks to any powers of restraint on my part, but rather to my realisation that I had a rival.

'Lord Ambrose, pray tell me if you know anything of Mr Sholto Lawrence, who is, I believe, a West Country neighbour of ours, in a manner of speaking. Have you heard the name?' enquired Lilian one day, and I could tell by the way that she spoke the name 'Sholto Lawrence' that she had an especial interest in its owner.

I answered her with generalities, praising his horsemanship, telling her that he came from a reputable and celebrated old-established Cornish family and so forth (I saw no need to cry up the young whipper-snapper in extravagant terms), and she replied with yet more questions, many that I could not answer, and some that were downright unanswerable, such as Mr Lawrence's opinion on the new fashion in small-brimmed bonnets.

I came rapidly to realise that she spoke for the pleasure of hearing his name.

Well, I had a rival, that was clear, a youth in his prime to whom Miss Westmorland was much inclined already. All things carefully considered, Sholto Lawrence would be a most suitable match for Miss Lilian in their shared liveliness and animal spirits as well as their tastes and station in life.

So I fought the temptations of the flesh, like St Antony before me, but unlike St Antony, I did not purpose to hold to this chaste attitude for evermore. At any rate, the metaphysical intervention of Mr Sholto Lawrence, so as to speak, prevented me from pursuing my ardours with Miss Lilian during our sojourn in the desert. I, Ambrose Malfine, failed to press for a conquest, a most remarkable circumstance, perhaps brought about by some unlikelihood of success.

On the fourteenth day of our self-imposed sequestration I gave thanks that good fortune seemed to have prevailed with the young woman. Anyone who reads these words may imagine for themselves the aching slowness of those two weeks, when Time's chariot seemed to be standing still. Every morning and evening I said to myself, 'One less night to endure', or 'One day fewer', and I counted off the sunsets with fear and longing, setting long scars in the rock-face to mark their passing; the longing was of course for the time to be up, but the fear was that this was the last day on which she enjoyed her health. I thought with horror of those dreadful pustules that had covered the face of the man I had seen dying in Casterman's house in Cairo: that the smooth face of this innocent girl should turn into such a mass of encrusted sores seemed too much to bear.

Yet at last my dagger made its fourteenth cut in the soft rock, and she had been spared.

'I will take you to my sister and her husband,' said I, as we sat beside a fire of dried palm-leaves and branches on the last night of her isolation. 'You can stay with them on the *Zubeida*, where they have sealed themselves off from the shore. You will be quite safe with them till the contagion in the city dies down – and protected from the machinations of that demon, Casterman!'

As far as Casterman was concerned, I had but one ambition: to hunt him down. I knew the full extent of the man's devious and cruel spirit and the nature of the wicked business in which he was engaged: I do not mean his purpose towards Lilian alone, but the other reason that had brought him to Egypt, the scheme which connected him with her uncle and made the two of them, Casterman and Micah Overbury, companions in evil-doing.

On that last day of Lilian's strange isolation I sat in my tent and scrawled a message to my sister, and then walked the some miles through the desert towards the river to where their boat was moored, near a site where some Bedouin were encamped. In my letter I asked Ariadne to take the girl on board. Not myself: I had dealings with Casterman which must be accomplished before I could allow myself the luxury of a safe place of refuge. There is always some obstacle to a quiet life, I find; some quittance that must be satisfied before I rest. Do I truly long for peace?

When I reached the bank of the river, I inserted my letter in a common small pottery vase and wrapped it securely in a piece of scarlet cloth, which was a signal I had arranged with Charles and Ariadne that the missive within came from myself and from no other. I saw their figures moving along the deck; the *rais* cast a line a shore to which I tied my missive, and I saw it hauled through the water and up into Charles' waiting hands.

I stood for a few minutes on the bank, while they unwrapped the cloth, a scrap of bright-red which was visible at a great distance, and smashed open the pottery vessel, and waited till I saw one of the little figures waving an arm in acknowledgement. I knew then that I could bring Lilian safely aboard the *Zubeida* and leave her in the care of those on board.

Then I turned into the great wastes behind me. Night fell. The fire threw up great flickering shadows across the canvas of my tent and the desert air seemed bitterly cold, the stars glittering, hard and remote.

CHAPTER 15

On the following day, I strode to the top of a dune, shaded my eyes with my hand and stared out across the desert in the direction of the river. Long soft crests of yellow sand stretched eastwards and behind me the sun was already starting to sink. Far off, in the distance, a solitary figure detached itself from the distant strip of bright-green vegetation that marked the course of the Nile, and made towards us, loping across the dunes with long strides and casting a long spiky black shadow that jerked behind it.

The figure wore a burnous that fluttered in the breeze, and held one end of the cloth across the face, to protect it from the sand that blew like faint smoke in the wind.

One of the Arabs, coming from the camp near the *Zubeida*?

What was it exactly that was strange about the picture before me? Had I not seen this a hundred times before: the figure of a lone Bedouin ranging across the sands, making for camp before nightfall?

So what was wrong on this occasion?

I stared for a few more moments. The figure continued to move rapidly up and down the sand-dunes, now steadily climbing, now descending, sometimes vanishing from sight for a few minutes, always reappearing.

There was something about the way the man walked. Something out of keeping.

The Arabs whose tents lay near the *Zubeida* wore a flat, broad type of sandal – the almost universal footwear for those whose life is spent walking over burning sands.

There is a difference between the walk of men who habitually wear such sandals – and have worn them from childhood – and the walk of Westerners, used to the rigid confinement of boots and shoes. When a Westerner walks across the desert, even if he is wearing flapping Bedouin sandals, he walks in a different way, conditioned by a lifetime of bringing his hard-shod feet down on solid ground, with a firm stamp of the heel that will not do amid the shifting element of the sand-dunes. The desert is not his element: he moves stiffly there.

This man was moving in the manner of a Westerner.

And why was he following his particular path? Every few minutes, he seemed to stop and check ahead.

With a sinking heart, I realised that the still desert air had conspired against me. Oh, for a sand-storm, a raging *khamsin*, that whirled the very grains of sand through the air and deposited them in different sweeping patterns and undulations, like the very waves of the sea, obliterating all previous traces.

All traces, such as the trail my footsteps had made in the sand between our hiding place and the bank where the *Zubeida* was moored.

I had been so confident we were safe! I cursed myself, for my relief that the painful suspense of Lilian's quarantine was so great that I had been blind to other dangers.

Casterman, I realised, would have found it easier to track us down during a time of pestilence. His contacts in that house in Cairo where Lilian had been imprisoned would have seen us flee together, and once it was known she was in my company, Casterman would eventually get on to the trail. I am, after all, a fairly distinctive creature, even in London or Paris. And here, we were isolated indeed; many Europeans had fled Cairo and there were no other houseboats now on the river – all had fled downstream to escape infection. The *Zubeida* was conspicuous, faithfully remaining at her moorings.

Casterman had but to keep watch on the boat – or easier still to pass a friendly word at the Bedouin camp nearby, asking whether they had seen such-and-such a stranger – and the game would be up.

Turning round, I saw that Lilian, unaware anything was wrong and wanting to know what message the stranger might bring, had followed me. She was some twenty yards behind me. I ran towards her, ducked down, running parallel with the dunes.

'Lilian, get back into the tomb – quickly! Go into the passage at the entrance!'

There was little time now. The figure moving across the sands was getting very close. There were a few minutes remaining before he came close enough to see what we were doing. With Lilian safely inside the tunnel that led down to the tomb, I dragged back the planks over the shaft just inside the entrance. Lilian watched me from the other side of the pit, understanding quickly what I was doing. She would be safe further inside, at any rate; even if he had a firearm, the twisting and turning of the passageway would make it impossible for him to shoot accurately.

In my tent, I found my pistol, checked it was loaded. The tent was partly concealed in the shadows from the rock behind the tomb.

Events now happened very quickly.

As he descended the last slope towards the cave, the man, the non-Arab in Arab clothes, began to run.

Casterman!

He was running directly to Lilian, who was still close to the entrance of the tomb, just on the other side of the mouth of the shaft. As he had come over the crest of the slope he could see her plainly, her white dress fluttering in the tomb entrance as distinctly as if it had been a flag.

Lilian retreated further into the tomb, and Casterman gave a cry of satisfaction as he flung himself the last few yards towards the entrance. He was so fixed upon her that he did not even look aside in my direction.

'Miss Lilian! Come out, Miss Lilian!'

He held something in one hand, behind his back.

A long, gleaming curve.

He had a knife.

At the mouth of the tomb, he paused, to let his eyes adjust to the darkness. I ran towards them; my footsteps were silent on the sand.

Then Lilian called out. 'You tried to kill me once! Well, come on then, murderer!'

She was actually taunting him, with a courage that seemed madness.

He was at the threshold of the tomb now. I saw Lilian's white dress retreating down the dark tunnel behind. I heard her call again.

'Come on then, if you dare!'

It seemed an absurd, forlorn, childish cry.

So Casterman must have thought, for he dashed forward.

His eyes must have been still unaccustomed, still blinded by the transition from brilliant sunshine to the black world within the tomb. So that he could not distinguish shades of grey, could not see the black rectangle, a darker patch amid the darkness of the tomb, that lay between himself and the fluttering patch of white that represented his prey. Nor could he have seen the outline of the planks that were now propped up against the wall instead of bridging the mouth of the pit.

He and I both were taken by surprise at that moment.

We had underestimated something – through lack of observation, or arrogance, or what you will.

That something was the depth of Miss Lilian's hatred towards him.

We had both thought, Casterman and I, and I confess that in this respect I was no better than he, that because she was a young and inexperienced girl, who had seen little of the world, that her feelings and actions would did not weigh significantly in the balance.

He had behaved with contempt and cruelty towards her; he had deceived her and he had not cared how much she suffered.

She hated him, as she later told me, in a way that she had never experienced hatred before.

'It was almost like love, Lord Ambrose,' she said. 'So strong!'

It caused her now to call out to him, almost like a girl to her lover.

I saw him hesitate for a moment.

I can still hear that young voice ringing in my ears.

'If you dare . . . if you dare . . . Here I am!'

He leapt forward.

There was a scream, a dull thudding sound as something struck the soft debris that had accumulated in the bottom of the shaft over the millennia.

'Stay there,' I called to Lilian. 'Keep well back!'

I had in mind that he could still be deadly, a wounded serpent in the pit below.

As I peered into the depths of the shaft, all I could see was a glimmer of light-coloured clothing.

I took no chances. I simply took aim and fired straight down into the pit, that trap where he had been caught. I cared not that it was like shooting a rat in a barrel: I wanted this creature dead.

The niceties of conscience are for those gentlemen who sit in their libraries and make fine judgements: I have fought men who would cut my throat with less pause for reflection than when they killed a hare.

I survived.

I cut their throats first. There was no time for anything else, as there was no time there in the desert for inquiring how many angels may dance on the head of a pin, or other delicate problems that moral philosophers may set before us.

Now the sound of my shot echoed round the rocky cliff.

I ran to my tent, grasped a rope and lowered myself into the pit. I fired another shot; the ensurance of death for this scorpion. Then Lilian began to sob – the reaction from stress and fear.

Later, when I had ascended, I pulled the planks down over the mouth of the shaft, put my arms around the girl, who was shaking uncontrollably, and got her to my tent, where I wrapped her in a blanket.

I fetched the Arabs from their encampment and we hauled him up, after I had got down into the pit on a rope and tied it under his arms. I was glad that, for Lilian's sake, there was not much blood to be seen. His eyes were open and staring as the body juddered up the shaft.

CHAPTER 16

'Oh, Lord Ambrose! I'm that glad to see your lordship!'

It was Jennet, whom I encountered outside the office of the British Consul in Alexandria, and great was my surprise when that lady fairly rushed into my arms, those very arms which she had clearly thought would embrace all the wicked temptations of the devil himsself.

But she was far from home and in a terrible fright. I was at least familiar, and English, and a gentleman.

'I've been coming here every day to try to make them search for Miss Lilian – I'm sure as eggs is eggs – Casterman's done something terrible, the wicked critter. Oh, whatever can we do?'

'Don't be afraid, Mrs Jennet. I've just arrived from Cairo and I can assure you that Miss Lilian is quite safe.'

'Lord be blessed! What's happened to her, the poor chick? And where is she now? Is she with you?'

'No, Jennet, but she is with my sister and her husband, on board their houseboat, and I am going to make arrangements for you to join them at the earliest possible opportunity.'

'Oh, your lordship – with Miss Ariadne – well, that's all right then, and I'm that grateful I can hardly speak – and it was a sad sad day I ever said anything against your worship and I say now I was utterly wrong and foolish . . .'

'Nonsense, Jennet, you were quite right – I am a terrible reprobate, you know – I just happen to have been of service in this matter.'

'Your lordship jests with me! But when can I see my mistress?'

'Very soon, for you can leave for Cairo today if you wish. The epidemic is dying down, and I'll help you get there as fast as possible. Why don't you return to the hotel and pack your things in the meantime?'

And Mrs Jennet actually flung her arms around me and embraced me then and there, before picking up her skirts and whirling down the street like a small black storm.

'All I know about him is that his name was Casterman,' I was saying to the Consul a few minutes later, 'that he was in the employ of a certain Mr Micah Overbury of Westmorland Park, and that he put Mr Overbury's ward in the most deadly peril of infection from the smallpox, with which, as anyone may see, he was himself afflicted at some stage in his life. As for his ill intentions towards Miss Westmorland, I believe a certain young Mr Sholto Lawrence would testify to that, for he rescued Miss Westmorland from a most perilous situation on a previous occasion, where she had been led into a dangerously decayed tower. And that was on a sight-seeing expedition in Alexandria which had been organised by Casterman. I freely admit that I shot the man, but I was convinced that in doing so I was saving Miss Westmorland from a fellow who purposed no good towards her. I am quite willing to make a statement to that effect and I am sure that Miss Westmorland will support my testimony.'

'There is a bullet-wound on his breast – it's all very dirty and torn, of course, but I could see the powder-mark on his shirt when I had a look at the fellow. Still, you assure me that was necessary to save the life of the young lady?' said the Consul.

'Or her honour, sir, her honour! I would plead that in any court of law!'

I could see that this semi-official jargon was greeted with relief. The Consul, to whom I had desired to make a statement concerning the body which lay in the next room, and which was at present causing His Britannic Majesty's Government a very considerable headache, gave a sigh – of relief, I thought – and then scratched away steadily with the nib of his pen. There were sticky marks of perspiration on the foolscap. Outside, in the streets of Alexandria, the cries and traffic of the Egyptian streets echoed relentlessly; in the room, the drawn shutters provided shade and a young boy pulled rhythmically at a punkah-style fan.

'Lord Ambrose, I accept your account of events – that goes without saying, as the word of a gentleman. But what are we to do with *him*?' There came an official outburst, as the Consul laid down his pen, wiped his brow, and gesticulated in the general direction of the room behind him. 'There are no relatives here in Egypt, I believe. How is he to be buried? Who is to pay the expenses? We have to decide these things without delay, in this climate.'

'Allow me to relieve you of the difficulty,' I modestly remarked. 'I am well acquainted with the Westmorland family, and will play my role of good neighbour. I will take upon myself the defrayment of the funeral costs – and make all the arrangements for the funeral itself. I will guarantee a solemn and fitting end, and will relieve the government of any expense or burden in this regard.'

The Consul poured some water from a jug that stood in a silver stand upon his broad desk. His broad, reddish face peered up at me hopefully. The words 'relieve the Government of expense' had their desired effect.

'Well, Malfine, if that is acceptable to you . . . it would certainly take a troublesome burden off my shoulders . . . But deal discreetly with it, will you? Can't have Europeans shooting one another – doesn't make a good impression on the natives, y'know. United front, and all that. Well, perhaps the least said the better – and I don't think I'll need to trouble Miss Westmorland. Where is she, anyway?'

'In the care of my sister, on board a houseboat. She is naturally very shaken, but will be travelling to Alexandria in a day or two. She asked me to book an early passage home.'

'Very well then, I'll not need to speak to her. I've already had her nurse here practically every day for the last month – a good woman, but my God, Malfine! I could get no sense from her – she has the vapours every two minutes. Some tale about this chap Casterman kidnapping a young lady, but there was no evidence whatsoever on which to proceed. Cairo is in an uproar as a result of the smallpox epidemic, of course, so who is to say whether he was not doing Miss Westmorland a favour by taking her into seclusion from infection? Though he's not a Britisher, of course. Still, Mrs Jennet can look after the young lady now – or rather, they can look after each other, for I don't know which of them will have the cooler head! At any rate, there's no need to cause Miss Westmorland any further distress. And you'll make all the necessary arrangements?'

The Consul pointed over his shoulder in the direction of Casterman's corpse.

'Oh yes, yes,' I answered in soothing, night treacly tones. And there's something else that needs attending to as well – there was a ticket in his pocket for a return to Southampton on board the *Arabian Lady* – she sails tomorrow, I believe. His luggage had probably already been taken on board and someone should inform the captain of the vessel that his passenger will not make an appearance and get the luggage off the ship – but you can safely place it all in my hands! And I shall have the assistance of my brother-in-law – he is waiting outside for me now.'

'Very good of you, Malfine. Well, I'll leave it all to you, then.'

Harassed officialdom conceded to the easiest course that presented itself.

I had thought it would. It always does.

'By the bye, Malfine, there's some mail for you. Came in with the last steam-packet.'

PART IV
The Arabian Lady

CHAPTER 17

The Contents of Lord Ambrose Malfine's Post-bag, Poste Restante, Alexandria

To Lord Ambrose Malfine, to be held at His Majesty's Consulate in Cairo until collected.

From R. Belos Esq, written at Malfine this second day of December, 1832.

My lord,

I have followed your instructions precisely, and send you this report by the fast steam packet, exactly as you requested.

Your apprehensions as to the death of the servant-girl, Maggie Dermott, were justified. As you desired me to do, I attended the inquest at Callerton on the poor wretch, where the old fellow who found her earthly remains gave evidence, along with Dr Sandys and some others. The case has had some publicity here in the West Country, owing to the extraordinary circumstances of the manacles, which were found, as it emerged at the inquest, not actually upon the girl's wrist, but lying loose within her garments. It is surmised in the newspapers that she managed somehow to extricate herself, for her wrists and hands were indeed very slender, and, breaking loose from her tormentor or tormentors, almost succeeded in escaping, but that they caught up with her, and silenced her for ever. It is assumed that the iron instruments of her suffering, which might provide a clue as to the perpetrators of her murder, were not retrieved, but left with her body, owing to the chances of darkness and urgency. I made notes of the Coroner's proceedings, and here present you with as full and careful a record as I can.

Dr Sandys was called first to the witness box. As you may imagine, the public benches in the courtroom at Callerton were crowded with avid faces, and the doctor's distaste for these ghouls ready to lap up the lurid details was evident upon his face when he stepped up to the stand. He spoke in his clipped, Scottish way, evidently wanting to give the onlookers as little satisfaction as possible, and his evidence was quite brief. He testified that when he first saw the body, life was beyond all doubt extinct. He observed the corpse of a young female, thin and not well nourished, as he described her, lying upon the ground, partly covered in dead leaves. The cause of death was plainly strangulation: there was a substantial mark around her neck. He did not think it was from a rope; it had not left the fibrous imprints upon the skin which would have characterised a rope. Rather, he thought it might have been from something such as the grip of a powerful hand, which could well have left the indentations he had observed. He had seen no other marks of injury upon the body.

The doctor later examined the body again, after it had been removed to the private laboratory in the grounds of

Lute House, and was able to testify that deceased was not with child, as he understood some persons had conjectured, and that she had been in fact *virgo intacta*. Dr Sandys said this in a very strong clear voice, as if to rebuke any who might have been spreading malicious rumours about the poor girl and her place in the Westmorland household; I am afraid that gossip of this kind has been circulating locally. Looking about him in a glaring sort of way, as if to dare those malicious tongues to go on wagging, Dr Sandys then left the witness box.

Several personages then testified that the deceased had been in employment until recently at Westmorland Park, as an under-housemaid. Mr Micah Overbury, trustee of the Westmorland Estate and guardian of its heiress, Miss Lilian Westmorland, then took the stand, at which there was much whispering in the public gallery, and he gave evidence that the deceased had been dismissed from her post, and had left Westmorland Park a week before her body was found. Asked what the reason for the dismissal had been, he said that the house was to be shut up as his niece was to travel abroad for her health, and he himself resided for business purposes in London. In any case, the deceased had not been fit to reside beneath the same roof as a gently brought up young lady such as his niece. He did not wish to speak ill of the dead, but he believed Maggie had some follower or other, for he had seen her indulging in some underhand and whispering conversations with a person of the male sex. Mr Overbury believed he had seen a stranger idling about in the vicinity of the house on the very day of the murder. In answer to the Coroner, Mr Overbury replied that this had taken place near the railings where the body had been found, and where the servant and her follower had evidently thought themselves unseen, but that he, Overbury, had been able to espy them from the upper windows of the house. Witness gave it as his opinion that the unknown man had strangled the girl, and left the body at their meeting place. Asked why the girl should have come to the house after she had been discharged from service, witness replied that he thought Maggie might have come to beg for her post back again which he, witness, would not have allowed, for he would not have had such an untrustworthy female in the household.

The mother of the deceased now took the stand; she was incensed and tearful, maintaining that Maggie had been unhappy and frightened since Mr Overbury had taken charge at Westmorland Park after the decease of Mrs Westmorland, and that she had referred to the comings and goings of a personage called Casterman, of whom Maggie had been especially frightened. Upon the Coroner asking her what was meant by this, she said she was unable to say exactly, for her daughter had never actually seen anything untoward. The Coroner thereupon commented that she must not speak ill of her betters when she had no proof beyond her daughter's tales, which were very likely fanciful, for Mr Overbury was known as a respectable personage of substantial worth.

Micah Overbury was then recalled to the stand. He stated that the man Casterman had been in his service for many years as his man of business; Casterman had been entrusted with the task of escorting his niece on her travels, so much faith did Overbury place in him.

One Patrick Hannigan, Constable of the Watch at Callerton, then gave his testimony. Here, your lordship will forgive an old Thespian for the observation, there was quite a theatrical interlude. I have played to the gallery too often myself not to recognise it in others, and you know, a courtroom is rather like a play; it has its roles and its heroes and heroines, and its audience, too. The audience in point of fact was hooting and shouting when the gallant constable made his appearance, for he was wearing the brave uniform of his constabulary, a tall top hat, together with a blue swallowtail coat and blue trousers, and this costume made the audience in the courtroom somewhat abusive, they giving many cries of 'blue devil!' and 'raw lobster!' and such pleasantries. But it was my impression that the new witness enjoyed his fame and stroked his whiskers quite complacently as he stepped into the witness-box.

Constable Hannigan's evidence did not, however, have a great deal to add to what we already had heard. He had been summoned to Westmorland Park by an old fellow who seemed very agitated and told him there was a dead girl as had been murdered, or some such words, and her body was lying under a hedge. On witness's arrival, Dr Sandys was standing beside the body and told him nothing could be done for the girl. This was in the grounds; the house itself appeared closed and empty.

Informant held up the manacles or handcuffs as he was speaking, and declared he had found them 'on the girl's body'. Witness had lifted the girl up and observed deep marks upon her neck, which Dr Sandys pronounced to be the cause of death.

Witness was at a loss to account for the manacles. He had never seen such a type before. They were not of the kind used by the constabulary for the restraint of prisoners and he had never seen such shackles. They were too small for a man, was the witness's opinion, and he caused something of a sensation in the courtroom by holding them up and demonstrating that the hoops would not meet around his wrists. This exhibition delighted the multitude, but the witness was unable to say anything more about the manacles.

The verdict was inevitable: murder by a person or persons unknown. Constable Hannigan was enjoined by the coroner to do all he could to find the man with whom Maggie Dermott had been keeping company, it being conjectured that he might have been responsible for this appalling crime.

There is nothing more that your servant can report in this particular respect; I made it my business next to investigate the circumstances of the Dermott family and to take careful notes of their situation and the conversation which I had with the mother and sister of the dead girl. Having obtained their address during the proceedings at the Coroner's Court, I made my way thither a few days later.

Garrison's Buildings, close to the docks in Bristol, consists of five storeys of leprous brickwork, built round a courtyard well into which the sun never penetrates. Four storeys are at least theoretically open to the air, being above ground; the basement, I was informed, contained two overflowing privies and innumerable rats.

On the third floor of this establishment, the Dermott family struggles to find a foothold for existence.

I made my way up the filthy staircase, holding a scarf over my mouth and nostrils. I had no choice but to be conspicuous, though I flatter myself I normally have the knack of blending in with the scenery, but I was not the kind of visitor who might normally call at Garrison's Buildings, to be sure. I had enquired the way to the Dermotts several times from various urchins who dogged my steps, and at length I approached a peeling wooden door, which attempted to protect, by means of skimped planks and a flimsy latch, the meagre possessions of a wretched household.

I knocked, gently, to spare the frail panels of the door. A woman opened it, and stared at me with eyes that barely seemed to register my presence. The lids were swollen and thick, shiny and glazed with much weeping.

She pulled a faded blue shawl around her shoulders. 'Yes?'

'Mrs Dermott?'

'What's it to you?'

'Mrs Dermott, I was at the inquest.'

She stared at me, seeming to see me for the first time.

'And what were you doing there? What was my poor child's death to do with you? You'll be the same as the rest of them – they don't care a farthing! There's lots of fine words – even the parson came round after he heard she were dead. First time he ever set foot in Garrison's Buildings, and then only when my child had been murdered. They doesn't care for us who lives in places sich as this – not that preacher, not that Coroner who prated away about my poor dead baby!'

Excuse me, my lord: I attempt to reproduce her speech faithfully as I heard it. We actors are quick students, you know, at noting the vagaries of accent and speech.

Mrs Dermott rubbed her eyes with a kerchief. 'So where are you from? And if you've anything to do with that Mr Overbury, you can take yourself right back to where you comes from! A real slave-driver, that Mr Overbury was!'

'No, I have nothing to do with Mr Micah Overbury, I assure you. I have been sent by one who is a friend to Miss Lilian Westmorland, to enquire into whether I might be of assistance.'

The woman's tone changed and she gazed into my

face for a moment or two, her anger ebbing away, as I could see.

'Miss Lilian? Aye, I heard Maggie speak of her – she treated her kindly, did Miss Lilian. That young lady were the only creature as ever offered her a decent word, you may be sure! Come in, though God knows, we have little enough to offer a visitor.'

This was patently true.

There were a few poor sticks of furniture in the room: a deal table, a bed, a makeshift shelf, a candle in a chipped saucer. It might have been furnished from the leavings of a rubbish heap.

It was clean, however. The uncovered floorboards had been scrubbed. There was a girl sitting on the bed, and her hair was tidy and her dress neat. The smell which imbued every step of the staircase outside was barely noticeable within this room.

Molly Dermott motioned me to a chair which had lost its back. It was the only object in the room on which one could sit, apart from the bed.

I remained standing, as I explained that I had been asked to express sympathy on the death of her daughter. I did not actually say that I was an emissary sent directly by Miss Lilian Westmorland, but I believe that Mrs Dermott and her daughter Sara (for so the girl on the bed turned out to be) understood me to have called in that capacity, and I did not disabuse them. I judged it better not to involve the name of your lordship in the matter.

'Molly were that sorry when she heard Miss Lilian would be taken off for foreign parts, she stood in this very room and cried. "Poor thing," she said to me and Sara, when she were allowed home for a visit. "Poor Miss Lilian, it'd break your heart to see her, she's got weaker of late!"

But then, of course, before Miss Lilian went, Mr Overbury turned Molly away from the house!'

'That is what seems so puzzling, doesn't it? Mrs Dermott, have you any idea why your daughter should have gone back to the Overbury household after she had been dismissed? Why she should apparently have been just outside the grounds when her attacker found her?'

'No, sir, I hasn't, but the only thing I think of was that perhaps she thought she might get to see Miss Lilian again and ask her for some help, for I don't mind telling you, sir, things are terrible hard with us, and that's the truth!'

Looking round the room, I could well believe this. The woman and the girl both had that sharp-featured look which suggested they never got enough to eat, and there was no sign in that room of anything to alleviate hunger. I have seen such poverty a long time ago, among aspiring actors, in my days in the theatre, but there it was bearable. Those garrets were lit with the bright clutter of stage flummery and bits of costumes, and the barely furnished rooms resounded with young voices declaiming passionate speeches, and supping on promises of fame, if I may express it so rhetorically.

Here in Garrison's Buildings there was the despair of grief, as well as the hopelessness of utter destitution.

The girl, Sara, broke in on my thoughts.

'But she never saw Miss Lilian when she went back.'

'How do you know that?'

She got up from the bed and put her arm around Mrs Dermott.

'I knows it because she was going to give Miss Lilian something. She said as Miss Lilian might give her some reward for it, but it were more than money our Maggie wanted. She thought as that Casterman might be doing something wrong – something that would hurt Miss Lilian.'

'Do you know what it was that Maggie was going to give to Miss Lilian?'

For answer, Sara bent under the bed and reached out a pair of grey woollen stockings, much darned at the toes and heels. At the sight of them, Mrs Dermott began weeping.

'Us got poor Maggie's clothes back from the Crowner. What she were wearing when some devil choked the life out of her. And she had the paper hidden in one of the stockings. Only they didn't find it, and they give us poor Maggie's clothes back. And we couldn't afford to . . . to . . .'

Sara Dermott struggled with embarrassment, but I could guess the rest.

This was something that I do not believe would occur to persons of your own station in life, my lord, but from my own experience when I was a struggling actor living amongst those who were truly the poorest of the poor, I understood what had happened. I had once had a landlady not much better off than Mrs Dermott: I know the shifts and strategies to which the near-indigent are driven.

The Dermotts could not afford to dispose of the clothes returned to the family by the Coroner's Office. So poor was this household that even the darned and repaired clothing of a dead sister could not be discarded.

'So you found something?' I said, quietly. We actors boom a lot, you know, but we know also when to speak softly.

Sara brought out a paper, much rubbed and folded.

'Us don't know what it says, sir,' she murmured, 'We can't read it, you see. Nor could Maggie – she were hoping Miss Lilian could tell her what it was.'

216

'So how did she know it was anything to do with the Overbury household?'

'Maggie heard them men going mad for having lost a paper. Carrying on terrible, they were. They was searching high and low and the whole 'ouse were in an uproar. Then that pockmarked fellow Casterman said best not to say more about it – that's what Maggie heard. But there were a paper lying in the hall, under where the gennlemen hangs their cloaks. Maggie found it while she were sweeping up the mud from outside as had tracked into the hall. She reckoned it had fallen out of a pocket or summa, and got blown out of sight wi' the draught, when the front door were opened, like. So she slipped it in her pocket.'

'Was it all that she gave you? Do you know aught of the objects – the shackles – that were described at the inquest?'

The girl started shaking. 'No, sir, and I've niver seen anything more horrible in my life than when them things were held up in the court. Evil, they looked, real evil. If ever Maggie'd said anything to me about them, we'd never hev let her go back there, I swear it!'

I have to agree with Sara. Those objects did bring a whiff of real wickedness into the courtroom. I still recall the obscene way they flashed in the light. 'The devil's bracelets' I believe they were called in the old slave trade.

'This is all she give me, sir!' Sara passed me the paper. As you may see, it is written in an elaborate and flourishing hand, with many twiddles and flourishes on the strokes.

'In Alexandria, this third day of December, in the year of our lord one thousand eight hundred and twenty-nine.

Received from Mr Micah Overbury through the offices of Messrs Capaldoni, of the Banca Prima di Venezia, the sum of five hundred guineas, in respect of the cargo which is described below.'

I puzzled over the words for a moment, before I understood them, so strangely out of place they seemed in that wretched attic room. And then I made out the description of the consignment: '*La Egiziàna*'.

Now, I have picked up a little Italian as I have traipsed around (never shall I forget that contralto from La Scala!) but I still cannot make much sense of this. The words would appear to mean 'the Egyptian', but the Egyptian what? It seems a nonsense to me, and of what it might import I have no notion, but I am sending your lordship an exact account of proceedings, as you requested me to do and therefore repeat the phrase *verbatim* and enclose the paper.

I am sealing this letter straightaway, as the messenger is come here in the room to take it to the packet. I trust your lordship is in good health. My compliments to Miss Ariadne.

Finally, my lord, I commend the Dermott family to your charity. They will have none, I believe, from Mr Micah Overbury.

I subscribe myself your devoted servant,

R. Belos

CHAPTER 18

From Miss Elisabeth Anstruther, Malaga House, The Downs, Bristol, to Lord Ambrose Malfine, care of His Britannic Majesty's Consulate in the city of Alexandria, poste restante.

My mother is well, and conducts herself most affectionately towards me, and I am happy to say that I am entirely re-established in the feelings of my family; indeed, our domestic circumstances here at Bristol are perfectly easy and comfortable. I take pleasure in our house on the Downs, with its tall windows, through which the clear light of day comes pouring in. All is freshly painted here, all well ordered and neat. It is peculiarly soothing to have one's life arranged with clockwork regularity, and nothing, my love, could be further from your extravagant, grand and gloomy Malfine.

Yet we live in a state of considerable excitement, for the town is in a ferment. There are many wretchedly poor creatures in the streets of Bristol and about the docks and shipyards, and it was hoped that some relief might be given them, more than is the usual custom, the autumn months coming on to be very cold. But their lives are more hopeless than ever, for no help is forthcoming. Indeed, things are like to become very harsh indeed, for the political reform for which they hoped has not been granted. The Bill before the House of Commons, to allow for Members of Parliament to represent the great and populous cities, was disallowed earlier this year. It is a sad blow against the recent agitations on behalf of democracy, and there is no hope of the people obtaining any redress against their misery, which inclines to real starvation, as I have seen for myself in some parts of Bristol, my mother being occupied with charitable work to relieve some of the suffering. I entered a house only the other day which you would scarce credit to be in a civilised country: there was a woman with her children, all lying beneath one ragged blanket, their limbs no better than mere sticks, and the air so cold that frost lay upon the floorboards around them. Of fuel: none. Of food: none. Looking round for the humblest possessions, or necessities to support life, I saw: none.

My mother's friend, Marguerite, accompanies us upon these expeditions of relief. Marguerite is of Negro ancestry and was stranded here in Bristol by the tide of events which ebb and flow in the great world beyond, for she and her parents were slaves awaiting shipment in the port when the judgement came through that the slave trade was abolished under the British flag. The captain of the slaving vessel, seeing his profits gone, cut off their shackles and turned them on shore, saying to them: 'You may fend for yourselves now! Eat freedom, drink freedom, see if your freedom will clothe and warm you, for I will not be at the expense of keeping you!'

So Marguerite and her mother and father were set down upon the docks to live as best they might, and a hard time they had of it at first, not knowing any in the place nor having anything but the rags upon their backs. But it was at this time that my mother, having cause to go down to the port with an urgent message for my father's man of business, saw the Negro child and her parents in wretchedness. She being of a gentle and pitying disposition, my mother took them to our house and gave them some employment about the gardens, till at last Grace's father was enabled to set up as a seedsman, an occupation which he managed excellently. Grace did his figuring and wrote his letters for him, and she has never left off her friendship for my family. Yet, she says to me, that we are deceived if we believe the Negroes to be free, for in the plantations they are still slaves to the owners, and labour under the whip of the masters. This I did not know, for I had always believed that, wherever the British flag may wave, all have their liberty and are free from that awful tyranny. But not so, for the slave-owners in the West Indies would not give up their property as they call their slaves, and could not be compelled so to do. There slavery still rules, under, to our shame, the British banner! And Marguerite believes that there are still slave-traders in our islands of Britain, carrying on their trade by smuggling human flesh as if it were so much dead contraband!

I go still with Mother into the town upon our charitable expeditions, but my father has said that he will forbid them if the situation should become more alarming still, and there be some real likelihood of an uprising. For myself, I do not fear, for when you and I are parted I care for nothing else: the rest of life touches me only as if it were a dream, but on behalf of my mother I must feel some alarm, and my family may remove to Bath for the remainder of the year.

The envoy you despatched from Alexandria, young Sholto Lawrence, arrived from Egypt at Portsmouth three days ago, and called here with your letter for me, which

I read again and again in my room overlooking the sea,
in this pale light which flickers and reflects off the water.
Sholto stayed here overnight and left yesterday for Malfine,
bearing your instructions to Belos. The task with which
you have entrusted the young man, who seems to be a
great admirer of yours, seems an almost impossible search,
that of looking for a needle in a haystack, yet perhaps
he may succeed. I am encouraged to believe he may on
two accounts: the first is that he can enlist the help of the
gypsymen, who go about over the whole county and have a
wonderful knowledge of such matters, and the second, not
to put too fine a point upon it, is that he has clearly fallen
head-over-heels in love with Miss Lilian Westmorland,
about whom he cannot stop talking! We had nothing but
Miss Westmorland for the whole of his visit, at every
opportunity. 'Miss Westmorland,' he believes, 'is a very
fine rider . . . Miss Westmorland does not care much for
reading the newspapers . . . Miss Westmorland has a very
charming shawl in just such a shade . . .' Clearly, the
briefest of acquaintances with the young lady has rendered
young Sholto her devoted slave, and he will leave no stone
unturned in the endeavour to assist her cause and restore
her happiness.

I break off now, for the candle on my table is guttering
in a wind that blows up from the sea; it will be a wild night
out there tonight. As the Psalmist says:

'They that go down to the sea in ships and do business
in great waters;
    These see the works of the Lord and his wonders in
the deep.'

But I myself desire only tranquility and safe harbour!

My letter is continued the next day, for there is some news to impart. Sholto Lawrence returned from Malfine this morning and begs me to go thither because he feels that my intervention may resolve his difficulties and bring him nearer to being inscribed in the 'good books' of his Miss Lilian. I doubt that I can truly be of any assistance in the matter but my father is of the opinion that Bristol is not safe any longer – there have been such rumours of riot – and the alternative is that I should accompany my mother to the tediums of Bath. If I have learned anything from your passionate spirit it is to resist the tyranny of tea and polite conversation, and my father's carriage is therefore to take me back to Malfine tomorrow. Do not think that thereby I am once more committing myself to you; I desire to be of some use to this ardent young man and to please my father, who will not be satisfied till his wife and daughter are safely removed from the scene of any possible danger.

This correspondence goes with a packet bound for Malta, whence the mail will transfer for Egypt. I see you in my mind's eye, with the sands blowing about you, unsealing this letter as you sit within your tent. Somehow I cannot picture you with any companions, for we are solitary creatures, you and I. Yet I fear some *imbroglio* for you; I know you to have a passion for justice that involves you against your will in the affairs of our fellow beings, taking you into dangers and entanglements. It was that idealistic hope for a better world which drove you to fight against tyranny in Greece, where you got so horribly wounded. It was the same passionate defence of the weak that made you intervene to save the gypsy from lynching at Crawshay's farm last year. And, in spite of all you say against the stupidity and cruelty of the world, of how you long to withdraw from it, I fear your quixotic streak of courage, for it may prove your undoing.

How can I promise to wait for you when any frightful enterprise might come between us, attracting your fervour as the flame attracts a moth? What, then, would be left for me? I want a living man, not a husk.

Write to me when you can.

E.

From Miss Elisabeth Anstruther, at Malfine in the County of Somerset. To Lord Ambrose Malfine, care of his Britannic Majesty's Consul in Alexandria, poste restante.

I arrived back at Malfine yesterday, but I do not intend to stay for long. Sholto called this morning – he is staying at the ale-house in the village, a place that can scarcely be called an inn, let alone an hotel, but it seems that the bed is cleanly enough and there he wishes to remain for the present. He may transfer to Lute House, for he has become acquainted with Dr and Mrs Sandys, and I expect they will ask him to stay with them if he desires to remain in the district. However, he has spent some time in the stables here at Malfine, worshipping your Zaraband, whom Pellers brought safely home from her exploits across Dartmoor. In the neighbourhood, it is truly considered a most remarkable feat and Pellers is near bursting with pride in his charge.

The task which Sholto Lawrence has imposed upon himself is a difficult one enough, although I understand he has had your advice upon the matter. But nevertheless the scent is so faint and the thread that is to be followed is so slender, that I doubt any traces now remain. But I will do what I can to help him. He rides out all around in the foulest of weather, across fields and byways, asking of every passing body, so that he is almost become like a village simpleton who can speak of one thing alone, and is regarded with a mixture of indulgence and exasperation by the good folk hereabouts so that he rarely receives a churlish answer. But Belos tells me that people mutter behind his back and would not in any event give him an answer to the question he so badly desires to have resolved on behalf of his Miss Lilian.

As for Westmorland Park, it remains quite deserted and shut up except for the lodge, but Mr Micah Overbury keeps a room there and visits it from time to time, though no one seems to know what lies within. On these occasions, Mr Overbury's carriage rolls up to the gates, the lodge-keeper is called for – the call always coming from the coachman, the occupant of the carriage not troubling himself to put his head out and speak with his own tongue – as I say, the lodge-keeper is called upon to open the gates for the carriage which arrives late in the evening and leaves early next morning. Mr Overbury has nothing to say to anyone, it seems, and when Mrs Sandys sent to enquire after his niece's health, he merely sent a reply to thank Mrs Sandys for her kind interest and say that he understood the climate of Egypt suited Miss Westmorland extremely well. I have heard also that nothing is known of the groom, Adams, though Dr Sandys did mention that he had treated Miss Adams for a bad burn on her hand. She was apparently quite silent throughout the painful business of cleaning and dressing the wound, coming to the doctor's house after dark as though she did not wish to be seen.

Young Sholto has been to the Park to try to speak to Mr Overbury, but either there is no one at home or Mr

Overbury regrets that he is too occupied with matters of business to entertain Mr Lawrence. So the young man learns nothing there – nor, I fancy, at Lute House, for good people though the Sandys may be, I cannot think they know anything that would bring Sholto Lawrence closer to his goal.

So he can learn nothing at Westmorland Park and nothing at Lute House.

The man he seeks, that is, the man you told him to search for, has not been seen these two months or more, neither him nor any of his family or tribe – they have the power to vanish into the countryside, almost as if a painter had just painted them out of the landscape a moment before! They may be deep within the woods even now – or on the move anywhere, for aught we know. At any rate, I am the person most likely to recognise them, since they lived here in the grounds over the last year. I will not close this letter yet, but will wait a day or two more.

And there is indeed further news. Yesterday morning Sholto rode over to say that he may have learnt something in the ale-house, and I understood why he had preferred to stay there. It was so that he might pick up any wayfarers' gossip that might lead him to that which he seeks. The young fellow is perhaps besotted with his Miss Lilian, but he is not a fool, after all!

He had learned from some casual talk that there was a gypsy caravan camped about twenty miles from here in the direction of Callerton.

When we got to the place, there was only the blackened ring of their fire and the scene seemed utterly desolate.

'Do stay in the carriage, Miss Anstruther,' said young

Lawrence, for we had driven in the Malfine coach. 'The day is raw, and it looks as if we are too late in any case. But I may as well just get out and take a look around.'

So I waited in the carriage on the road next to the rough unploughed field where the gypsies had been encamped, behind a screen of scrubby hedge and trees that tempered the cold wind which was blowing across the deserted spot.

There was a small trench neatly dug at the side of the field, with clean water that must have seeped therein. Sholto walked over to look at it.

'They were the old Romanies, all right,' said a voice from the hedge.

A man emerged, young and sleepy-eyed, rubbing his head, and he bent down over the trench, cupped his hand and splashed some of the water over his face. 'I was drinking in the tavern with them last night – and by God, they are good men for a wager and a yard of ale!'

He felt his pockets and laughed. 'Well, I had nothing more to take! I woke up this morning and they were gone clean away, like birds from the nest!'

He bent down once more, giving a groan as he did so, and again splashed some drops of water over his face.

'Aye, they were true gypsies, all right. See this water here? That was their bath and their basin. They would not wash except in a hole in the earth. Would not drink out of another man's mug, lest it were defiled by one of us *gorgios*!'

Young Sholto leaned forward eagerly.

'Do you have any idea of where they are gone?'

'Who is asking for them?'

'My name is Sholto Lawrence. I have a most particular reason for finding them – I assure you, I mean no harm to them.'

'Well, there's precious few folk come looking for the gypsies for their pleasure, young sir! Unless it be some fool like myself, wanting companions for an evening in a tavern! I'm part gypsy myself – but I married out of the life and the old ways are dead now – or almost dying. I have no wish to live upon the road – but still, I wish them no harm, and so why should I tell you what I know – if I know anything, that is?'

'I can reward you.' Young Sholto clinked a purse.

'Aye, but can you protect me from vengeance if they say I have betrayed them? They can track a man down, you know, from one end of the country to another, if they have sworn to do it.'

'That is exactly what I want from them – to track a man down – but not for any harm to him, I promise you.'

The fellow still seemed reluctant, passing his hand across his mouth as if thinking upon things, but he was suddenly startled into speech again. The horses of the carriage in which I was sitting, wrapped in my thickest cloak, as this encounter took place, shifted slightly, moving the coach forward a foot or two, and I saw the eyes of the new acquaintance fall upon the black wolf's head coat of arms painted upon the door.

'That crest over there – what's that?'

'The coat of arms of Malfine. Do you know it?'

'Never seen it before in my life,' replied the other, maddeningly, yet I could tell somehow it was the response of a perfect automaton, which he would give on any topic to any person who might have some connection with authority.

Then he came across towards the carriage and peered at it with his bleary eyes for a few minutes, as if scrutinising it carefully. 'But I've heard something about it. If you come on behalf of the man who has the right to use that crest, I'll help you to the Romanies and you can keep your money. There are times when it's bad luck to take money, strangely enough!'

We never learnt his name.

That is all that I can tell you so far and I will leave all further enquiries to Sholto.

I have given more thought to the matter of which we spoke before you left. Are you not likely, after all, to make a match with someone of your own status in life, some lady of aristocratic breeding who will make a suitable mistress for Malfine should you desire one day to re-open the full glories of your mansion? A lady who would provide you with a suitable heir to the Malfine estates? My family is untitled stock and not such as grand personages of your own rank would find acceptable as a match for you.

At all events, I am not going to stay here at Malfine and mope till your return, like some wailing queen in a tragedy! You would not respect that, and I do not wish to experience it!

Elisabeth

CHAPTER 19

The Further Narrative of Lord Ambrose Malfine

The *Arabian Lady* was at anchor, her sails flapping gently in the breeze that drifted unseriously through the harbour. The pearly, scummy, dirty waters of the Mediterranean lapped at the old stone masonry that had probably seen Cleopatra's ships set sail for Actium.

The ship was a fast schooner, however indolent the scene in which she might now appear. She had a high, sharp keel that would slice through the water like a knife, and the look-out on her deck knew his business. He challenged me as we stepped onto the gang-plank.

'We desire to see the master of this ship, if it is pleasing. And possible.'

The sailor looked me over, took in my obviously European appearance which must have made somewhat of a contrast with the Arabic with which I addressed him, and came to a decision. 'It is possible.'

He swung down into the depths of the vessel.

The man who came up to greet us was clearly not a sailor; he was dressed in elaborate brocaded robes and was bare-headed and had pomaded hair, Western style.

'I am the owner of this vessel – the captain is not aboard at present. You have business with the *Arabian Lady*?'

'A morning of light to you!'

'A morning of roses!'

'A morning of jasmine!'

We exchanged the traditional courtesies warily. Then I judged it possible to explain the purpose of my visit. The wind was blowing more strongly now and the gorgeous robes fluttered as my host bowed and ushered me on board.

'We have come on behalf of one of your passengers – well, that is to say, in a way on his behalf, but it would be truer to say on behalf of his heirs, if he has any. He died yesterday, near Cairo.'

I held out the ticket which had been found in Casterman's pocket.

'As you see, this man had a passage booked with you. I am here to represent the British Consul and to recover any effects which Casterman, for that was his name, may have had transferred to your vessel for the voyage.'

'I deeply regret to hear of such misfortune. What were the circumstances of his death, may I enquire?'

Here I coughed and paused. 'His Majesty's Consul is still enquiring into the circumstances of the death and I am not yet at liberty to reveal anything – but I have heard that it was an accident occurring at one of the old tombs near the Pyramids.'

'Ah, I am not at all surprised, though very sad, of course to hear it! But there are old shafts there, going deep into the ground – deep amd treacherous, still guarding the passages into the tombs!'

'Yes, I believe there was a fall down into one of the shafts.'

Well, I reasoned to myself, that had certainly been a contributory factor.

'My dear sir, such accidents occur if people do not take every precaution and are not accompanied by experienced guides. But Mr Casterman was more at risk than most, I believe, for he had a great interest in antiquities.'

'Indeed?'

'Oh, yes – allow me to present myself – I am Signor Moroni, a dealer in antiquities in my modest way. You may have heard of my little enterprise perhaps – I have an antique shop in the Khan el-Khalili, the souk in Cairo. We have curios, antiques and so forth – just exactly the sort of thing that appealed to poor Mr Casterman! He took such a keen interest in ancient Egypt – I daresay he was pursuing his hobby when the accident occurred.'

'I daresay.'

Casterman had, it transpired, indeed booked a cabin for the voyage to Europe. 'But none of his possessions has been carried aboard. Oh – I believe there is one exception – it is an antiquity he purchased from me – but that will not be of any interest, I take it. You will be wanting his personal effects, papers and so forth, I expect.'

The man's manner was very smooth and friendly; I supposed Casterman had purchased some trinket, a faience necklace or some such gee-gaw. Yet the account of Casterman as a dabbler in the antique somehow did not hold water.

And I suddenly recalled the tattered and grubby paper enclosed in the packet of letters that I had collected at the Consulate that very morning – letters three weeks old, addressed to me Poste Restante – for collection at Alexandria. *La Egiziàna*.

'The Egyptian what?' Belos's letter had been impatient.

Perhaps I was about to find out.

He tried in every way possible to keep us from going down to Casterman's cabin. First politely, then barring our way, then I saw him opening his mouth as wide as a carp, probably as a preliminary to summoning help.

I had a simple answer. I seized him, twisted his brocaded silk-sleeved arm behind his back and held a knife to his carotid. Nothing expensive, none of your damascened inlaid blades – just something very functional, which I held up before his eyes for a moment, so that he could see what it was. A common cook's knife, such as is used to slit throats.

'Hold your tongue.'

I lifted him off his feet and spun him around.

'Set your foot on the first tread of the steps down to the cabins. Now the second. Now we'll follow you – and if you give me the slightest bother I'll slit your artery and throw you down those steps.'

There were two cabins opening off the bottom of the steps down from the deck. He indicated the one on the right with a jerk of his head.

With my arm still around his fat neck, I flung open the door.

The cabin was almost empty, save for one strange object.

I pulled my hostage back again through the door and flung him into the other cabin; with the sash of his robes I tied him to a bunk bed and thrust his satin kerchief into his mouth. 'Don't struggle – you'll smother yourself. Charles, look after him for the moment, will you?' Charles willingly busied himself with the makeshift bonds.

Back to the other cabin.

And I feared I was too late. I had been a fool in not realising how malign Casterman was – and how determined were those he served. If there was a death on my hands it would not be that of Casterman, for I felt no guilt over him, but that of some poor innocent whom I was too late to defend from the cruelty and evil that the Castermans of this world can unleash – and which they will justify in the name of their damnable unholy naked greed.

The seconds that it took to fling myself across the passage between the cabins, to hurl myself into the right-hand cabin, knife in hand, seemed almost an eternity, as long as it took to build the pyramids themselves, or as long as the time that had elapsed since the Sphinx was young. My movements seemed heavy, dragging – yet every second counted.

I dashed across to the object in the middle of Casterman's cabin.

An Egyptian coffin, brilliant, exotic.

And tightly lashed round with ropes.

There was an old cutlass lying on a filthy bunk next to the coffin.

The girl was blinking up at me. In a moment I had slashed through the ropes and lifted her – for she could not stand – out of the depths of the coffin where she had been confined. She was pale and her eyes were glassy – she had probably been drugged to keep her quiet. And her wrists and ankles were fettered. She was still alive, for air holes had been contrived unobtrusively round the base of the coffin.

La Egiziàna! A slender Nubian; she was black and very beautiful, with blue tattoos on her cheeks.

She was still alive, thank God, and we were able to convey her safely to Cairo, where we took her on board the *Zubeida* and it was touching to see the affectionate reunion between Lilian and Rahaba, who was delighted to see the companion of her imprisonment safe and sound, for she had thought that Lilian was sure to perish in the epidemic from which she herself had been saved. A slave-girl was of course far too valuable a piece of property to risk in an outbreak of smallpox, for even if she were to survive, the inevitable pock-marked scarring would reduce her price to a fraction of her worth if she were unblemished goods.

At all events, they are both safe now. Ariadne and Charles are to take Rahaba south, back to Nubia when they sail for Aswan – she will return to her family there.

But how many other innocents have been sent to a life of hell and servitude on the other side of the world? How long will our government go on allowing rich planters to be slave-owners – because, after all, you cannot expect a true Briton to give up his property, even if that property be human flesh?

And as long as they are permitted to keep slaves, so long will there be an unlawful trade. For although it is too dangerous to supply huge numbers of men for agricultural labour in the cane-fields of Jamaica and Barbados, yet it is perfectly legal to own slaves there – perfectly legal to keep a woman as a whore even if she has to be kept chained up in the house of some rich planter. And they are rich, those plantation-owners – so rich they will pay sky-high prices for a woman house-slave whom they can use as they wish. Why, it is not illegal to own her, is it? Merely illegal to own slaves in England! But on Jamaica slavery is so necessary to the economy of the island that we dare not do away with it – and nor do the British judges dare order us to liberate our slaves, so much does that motherland depend on the flow of gold we deposit in her coffers. No, no sir, slavery is perfectly legal here in the West Indies! And I am the legal owner of this woman – why then, sir, how dare you assert that I have broken the law of the land! I am merely exerting my due right of possession!'

For such a woman, a fortune could be paid. The rich

planters of Kingston compete with each other to show off their slave-girls and if later on a man should cast a girl off when she is diseased or too dulled with beatings, well then, there are plenty of brothels in the West Indies to which she can be sold to end out her days, fettered if need be. Who would ask and who would care?

So the slave-trade continues, although you may say that it has taken on a different commercial aspect, for now it deals in small consignments of very valuable and high-quality merchandise . . . that is how the slavers would see it. A beautiful girl, a virgin, of high birth and trained in the social graces . . . such a woman would bring enough money to make the whole expedition worthwhile, like a rare and exotic animal brought back to exhibit in a fashionable menagerie.

Then and there, we worked out the details of Casterman's scheme, aided by reluctant responses from Morino whom I was kicking at intervals. The girl was to be transported on board the *Arabian Lady* in the coffin – as I surmised, she would first have been drugged, to ensure her silence. Outwardly, a respectable gentleman would be shipping back an interesting antiquity, a piece to add to a collection, and a parcel of the ancient world that proved the refinement and curiosity of his taste. The coffin would be placed in Casterman's cabin to await his pleasure.

Once they were at sea, the girl would be released. The crew would have been bought, and the coffin provided in advance with a false bill of shipping by Morino. *La Egiziàna* – it was in the feminine form in Italian! The Egyptian woman!

This document would have been sent by the fast steam-packet to Overbury in England, to warn him of what to expect and allow him to meet his most interesting import at the dockside.

Would there have been time for all this? Yes – Morino

had the plan ready in advance, and sent the bill of shipment which that sad and courageous servant-girl had found at Westmorland Park. No doubt they had not at that time decided on a suitable victim, merely an appropriate means of smuggling. Thank God for the fast steam-packet, which had allowed Belos to get the tell-tale document to me in time!

Meantime, on board the *Arabian Lady*, Rahaba would be allowed the freedom of the cabin, until they were again in sight of land, when she would once more be forced into the hiding place, and when Casterman disembarked, the Egyptian Coffin would accompany him, as a rarity which he was bringing home, and of which every possible care must be taken. It would travel with him to some safe place – such as a barred and shuttered room in a country house, somewhere not far from the coast and a port, somewhere where the servants had been dismissed so that there would be no gossip. Somewhere like Westmorland Park, for instance.

Then some means would be found to get the girl to the shore again and on board a ship for the West Indies – and then her fate would be sealed indeed.

Questions remained in my mind. Casterman was evidently but one link in a chain of hidden slave-dealers, who must stretch across the Atlantic, for payment must somehow be arranged at the other end of this chain. How deeply was Overbury involved? What was to be his role in the scheme?

He would be wary, no doubt about it. But I thought I had a way to smoke him out.

The *Arabian Lady* at last dropped anchor at Bristol docks and I glimpsed a tall figure on the quayside, pacing up and down as the gang-plank was slung out to the shore. The sailors bustled about the decks, furling sail, making all ship-shape, and if they were not the same captain and crew as that with which the ship had left Alexandria, there was nothing outward to show that new hands had been engaged shortly before she had sailed.

So anxious was Mr Overbury to get aboard as soon as the gangplank dropped down that he rushed up on deck immediately it was possible.

'I must see the captain of this vessel straight away. There is a very important item which has been shipped for me from Alexandria – a most rare and fragile antiquity! My man of business, Casterman, should have it in his cabin. My name is Overbury, Mr Micah Overbury of Westmorland Park.'

He was so preoccupied with anxiety about his precious cargo that I think he did not observe a tall skinny-legged fellow in a tattered cloak who slipped past him on to the shore and stood for a few moments watching events from the shadowed doorway of a small tavern at the edge of the dock.

The captain emerged from his cabin. 'Overbury, did you say? Well sir, I regret that Casterman was unable to take up his berth – but no cause for alarm, sir, Mr Moroni got your shipment safely on board and he has arranged for everything to be taken care of as you would have wished.'

And here the captain nodded discreetly at Overbury, so that the latter understood his meaning and seemed to relax.

'You will be well rewarded, Captain, if you can get my property unloaded straight away – I have a coach waiting to take it to Westmorland Park. We can be there in a couple of hours.'

The captain showed no surprise at this feverish haste and called out command to half a dozen members of the crew, upon whom he laid many injunctions to fetch the old coffin standing in the first-class cabin.

'And they'll be glad to get it off the ship, Mr, Overbury, for 'tis said a coffin means bad luck to any vessel that carries it, and it's no good telling sailors that this one is but an ancient, empty old thing – they're a superstitious species! Look careful there, you lubbers! The thing is most odoriferous! In a word, sir, it stinks!'

The coffin, which seemed quite absurdly bright-coloured against the slimy grey-brown timbered background of a British dockside, was swung out on ropes over the heads of the waiting men and then Overbury made a signal and a coach clattered on to the dock and drew up alongside. Gradually, with many shouts of 'Steady there!' and 'Gently, gently now' from the captain, and with Overbury fussing about as if he were organising the transport of a coffin made out of glass with a sleeping princess inside, the object was lowered on to the roof of the carriage and secured carefully with leather straps, which Overbury insisted on testing before he finally climbed inside and the horses moved off at a careful trot. So cautious was the pace that there would have been plenty of time for a fast horse, hired perhaps from livery stables close to the port, to get to his destination well ahead of him – assuming, of course, that the rider knew the road that the exotically laden coach would follow.

The carriage swept up to the gates of Westmorland Park and the coachman called to the lodge-keeper as usual. The iron gates swung back, and the carriage, with its strange cargo of bright blue and gold in that long sinister shape, moved off up the drive.

At the entrance, Micah Overbury sprung out as the coach slid to a halt. He was calling to the coachman to get down and fetch the lodge-keeper to help unload when two figures emerged from behind one of the pillars of the portico.

'Good day, Overbury! May we be allowed to welcome you home?'

'Malfine! Good God, sir, what are you doing here? And you, Sandys?'

'Thought I was on my travels, didn't you? Well, Overbury, I'm pleased to report that I've just returned from Egypt and you'll be delighted to hear that your niece is in splendid health! Dr Sandys and I were just strolling over to Westmorland Park to acquaint you with the good news!'

It was quite interesting. I'd never seen anyone's jaw drop before. I thought it was merely a literary term, but I saw that incongruously fleshy red mouth fall open and a trail of saliva slid unhindered from its lower lip on to Mr Micah Overbury's cravat.

'Shall we give you a hand with that curious object – ah! – it's a coffin! Heavy, too. Who've you got in here, Overbury – Ozymandias?'

By now, with the combined efforts of the coachman and the lodge-keeper who hauled upon the leather straps, the coffin was sliding in gentle and controlled fashion to the ground; I stepped in to support it before it bumped down.

'There's something wrong, here, Overbury. What have you been buying in the Orient – not all the perfumes of the East, for sure! Fortunately I've got a knife in my pocket – shouldn't we take a look inside the coffin straight away?'

Overbury rushed forward as I cut at the ropes around the coffin shouting that it was his property, that I should keep my damned hands off . . .

'Your property, eh? Well, you've acknowledged that in front of these witnesses here – three good men and true who can swear before a jury that this coffin has been claimed by Mr Micah Overbury as his very own property! Faugh – disgusting, ain't it?'

I had hacked through the ropes by this time, while Sandys pinioned Overbury by the arms and held him back.

I pulled up the lid. The coachman and the lodge-keeper, who had craned forward, started back with cries of disgust. The coachman turned aside from the path and I heard the sound of vomiting.

Gaping from within the lower part of the coffin was a hideous face, swollen and black with decay; the teeth gleamed through the shredding flesh of the cheeks and the eyes were liquified and putrescent.

I tipped the coffin forward and the body rolled out, filling the clean country air with foulness as a viscous dark liquid ran into rivulets across the drive.

'Looks like someone tried to do a spot of preservation but their attempts at mummification weren't very successful – they probably didn't have much time. And he's been at sea for a month or so; the *Arabian Lady*, I believe, ran into storms off the coast of Malta. Still, here's your coffin – do you recognise him, Overbury? You are in the most suspicious of circumstances, you know, claiming a coffin containing a dead body as your property? And no ancient Egyptian, neither! Have a good look at his face now – you two, hold Mr Overbury close so that he can see the face – what once passed for the face, at any rate. Get a good look, Overbury – closer! Don't you recognise it? Why, I do believe it's your man of business – your confidential adviser!'

'Yes, yes,' shrieked Overbury. 'It's Casterman. How in hell's name did this come about? I deny it all – this has nothing to do with me!'

'Oh, come, come, Overbury,' said Sandys. 'Not only did you openly claim this coffin as your property, but Lord Ambrose has a piece of paper on which the shipper expressly sends the consignment to you!'

'Malfine, how did you get that?'

'There was a child, for she was little more than a child, whom you killed, Overbury – you or Casterman at your bidding. The servant girl, Maggie Dermott, who tried to warn your niece of the evils she suspected – and who paid for it with her life. But her sister retrieved this tell-tale piece of paper that links you with her death and with this shipment.'

I held up the paper and read aloud. 'To Mr Micah Overbury at Westmorland Park . . . *La Egiziàna.*' The Egyptian what? The Egyptian Coffin? It would have contained something else – a living, breathing human being – the Egyptian slave-girl, shall we say? Other people's lives mean nothing to you, do they, Overbury? Neither poor Maggie Dermott, nor your own niece, nor the girl Casterman strangled in Cairo lest she, too, should try to aid Lilian Westmorland. There is a pattern there, Overbury, is there not? Young women, especially – they have no importance at all. And that is why you can trade in their flesh, you and your fellow slavers! That is why the girl would have been brought here and kept prisoner till she could be sold on at a profit and smuggled out of the country! As for your niece, you did not dare to harm her openly here, where she had friends and neighbours to watch over her! But you knew that if you sent her to the East there would likely be many opportunities for her death to occur – by a seeming accident, perhaps, or else by Casterman's unusually resourceful methods. He didn't succeed in contriving another accident – but he tried to take her into the heart of a raging epidemic which was almost bound to infect her with a deadly disease! Was that your idea or did he plan that on the spot? I had no opportunity to ask him and it's too late now!'

Overbury was struggling frantically and would almost have broken free, but Sandys stepped forward, putting a hand into his pocket, and held up something that glinted in the light.

'You're a cunning devil, Overbury, but Malfine arrived before you – as a matter of fact, he was in time to alert me and we got here together. We found these inside a room at Westmorland Park. In a room next to yours, but windowless, with a padlock on the door. But I think they will go round your wrists. We'll use them on you, Overbury – and it's less than you deserve. And if you don't stop struggling, we'll use the other tackle we found here, as well. The whip, for instance. Ah, I thought so – that's quietened you down!'

And Sandys snapped the manacles on Overbury's wrists.

PART V
Malfine

CHAPTER 20

The Further Narrative of Lord Ambrose Malfine

I strode at last across the fields from the direction of Westmorland Park, towards home. So I speak of Malfine now, if I have any such place in the world; if I have to describe where I am from, as a traveller is so often asked to do by some passing acquaintance, I answer 'Malfine; that is my home.' Yet how can anyone call Malfine, this immense heap of slate and marble, this absurd and beautiful monstrous burrow in which I have the right to lay my head, home?

Nevertheless, as I grew closer, my pace quickened when I saw the white columns soaring up and the long sweep of the carriage drive. I had forgotten how fragile the vast house appeared, how it had a trick of floating above the earth, with its fragile boundaries of trees and lake, to seem like a vision in a dream.

Thus my Greek mother must have seen it, when my father had first brought her to his home, this fulfilment of a cool vision, in a setting so unlike that of her hot and stony homeland. How many deserts had I crossed now, to come here once again to these green fields where I had once, in my benignly neglected youth, run wild?

But even as I hurried towards the house, I knew that I should never come home to a mere place, not even this. My pulse was racing and I yearned now for my journey's end – but as I ran up the driveway of Malfine, my longing was still unfulfilled. The stones were bloodless stones merely, the marble had no voice.

I had no news now for two months or more – since the last letter had reached me as I sat in a tent beneath the burning skies of Egypt. What I hoped for was impossible – there was every likelihood that she had returned to her family – that her mother had persuaded her into a sensible and decorous life and that her parents were even now contriving for their wayward daughter to meet some suitable middle-aged suitor. I myself had advised that course and counselled her to abandon her relationship with an eccentric and rebellious aristocrat. Of course she would not be here!

It was impossible. Yet I could not prevent myself from hoping.

And then suddenly, on the white steps of the portico, was a woman with her hair down around her shoulders, staring as if she could not believe her eyes. And then she was picking up her skirts and running. Running towards me.

Behind her, a manservant was calling out, 'Miss Elisabeth, pray take care! Miss Elisabeth, who is that ruffian in the drive!'

CHAPTER 21

Record of a statement made by the gypsy, Shadrach Lee, and set down by the hand of Lord Ambrose Malfine

My lord asks me to say what I know about the business at Westmorland Park, and that he will set it down as I speak it, for I have no letters, neither in English nor in our tongue of Romany.

It is not much I can say. I was sent for, together with another Romany man of our family, by name Trito Hearne, he being what is called among us a *gryengro*, or horse dealer, that is a man who knows the ways of those beasts – and the ways of those who deal in them. Trito has told me some of the artful ways of tickling up a beast for the buyer – that a dull horse can be made to look lively by tipping a live eel down its throat, for example, or that if the creature is too frisky and bucking about, that a gallon of strong ale will make him most agreeably placid and dozy till the deal is done and the buyer rides safely off upon the back of his new purchase.

But I don't know if any such tricks were used that night – Trito never told me, if they were.

We were never told the name of the man who sent for us.

I was with my wife and children living in our *keirvardo*, a caravan, in the grounds of my lord's estate at Malfine, as he has permitted us to do. [Note: I will bear witness that this is perfectly true: these gypsies have done me good service in the past and have permission to camp on my land – A.]

But at night comes a carriage, driven by a man with a cloth over the most part of his face, save for his mouth and eyes.

I steps out of the caravan, cautious, and waits for him to speak.

'I have a horse I desire to sell,' says he.

Well, no honest man comes horse-dealing in the middle of the night, so I guesses this is a case of *gry choring* [horse-stealing – A.] and he purposes to dispose of the beast with all speed – and hopes that a gypsy might spirit it away for him.

'Sir, if you have a horse to dispose of, you want old Trito Hearne from Callerton way,' says I. 'He's the horse-man in these parts.'

The man with the cloth says there will be a guinea in the palm of my hand if I will go straightaway with him and fetch Trito. He says the matter cannot wait till morning and I knew full well why – because the horse must be got far away by daylight. At any rate, that is usually the reason in such cases!

So we goes over and fetches Trito, then and there in the middle of the night, and the stranger took us west – I would say a distance of about ten miles – to a big house built of brick, and we creeps round, the man we did not know motioning to us all the time to be silent, to the stables at the back.

Then he leads out of a stall a horse with sacking tied round its hooves, so it makes no sound on the cobbles. I could not rightly see it in the night, but it looked to be a darkish colour:

it may have had a small white blaze upon its forehead, but that I cannot swear to. I saw the creature only in the darkness: Trito went close, with a lamp.

Anyway, to return to the tale: I am taking fright, for leading away such a beast from the very stables of the house cannot be less than a hanging offence, and I whispers to old Trito to come away and leave off such games, but then another man appears, a tall gentleman, very well-dressed and with a long beard and a high black hat. Something like a parson, he looked.

'Can you dispose of this animal for a price?' says he.

Well, Trito searches the beast over, and looks in its mouth and runs his hands over its legs. Then he rubs its back and fetlocks with a bit of wet straw. He's looking for dye covering up the beast's markings, you see, berry-stain or suchlike.

'This is the finest mare I ever do see!' says he to me, in our Romany tongue to keep it secret, but they knows what a valuable animal they has got there, of that I am sure.

Trito says to them, 'I'll get you a price for it, and a good one. It has a cut on yon foreleg, with some tarry muck around, but that'll heal soon enough. I'll not ask you why a fine thoroughbred mare is being sent off – but that's what she is, gentlemen! There's no disguising the quality of this piece of horseflesh – no sir! Thirty guineas is the price I can get for you, if I take her far enough away.'

Far enough – they knew what he meant. Far enough so she wouldn't be recognised, that's what they wanted. He took their wishes, you see, old Trito, without they said a word. He's seen a lot of this horse-dealing, has the rogue.

'Thirty!' says the second gentleman. 'Why, she's worth a couple of hundred!'

'Why, sir, advertised at leisure among the quality, and with a docket of her breeding, I doubt not she's worth a hundred or more. But taken out of the stables at night and led across half the countryside, I'll put it no higher than thirty. I can find a buyer at that price, and quick enough if you want her taken off your hands.'

'Can you give me the thirty in my hand now?' says the man in the tall hat.

Now, to look at him you wouldn't think old Trito had so much as a penny-piece to his name, but as he said to me afterwards, 'Us horse-dealers must be ready for any emergencies that may arise in the course of our profession.'

The old gypsy man carries round more than you would think. You know, one time I sees Trito pull a silver tankard out that he kept in the pocket of his old tail-coat, and he said he carried that tankard around so that he might never have to drink his ale out of the same cup as a *gorgio*, (which persons, being not Romanies, begging your lordship's pardon, we do not consider clean). That was how much Trito clung to the old Romany ways.

But to return to this business of the mare, the two men are waiting and Trito pulls out an old knotted kerchief that was slung inside his trousers, and a bag that is hung under his armpit, and another that is tied round his neck beneath his kerchief. And from every little bundle and crevice as we might say, there comes the chink of guineas here and groats there, of bits and bobs of coin so that old Trito must have been a walking bundle of fair old horse-currency. Then and there he counts out the price of the mare, and as he was pulling the money out so the fellow in the tall hat was peering at the coins and weighing them in his hand.

'I'll get you hanged if there's a dud!' he says to Trito.

'All coin of the realm, sir,' says Trito. 'You'd best count it again in daylight to satisfy yourself!'

The man gave a grunt, as if to say 'Well, that's to come' and turned away towards the house.

'Remember, far away!' says the other man. And he gives me the guinea for fetching Trito, as he had promised.

And that was all we saw of them, for we led the horse out of the stables, and once we were a half-mile or so beyond the house Trito jumps on its back and pulls me up behind, and they left me near Malfine, horse and rider going like the wind. And I've never had a ride so fast before, for all that mare had a cut on her leg.

But my woman, when I told her, was greatly feared, for she knew that the horse must be stolen, and thought all was contrived to put suspicion on us Romanies. So she went with our child to Malfine mansion house at night, and roused the *raia*, and told him of the dealing with the two men and old Trito.

And all of what I have said now is true, and may my ancestors curse me otherwise with these words: The curse of our souls light upon him and his for ever – may our spirit be deep upon him in his life and in his death – may his thirst be unquenchable – may he dwell in the darkness of his own heart – may his last food be the bread of his enemies – we, the ancestors, have spoken!

And if what I have said is untrue, may my children bury me in a churchyard.

The mark of Shadrach Lee

CHAPTER 22

The Concluding Narrative of Lord Ambrose Malfine

Yet there was a mystery still to unravel. We were in the dining room at Malfine, setting our brains to work to solve this final puzzle.

My dining room is somewhat unusual as to its furnishings – it was designed as a salon of immense grandeur, for the banquet of a prince, literally, for my grandfather had thought he might entertain Prinny himself beneath his roof. But it would have been an arrangement against my grandfather's interests, for the Prince was heavily in debt and my grandfather was not, and besides the expenses would be quite monstrous – a twenty-course dinner would be a mere bagatelle. In any case, Grandfather Hedger had got wind that Prinny was looking for loans.

So the visit never took place, but there was a magnificent room with a table forty feet long and candle-sconces all around the walls, and somewhere in the butler's pantry was a blue-and-gold Sèvres dinner service, every plate painted with a naked deity, that old Hedger's Paris agent had got cheap after the sale of Madame du Barry's effects, following the unfortunate revolutionary events in France. It would, perhaps, have been a tactless reminder to set before poor Prinny.

Such, at any rate, was the dining room, which now in early spring was beginning to be just warm enough to use on a sunny day, provided we sat at the fireplace end of the table. And there we were early one evening, surrounded by a comfortable jumble of earthenware plates, nutshells and the Paul de Lamerie silver that Belos insists we must use, so that he can be a proper butler and polish the silver with his thumbs, or whatever butlers do when they buttle.

There were three of us: Elisabeth, Sholto Lawrence and myself.

'I think I have made some progress,' said young Lawrence. 'After you warned me in Alexandria that I might appoint myself Miss Lilian's guardian, because you could not accompany her without arousing the suspicions of Casterman, I have been determined to protect her as much as is within my power – but I most earnestly wish to do more than that, and to restore to her something that was very precious to her.'

'There are one or two points to consider before you embark on that search,' said I. 'When I visited Westmorland Park shortly after Miss Lilian's accident, I walked the ground which she had ridden over and that was where I first thought there was some cause for suspicion. There was a mark around the trunk of one of the trees which could have been made by a length of thin rope or twine which had bitten into the bark, and there were some dark smears around the scar on the tree trunk, for which I could not account.

'But then, when I saw in the stables that there was a length of twine soaked in tar which was lying on top of a heap of rubbish – disgraceful, to allow such disorder to accumulate in a stable, by the way – in the stall next to that of the old pony, Dobbie . . .'

'Barbary!' said a reproving boom. Belos was placing a decanter of port on the table.

'I'm sorry, Belos – the stall next to that of . . . er . . . that magnificent animal, Barbary. Now, why had the twine been soaked in tar? Two reasons came to mind. Firstly, it would be much more difficult to spot a length of rope across the path if it had been blackened to be inconspicuous among the shadows that lie across that spot at the time of day that Miss Lilian's accident occurred. I made a particular note of the way the trees cast the path into shadow just at that place, but did not think that alone could account for the accident.

'Secondly, if it had been desired to make the rope black, why use tar, which is not so easily available lying around in the average household – lamp-black or boot polish or ink are all substances which would come to hand much more readily in the normal course of events. No, tar suggested one thing – the sea! It is commonly used on sailing ships to coat twine and rope, protecting them against rotting and salt damage. So then, when I heard that Casterman and Overbury had done business at Bristol docks, I was immediately alerted to the possibility that one or the other of them had simply picked up a convenient length which was lying about – perhaps thinking therefore to avoid the problem of blackening a piece of rope at Westmorland Park. That might have been a conspicuous sort of procedure – and there at the docks there was no doubt an amply supply of cast-off bits of rigging lying around. I suppose it's something we will say farewell to when the new steam-ships take over from sail.'

'So you knew that someone had contrived Lilian Westmorland's accident?' asked Elisabeth.

257

'I suspected it. And then the other circumstances – the dismissal of the groom, for example.'

'I suppose that was in case he had noticed the twine stretched across the path,' commented Sholto.

'More than that!' I replied. 'There may have been marks on the horse itself, which would have meant that the horse had to be disposed of, lest they give rise to speculation. A cut on the foreleg – well, that could have been passed off as a result of the horse perhaps rolling on the ground – something like that. But a cut in which there were traces of some blackish substance – something with the characteristic smell of tar – now that would have been a very strange injury, would it not? That might have set people's minds a-working – even here, in the countryside.' I paused, tempted, but refrained from comment, and continued with my analysis.

'So the horse must be got rid of as fast as possible, and how is that to be done?

'Now, here we have to consider the mentality of Uncle Micah. The most obvious answer would have been to shoot the horse and send for the knacker to take the carcass away – pleading, perhaps, that the sooner the creature was put out of its agony, the less distress there would be for Miss Lilian. But this particular animal, the mare Selene, was a rare piece of horse-flesh. She was worth at least five hundred guineas – at least, Micah knew that was what Mrs Westmorland had paid for her. And was there nothing to be gained from this creature, who was, after all, only slightly injured with a cut that would soon heal over? Was such a valuable animal to be thrown away, as it were, with no advantage to Micah Overbury?

'That is how misers are entrapped, you know, by their own petty greed. The hope of selling Selene for whatever sum he could get made Micah blind to the advantages of eliminating all trace of the crime. For the miserable thirty pounds that he got from the gypsy, Trito Hearne, Overbury was willing to forgo his long-term advantage.'

'Which was the Westmorland estate, I suppose!' exclaimed Sholto angrily.

'Not only that. The same mercenary and callous attitude he displayed towards horseflesh he displayed towards human beings. Selene was something to be sold for whatever he could get, and so was Rahaba, the Egyptian! Micah had no moral objection to slavery, provided it benefited him. But there was a practical difficulty. The slaves were to be brought from Egypt, a country well known to Casterman and where he had many business contacts. Then they were to be shipped out to the West Indies. But in the meantime they must be kept somewhere in Britain – somewhere discreet, where they could be imprisoned well away from any prying eyes. And that, of course, Micah thought to do at Westmorland Park. But his niece was an inconvenience – she might get in the way, make some discoveries of her own, perhaps. So she was to disappear from the scene and leave Westmorland Park completely in Micah's control. Thus there would have been an isolated hiding-place which was perfectly situated – in the depths of the countryside but not too far from Bristol, a port to which much shipping was bound. Uncle Micah was in the act of furnishing his slave-quarters suitably, equipped with manacles, when the girl, Maggie Dermott, became a nuisance.'

'Oh, yes, she was found with manacles, was she not?'

'Yes, but I was misled there, for I thought at first that had she been manacled herself – had been confined somewhere in the house and was trying to escape when they killed her. Then I took note of the fact that the manacles were not actually on her wrists when we found the poor child – they fell out of her skirts when we lifted her up. I think that she went to Westmorland Park to warn Miss Lilian, did not find her, but perhaps crept into that horrible room which Sandys and I discovered, the one Overbury had prepared for his victims, and she found the manacles there and slipped them into her pocket as evidence. But as she was running to the gate to raise the alarm, they overtook her.'

'Casterman and Overbury?'

'Perhaps Casterman, acting alone. That quick and efficient strangulation was his particular mark – it was much the same method as he used on the servant girl who tried to run away in Cairo. She was trying to reach me in order to alert me to Miss Lillian's plight. In fact, the pattern of the second killing was very much the same as the first – once more a girl shows sympathy for Miss Lilian Westmorland, tries to do something to help her – and dies for it! Murderers have their characteristics, you know, and that decisive ruthlessness was Casterman's.'

'I suppose he was likely to make a great deal of money out of Micah Overbury's dealings,' observed Elisabeth.

'Yes, but I don't think he was involved just for money. His motive for taking Lilian into the heart of the epidemic of smallpox, for instance. I suspect that was a form of revenge – why he should he be condemned to wander the world with those terrible disfiguring pockmarks, accompanied by a smooth-skinned young woman whose every public appearance must be a counterpoint to his ruined face? I believe that he probably desired to maim Lilian Westmorland as much as to kill her. She might have survived the smallpox, as he himself had done, so it was not a sure way of contriving her death, but it was a sure way of destroying her good looks, and that would no doubt have given him great satisfaction. As long as she was away from Westmorland Park, he could

ake his time over her death. Before that occurred, he could
ontrive much enjoyment from watching her suffering.'

Elisabeth shivered and drew her cashmere shawl about her
houlders. 'What an evil creature he must have been! But
suppose the sooner we can forget about him, the better
_ilian Westmorland can recover from her experiences. I
m afraid that some terrible losses have befallen her in her
hort life.'

'There is one loss that we may mitigate,' said I. 'Sholto,
an you accompany me?'

here was a small stone cottage at the very end of the village.
Although it had at one time been rather better than most of
he village houses, which were built out of mud and wattle,
eglect had clearly befallen it so that weeds sprouted even on
he shingle roof and the door and window-frames had long
go lost their paint or varnish to the weather.

There was a cleared patch in the garden, where some
vorkmanlike rows of beans had been recently hoed and
ied up to stakes. We made our way along the path beside
his evidence of habitation.

The door swung open a few minutes after Sholto had
apped upon it with the handle of his whip.

The woman who opened it was tall and wiry, with an old
·oke-bonnet and a scarlet petticoat. She had the eccentric
ouch of a man's old jacket draped around her shoulders.
he garment was green with brass buttons; it was oddly
aunty.

'My name is Sholto Lawrence and this is Lord Ambrose
. .' began my companion, but he was interrupted before he
got any further. The sharp eyes took in every detail of our
ppearance.

'Yes, I knows both of you, who ye are. And I don't

know I cares a great deal for either of ye. Not a fig, as th
saying goes.'

'We've come to ask you a favour. Will you allow us t
come in?'

'No, I won't. I don't want folk thinking I've got to
friendly with the gentry. Yez can speak on the doorstep
can't ye?'

'Miss Adams, we do need some information from you
if possible. There has been a very grave wrong – and
wicked crime, too – committed, and there may still be som
possibility of putting things right.'

'Yez can never make up for what happened to him
Never!'

'You know, then what we are talking of?'

'Yes, of course. Soon as I saw the two of you coming along
here – why else would you come, except about summa tha
happened to the young lady? You wouldn't have come to se
the likes of me for my own sweet sake – not unless it wer
about some of the gentry, and what have we to do with th
gentry except for them at Westmorland Park? So that's hov
I knows what you was coming here for.'

I thought it was time to add my voice to that of m
companion. This lady was too shrewd for anything but th
direct approach.

'Can you tell us where your brother is?'

She seemed startled. 'Ah, you come out with it straight
away! And what kind of answer do you think you'll get?'

'Miss Adams, I have an invitation for you. You are invite
to a funeral, to take place at half-past two o'clock next Frida
afternoon. The parson is doubtless even now fudging u
some platitudes for the occasion. The name of the decease
is Casterman.'

There was a long pause. She sank into a chair with a sig

of amazement and relief. Then she spoke. 'Well, I'll come and dance on his grave all right, the wicked bastard, excuse my language, my lord. But he were only part of it – I'm still afeared of the other.'

'Micah Overbury? Why then, you have no cause for fear. Let me give the news of Mr Overbury. It's bad news – at least, for him.'

She asked us in at last, after I had told her.

'I cannot say it is a sad end. Casterman dead and Overbury in prison.'

'No indeed, my lord – let me get a drop of dandelion wine out to celebrate.'

'Er . . . no, thank you, Miss Adams. Mr Lawrence and myself are reforming our ways of life, you know – we are contemplating taking a vow against strong drink, are we not, Lawrence?'

'Confound it, Lord Ambrose, why d'ye kick me in the ankle so?'

'I do apologise, Mr Lawrence – it was utterly accidental, I do assure you. No, madam, we will trespass no longer on your hospitality – all we would ask is that you will tell us where your brother is.'

'Oh, Lord Ambrose, I have not told a soul! For on the day after the young lady's accident, my brother Robert came here after dark, skulking along as if the hounds of hell were after him. Which, in a manner of speaking, you might say they were, for Mr Micah Overbury and that Casterman – they were on his track all right. They'd turned him away, you see – him as had worked there at Westmorland for twenty year or more! But he thought there were summa wrong, all right.'

'What did he say?'

'There was never any dead horse there. Where it was shot, supposedly – the young lady's mare that Mr Overbury said

263

was so badly injured she had to be killed! Robert heard the sound of a revolver all right – he reckoned Casterman had fired a gun near the place where the horse fell. But Robert ran up through the trees and saw the horse alive and moving. Then when old Overbury dismissed him, he guessed there was something wrong. But what, Dotty? he says to me, what can it be?'

'Did he stay with you after the incident at Westmorland Park?'

'Only the one night. Then he insisted on leaving – he said it weren't safe to stay anywhere near them two at Westmorland – and he told me to say that I'd never laid eyes on him after the accident. And that I did, when Casterman came to ask where my brother was. "I'll send some extra wages after him," he said, the smooth-tongued devil, "to compensate him for the loss of his position. Mr Overbury acknowledges that he was a trifle hasty in dismissing him!" But I knew that Casterman meant no good to my brother and I never said a word, just stared at him, when he says, "You'll have to tell me where he is if you want me to send the money, Miss Adams."

'"I don't know!"' says I. "Not if you was to offer a thousand pounds, I still wouldn't know!"

'He looks at me for such a long time, and I could feel myself getting frightened till I was shaking here on this very doorstep, like a willow branch in the wind, I was. And then he pushes me inside and he . . .'

She held out her hand. There was a long red puckered scar running across the back of it.

'He thrusts my hand down on the edge of the stove. I screamed, but we're at the end of the houses here – no one heard. Anyway, 'twould have been my word against his – he'd have just said I burnt meself by accident. "Now," he says, "You can remember me by this. Every time you look at the scar, think of your brother – and tell me if you know aught of him! For if you lie to me I shall find out – and that burn upon your hand is a little taste, a very little taste, of what you'll get!" And with that he makes off.'

'But do you know where he is, Miss Adams? And will you trust us? For your brother's evidence will help to bring Micah Overbury to justice.'

'First show me Casterman's dead body!'

She meant it. She enjoyed it, too. This was a woman with a strong stomach and I cannot say I exactly blame her.

Micah Overbury never did come to justice, if by that word is meant the usual flummery of our law-courts. Overbury had blamed all the deaths on Casterman, of course. He was imprisoned awaiting trial on a charge of slave-dealing and a lesser technicality involving unlawful possession of a dead body, which the authorities had dug up from somewhere, but which even I thought was undeserved. He had wanted to be in possession of a beautiful living slave girl, not a nasty smelly male corpse.

He did not stand trial. Word went across (by fast steam-packet!) to Kingston and his fellow slave-dealers, fearful that he would betray what he knew and interfere with their profitable business, made some arrangements. They had plenty of money and the goal turnkeys were poor.

One day Micah Overbury had supped up his customary prison breakfast of gruel. Perhaps it tasted a little strange, perhaps a bitter scent arose as he set the first spoonful to his lips, but no doubt the prison fare did not encourage delicate behaviour at table, and Micah gulped his breakfast down.

It was his last.

He had a painful death.

'His eyes were fixed, glistening, the body leaping and

twitching, the breath coming in great sobs or gasps. His jaws opened or closed two or three times, and so he died, within a few minutes of supping his gruel. Yes, there was a strange smell about it. Yes, it was flung into a corner and I saw some dead rats in that place afterwards.'

The symptoms described by the turnkey corresponded well with those of poisoning by prussic acid. I believe Sandys mentioned this at the time.

No one cared.

CHAPTER 23

The Further Narrative of Miss Lilian Westmorland

It was a great good fortune to be returning to England as spring arrived. Reunited with Jennet, I had spent the winter in Egypt with Ariadne and Charles on board the *Zubeida*, where she was moored at Aswan in the dry scented air of Upper Egypt, where not only my troublesome cough had disappeared, but so had the fears and nightmares from which I had suffered, dreams in which Casterman, his scarred face monstrous big and swollen, lurched after me as I tried to run. And Jennet too had got over her frights and alarms, for, as she said she had feared me dead and that she would never see me again. 'You vanished into that city, Miss Lilian – just think of it! All that great crowded Cairo – and you disappeared into the midst of it! They set me down on my own – and I found some great fellow in a turban and got him at last to lead me back to the Hotel, and no one knew anything of you – most of them were packing, for there was rumours of disease starting to fly about! So I got a conveyance with Mrs Cornwallis to Alexandria, for she was to leave for India, and there I hoped the authorities would do something. But could

I get the Consul to stir his stumps to find you – not he! Not till Lord Ambrose came – and Lord forgive me that I ever said anything against his lordship – not till then did I have any hopes of ever seeing you again, Miss! Oh, my blood runs cold when I do think about it!'

But a tranquil warm winter assuaged our fears and we were willing to set out for home – indeed, Jennet was begging to return. Charles counselled prudence, and it was not, I believe, till he had received certain papers concerning my uncle from Lord Ambrose that he was willing to let us return to Westmorland Park, and booked our passage on board the *Great London* from Alexandria to Portsmouth. But then a few weeks later Ariadne came very gravely one day and told me that my uncle was dead; I tried to grieve for him and might have pretended that I did, but could neither regret his passing nor force myself to a false display of mourning. I have known true loss in my life and that does not incline one to false tears.

At any rate our passages were booked and we had an uneventful return voyage, except that poor Jennet was sea-sick again, which she had hoped would not occur, believing that one attack of sea-sickness vaccinates you against another, as it were, though I tried to explain that happened in the case of smallpox, not *mal-de-mer*. I fear she had misunderstood some of the conversation.

Jennet was wondering all the way from the docks to Westmorland Park how we should find things when we got home. 'I'll be bound there's no beds aired for us to lay our heads, Miss Lilian, nor crust nor crumb to eat. I'm afeared the house will be all deserted.'

So as the coach turned into the drive we were at any rate pleased to see the old lodge-keeper coming out to open the gates. Here at any rate was a sign of life. And we were even better pleased at what he told us.

'Lord Ambrose asked me to get the house prepared for you, Miss. My daughter has been putting things in readiness and you'll find she's made up a good fire, for 'tis a chilly spring and right enough, though the daffs be out on the lawns – well, you'll see 'em as you goes up to the house.'

See them we did, acres of pale golden trumpets in great drifts below the house, just as they had always been. And there was my mother's magnolia tree, its branches shooting out leaves of that light spring green that presaged the white and purple streaks of flower-buds.

As we got down from the coach, there came the sound of footsteps from the side of the house.

I had not allowed myself to hope nor to speak of Mr Sholto Lawrence. An interesting acquaintance, and I was greatly in his debt. That was all that could be admitted, to myself or to any other.

So I was not really prepared for the depths of my feeling as I saw him emerging from the path that led to the stables at the back of the house.

'Why, Miss Lilian, take care!'

'I'm sorry, Mr Lawrence – I stumbled somewhat on the steps! How good to see you again! Are you visiting the district?'

'Yes, Miss Lilian, and so is another old companion of yours!'

'Why, who could that be?'

'One moment, I beg you.'

Mr Lawrence dived round the corner for a moment.

He re-emerged, followed by a stout fellow in russet jacket and groom's britches, holding a rein.

It couldn't be! That was surely Adams, our groom, whom Uncle Micah had dismissed after my accident.

And there was something utterly incredible! I could hardly believe the evidence of my eyes!

Yet there was the familiar soft whicker, and there, yes, beyond doubt, was the distinctive mark upon the forehead – the white crescent moon blaze of my own dear Selene, for whose death I had wept!

I could say nothing, only rush towards her and fling my arms about her neck.

'There, I beg you, don't take on so, Miss Lilian! Malfine and I had the devil's own job to wash the dye off that blaze of hers – the gypsies had disguised her mighty well, you know! But we found her – well, Malfine did – at least, Malfine and I found her together, y'know.'

'How – how on earth?'

'Malfine figured it out, y'see. Got a statement about that gypsy fellow who bought her. Ambrose said the gypsies would never have sold her – they'd have been accused of theft straight away. It was much too good a horse for them to have come by honestly; he thought they'd have kept her themselves. So what would they have done with her? Not have her pulling carts, not this one. No, they would race Selene themselves – that's what your Lord Ambrose Malfine figured out, anyway, so when I heard there was a great gypsy meeting on Exmoor I just went round watching the races and looking out for a horse that might just have a scar on the foreleg and a spot of walnut-oil or some such trickery that might be covering up a mark on its forehead. And there was a fine winner that seemed to leap like the wind itself and there was old Trito Hearne laying bets out on this mare and raking it in whenever she sailed past the winning-post, which was pretty often, I can tell you! Miss Elisabeth and I found a fellow who'd been drinking with the gypsies – he told us where old Trito was likely to be.'

'I don't think I'll ever be able to thank you!'

'Thank me? Oh, well, it don't matter – I'm a bashful sort of chappie, you know. And the groom, Adams, he's come back from Ireland. That's where he took himself off to, and now his sister's sent to tell him it's safe to come home. So perhaps you'd take him on again?'

Of course, it went without saying that I did. I think often and again of my good fortune in the devotion of my future husband (for we intend to marry in the summer). And in another respect: to how many of us is it given, as has happened to me with Selene, to have something one loves come back from the dead?

CHAPTER 24

Unsigned Copy of a Letter from Lord Ambrose Malfine

Malfine, Christmas Eve, 1832

You wrote to me once that you thought one day some aristocratic lady might rule by my side at Malfine.

Well, it has come to pass!

The nobly-bred lady in question has an exquisitely long and aristocratic jaw, a sharp row of white teeth, and a pluming and feathery tail like the foam of the sea.

In short, she is a Seluki, one of the fabled breed said to have been the hounds of the pharaohs – and that, judging by her likeness to those beasts I have seen following their master's chariot on the carvings in ancient tombs – that is probably quite truthful. The species has been preserved by the Arabs, who took them everywhere they inhabited. And when Lilian Westmorland arrived back in England, she brought two puppies with her. They are a gift from the father of Rahaba, the Nubian girl whom we rescued, and a gift which I cannot possibly refuse! They are of a pale golden buttery-white colour, and move as if 'borne by the wings of the air' as the old Arab poem about a hunting-dog has it; the Arabs say a Seluki has ears like the flower of the hyacinth, a claw like a cobbler's awl and eyes as clear as drops of water.

The dogs cause much amazement in the district: as if I were not a sufficient cause for wonder, as if Zaraband were not enough animal excitement for their spirits, these young Selukis will seal the strangeness of my reputation! They have nothing in common with any familiar obedient whippet, Jack Russell or terrier; they would certainly give the Master of Foxhounds nightmares if he should ever encounter them, for they are simultaneously the fastest and laziest specimens of the canine kingdom that ever graced a palace! In short, they are throughly at home here, part of Malfine already, and will greet you with many leaps and cabrioles when you arrive, and never leave your side if you wish them to guard you, not even if they were to be cut to pieces.

And now, my dear Elisabeth, I look forward to your return, you and the boy, from the Christmas merry-making at your mother's house. I have spent the last few days, as I intended to do many months ago, in putting together the documents that will lay bare the bones of this affair of the Egyptian Coffin.

But there is one question that they do not answer. As you, with your customary powers of observation put it, 'But who killed him?'

He, of course, being Casterman.

Now, if your question were 'Why was he killed?' or 'Where?' these papers would of course have answered it. But 'Who?' is a different matter.

And a much graver one. The burden of murder – even such a specimen as this – the knowledge of having sent a fellow human soul into eternity – that is a dreadful load, truly the curse of Cain!

Yes, it was Lilian Westmorland. For when I descended to the body of Casterman in that pit, his neck was already broken. He had been dead when he hit the bottom of the shaft and I put my bullet through a lifeless man. I knew that when I saw him lying there, with his head twisted down. And there was one bullet-hole and a trace of powder upon his shirt, because my first bullet had missed and my second, which I discharged after I had got down into the pit, was fired a foot away from his heart – or whatever substitute we may suppose he had for the seat of his emotions! That is why there was very little blood. It was fortunate that the Consul in Alexandria left all the arrangements concerning the disposal of Casterman's remains to me. I tried to make it as easy for him as possible; that there were two shots fired and only one wound in the body went unremarked. If Lilian had noticed at the time of Casterman's death that there seemed to be two explosions, why it was but the effect of echoes coming off the rocky cliff behind the tomb. My first bullet lies hidden deep within the sands of Egypt. My second struck a corpse.

Lilian had beckoned Casterman on, and called him to his death, as he had once tried to lure her in that tower at Alexandria, to her near-certain destruction.

But I shall not tell her that and you, too are sworn to secrecy. Consider, a tender young heart, a conscience as fresh and delicate as hers – why, to be saddled with such a thing as death. I know how I suffered after the death of her father. I cannot make reparation to him, but I can spare his daughter the visions of death and guilt which I fear would visit her. I can still hear her voice, ringing out across the desert:

'Come on, then! Come on if you dare!'

And across the years I hear still my own voice, calling out to her father as we stood at the side of the river, 'Come on, then! I dare you!'

So, as the world thinks, the death of Casterman was but one more killing for Ambrose Malfine to take upon his broad shoulders – and a well-merited death in any case. And the coffin stands in the hallway at Malfine – for though I told Lilian Westmorland it was certainly her property, as she was Micah's only heir, she begged me to remove it from Westmorland Park.

Belos has my instructions that the other documents, the narratives of myself and Lilian Westmorland, the statement of the gypsy, Shadrach Lee and the letters which I received in Alexandria, are to be placed under seal in the muniment room at Malfine. With them will be placed a copy of the most shameful decision ever made in British legal history, which condemned thousands to remain in slavery.

But all evidence of Lilian's part in Casterman's death is to be destroyed. Burn this letter, I pray you, when you receive it.

Belos will take it to the post for me in a few minutes.

I hear his footstep now and trust him never to read this.

Appendix

Legal decision: In the Matter of a Slave Woman named Grace.

Grace was a slave in Antigua who had accompanied her mistress to Britain. The question was whether she was a free woman once she had set foot on British soil.

The Judgement of Lord Stowell in November, 1827

[Note: 'his lordship in consequence of infirmity of eyes and voice, found it necessary to devolve upon junior counsel in the case the task of reading his judgement.']

'It was never intended to put any restraint on a domestic slave accompanying his or her master to Great Britain or on being taken back from Great Britain to the colonies. The purpose of the law was to prevent the introduction of *new* slaves into the colonies. In the eighteenth century the personal traffic in slaves resident in England had been as public and as authorized in London as in any of our West India islands. They were sold on the Exchange and other places of public resort by parties themselves resident in London and with as little reserve as they would have been in any of our West India possessions.

'In 1772 a judgement established that the owners of slaves had no authority or control over them in England nor was there any power of sending them back to the colonies . . . this judgement was made by Lord Mansfield with many delays and great reluctance.

'Lord Mansfield said "slavery is so odious that it cannot be established without positive law" . . . but ancient custom is now recognised as a just foundation of all law. The practice of slavery was founded upon a similar authority . . . the arguments against slavery do not go beyond Britain. There has been no act of ceremony of manumission nor any act whatever that could even formally destroy those various powers of property which the owner possessed over his slave by the most solemn assurances of law . . . the slave continues a slave as far as being in the colonies is concerned.

'It would surely be a gross abusing of all principle to say that they [the West Indian slave-owners] should be deprived of their commerce. Slavery was a very favoured introduction into the colonies; it was deemed a great source of the mercantile interest of the country, and was, on that account, largely considered by the mother country as a great source of wealth and strength . . . it has been continued in our colonies, favoured and supported by our own courts, which have liberally imparted to it their protection and encouragement.

'It has been said that the law of England discourages slavery, and so it certainly does within the limits of these islands; but it uses a very different language and exerts a very different force when it looks to its colonies, for to this trade, in those colonies, it gives an almost unbounded protection.

'Is it not most certain that this trade of the colonies has been the very favourite trade of the country and so continues?'

*   *   *

[The conclusion was that the woman, Grace, was not entitled to her freedom and had to return to Antigua as a slave.]

In 1807 an act had been passed which forbade ships to carry out any slaves from a British port, but slavery was not abolished in the West Indies till 1838, after Parliament had voted the sum of £20 million as compensation to the planters.

Jane and the
Unpleasantness at
Scargrave Manor

Stephanie Barron

To Jane Austen's surprise, her visit to the estate
of young and beautiful Isobel Payne, Countess of
Scargrave, is far from dull. She has scarcely arrived
when the Earl is felled by a mysterious and agonizing
ailment. His death seems a cruel blow of fate for the
newly married Isobel. Yet the widow soon finds that
it's only the beginning of her misfortune . . . as she
receives a sinister missive accusing her and the Earl's
nephew of adultery – and murder.

Afraid that the letter will expose her to the worst
sort of scandal, Isobel begs her friend Jane for help.
Which is how Jane finds herself embroiled in an investigation that will have her questioning the motives
of Scargrave Manor's guests, stumbling upon the
scene of a bloody murder, and following a trail of
clues that leads all the way to Newgate Prison and the
House of Lords.

'Succeeds on all levels. A robust tale of manners and
mayhem that faithfully reproduces the Austen Style –
and engrosses to the finish' *Kirkus Reviews*

0 7472 5375 7

HEADLINE

A Word After Dying

Ann Granger

Superintendent Alan Markby and his girlfriend, civil
servant Meredith Mitchell, are in need of a holiday
and the Cotswold village of Parsloe St John seems the
perfect choice. Their neighbour, retired journalist
Wynne Carter, is as convivial as the village itself and
over a glass of blackberry wine, indulges in her latest
obsession, Olivia Smeaton, a racy old lady whose life
and death – she is convinced are not all they seem.

Markby is more interested in buying Olivia's house
than the circumstances of her vacating it, but Meredith
is intrigued: by the old lady, the death of a cherished
horse and a dusty junk shop run by a white witch.
When another fatality – of a very grisly nature – is
discovered, it seems her suspicion is justified. Clearly
Olivia isn't the only enigma in Parsloe St John . . .

'Probably the best current example of a crime-writer
who has taken the classic English village detective
story and brought it up to date' *Birmingham Post*

'Classic tale . . . a good feel for understated humour,
a nice ear for dialogue' *The Times*

'Deft plotting and elegant descriptive prose . . .
delicate comic touch and endearing eccentric
characters' *Publishers Weekly*

0 7472 5187 8

HEADLINE